A SIMPLE THOUGHT
of Sanity

C E HUNTINGDON

Copyright © 2021 by Christopher & Ellen Huntingdon
ISBN 978-1-7366237-0-1
C E Publishing

First printed edition.
Authors' website: www.cehuntingdon.com

Acknowledgments

Thank you to Don and Alex for reading our first terrible draft. Thank you to our friends at Ternion for giving us the confidence to continue. Thank you to Rick for finally reading. Thank you to Jack and Jacqueline for not only reading and editing but giving us the critiques we needed to hear. Thank you to Anna and Jane for all your motherly support.

"When we penetrate into the human secrets…the madness discloses the system upon which it is based, and we recognize insanity to be simply an unusual reaction to emotional problems which are in no wise foreign to ourselves."

–C. G. JUNG

ACT I - PRODROMAL

"I've never not known who I was, even though I haven't always been me."

1 | THE CITY

Like all places, our surroundings become a reflection of ourselves. The City was no exception. A sterile and vaulted place, its complexity was not in its design but in its breadth. Born from an evolution of ideas that had bred structures and places to suit its people, the City grew and grew until its manifestations outweighed its capacities. So then the people made their lives busy to fill in all those places that had been created, and in doing so, forgot about the self, and the shadow cast by such magnificent edifices.

2 | Me

Billy, that wasn't his name. His name was Bill. It was simple, it was short, and it didn't need a nickname which added to the length of it. Yet, nobody called him Bill. *Why was that?*

His train of thought was interrupted as he stared out his window into the alley down below. He cocked his head as he watched a stray cat prowl the asphalt street. The cat moved out of sight, and he began to think again on what had entertained him before this moment as the reflection of his mother caught his eye in the window. She was setting down the evening meal and would soon call him to join.

"Billy," her voice called out through her motherly mask. A twisted version of the service industry smile, no doubt designed by someone who had never had a mother. She leaned over the counter to collect the family's meal as it ascended from its pedestal in the kitchen. Her dress was covered by an appropriately sterile cooking apron. An apron that had never once seen a speck of food.

As the rain flecked the window, Bill returned his gaze to the alley, secretly waiting for the cat to appear again.

"Have a good day at school." She didn't mean it, she never did. It was one of those expected lines that everyone was so fond of. Bill simply looked up. His mask's built-in smile prevented him from having to pretend to care. She left him on the street corner with the other children like she always did and marched off to work without a look back. Bill always watched, hoping that she would turn around, hoping that she would demonstrate something that wasn't expected of her.

Sure Bill hated her, just like everyone else with a mask, but that didn't change the fact that she was his mother. Instinct compelled him to love her and wish for her affection. Deep down, he wanted her to turn back.

She never did.

The shrill whistling of the crossing guard indicated that it was safe to pass, and other children his age marched in unison across the street. Bill, however, was already in the alley outside his window. He'd marched along solemnly kicking cans, deriving amusement from the chaos caused by strewing litter across the pavement. As Bill got closer, he stopped kicking cans and started looking. He had seen it duck in here last night, where the walls met to form an alcove for the dumpsters that lined the alley.

Curled up behind the metal box, he found the cat from last night. It was an ill-fed and unhygienic-looking creature. Its fur long since matted or sloughed off by the natural sludge that collects in the crevices of the world.

That didn't matter to Bill as he picked the cat up by the scruff of its neck. Barely a yowl escaped as he held it up. It was a thing. Sure it was living, but it was just a thing. A thing neglected by the world, a dirty secret left for the Cleaners to burn away. As Bill stared into its eyes, he felt a connection he'd only dreamed about with his mother. He saw the same look in that creature's eyes as he felt in his heart, watching his mother walk away. He was better than her, he knew this, and this would be his chance to demonstrate it.

Pulling the cat in close, Bill gripped it in his arms. The movements came naturally as he stroked its back, blackening his hands and shirt as he stood there wiping away the filth of the City.

The two spent the rest of the day together. Bill fed the cat milk from the kitchen's pedestal and spent every second afterward stroking its back. The act brought him pleasure, though he couldn't explain why. The lick it gave him as he rubbed its throat sent a tickle down the small of his spine. A smile grew across his face, and he ripped his mask off to experience the moment, holding the cat close to his chest. This creature had shown him more affection in one day than his mother had in a lifetime.

Bill heard the familiar clicking of his household door opening. Struggling to his feet, he raced to show his mother, compelled to share the experience with her.

"Mother, look!" he said as she entered.

In the moments after, Bill imagined that his mother's face, her real face, had been wretched in horror as she witnessed her son without his mask, covered in filth and holding a cat from the street. But her Face would never change. It would always be the same fake smile.

"Billy!" she screeched, her tone betraying the visage. "Your Face, your uniform! Cleanse and mask yourself."

She didn't even mention the cat. It was so far gone from her understanding, beyond what was ever imagined or experienced. She simply took it from his hands, went to the incinerator, and disposed of it like the family's nightly meals.

Bill looked on in horror.

"Have a good day at school." She didn't mean it, she never did.
Bill simply looked up. His mask's built-in smile prevented him from having to pretend or care. Even so, he realized there was no Face in production that could portray his emotion.

As Bill's mother started to walk away from the street corner, he called her name.

"Mother, my shoe's untied."

It was a diversion from their daily routine, but not one beyond the realm of comprehension. His mother returned and bent down to correct her son's wardrobe.

"Mother," Bill said again. Their false smiles met as she looked up.

Extending his arms abruptly, Bill pushed his mother into oncoming traffic. She didn't cry, she didn't scream, she just disappeared. A stream of vehicles crushed her body, each a little bit more than the last, until there was nothing but a stain on the pavement.

3 | RECOLLECTIONS

"Well, I'll be damned." Thomasson had heard the phrase on his favorite show, and he was glad he had because he was more than surprised by what he was looking at.

He'd been walking to work when his handkerchief had blown out of his breast pocket. The largely ceremonial object had danced quickly past his head and floated off behind him. Like every morning, the streets were shoulder to shoulder, which meant turning around wouldn't be easy. The handkerchief wasn't special in any way, but it was his, and he'd be expected to have one.

"Excuse me—I'm sorry—pardon me." The simple excuses were all he needed for his aberrant behavior, allowing him to get to his possession and quickly return to his day.

Thomasson managed to exit the stream of people who steadily flowed across the sidewalk like a simulated current. He scanned the streets and soon found that his handkerchief had blown into an unused corner of the path. A slight deviation in the protruding office fronts had left a small hidden gap where the current of Faces had failed to conform to the contours of their concrete stream.

Thomasson rushed over to reclaim the escaped object. He was going to be late if he didn't hurry. Shaking his head, he bent down to pick up his now slightly less immaculate handkerchief and was just tucking it neatly back inside his pocket when he almost dropped it again in surprise. What he thought was an abandoned corner of the sidewalk was occupied by the strangest structure he'd ever seen. Wedged between two cloud scraping towers sat a small wooden building with rounded ceramic tiles clinging to its sagging roof.

Like a forgotten spec or a hidden stain, somehow this building had survived the City's renovations, tucked into its little corner, concealed out of sight. His handkerchief all but forgotten, Thomasson felt drawn to the strange structure, and he approached, ensnared by its absurdity.

As one foot advanced forward, he turned his head in surprise. Someone else must have surely seen this, but all he saw was a steady flow of Faces whose path never showed them the quiet corner with the little building. If one had chanced a glance over their shoulder at just the right moment, they might have discovered the shrouded and sagging structure. Yet given the state of the dusty old thing, it seemed no one ever had, save for today.

"This can't be real."

As Thomasson took another step closer, his head ducked instinctively to the side, as if protecting itself against an unknown thing, where danger might explode from at any given second. Though as he continued to draw near, the building remained as it was, ominous yet quiet.

"Hello?" No one answered. "Hello!?" Still just a building.

Thomasson shook his head as he crept forward. He knew this was a bad idea, but something deep down drove him closer and closer until his hand was turning the knob of the door and sliding it open. Veins of dust ran down, scattered by the breaking of the building's seal. The door stuck for a moment in the sagging frame before giving way.

Thomasson fumbled briefly before finding a switch. A satisfying click brought the sleeping room to life. Scattered about were the dusted contents of a foreign interior, which made a kind of consistent sense.

Thomasson coughed and raised his hand to cover his mouth. The gentle fabric of his handkerchief brushed lightly against the nose of his Face, filtering the dust before it reached his lungs again. He was surprised not only by the fact that he had forgotten the previously useless swatch of fabric which had led him astray but also that he'd finally found a use for the damned thing, other than adorning his pocket that is.

Squinting through the antique lighting, he noticed the floor was littered with more than just dust and dirt. Kneeling down, with handkerchief still in place, he picked up a small round object. It was heavier than he'd imagined, with red protruding stitching that paralleled across its surface. He tossed it up lightly, catching it as it came back down, and felt the strong urge to continue doing so.

"What have I wandered into?"

His muffled words expressed his deeper thoughts.

Curiosity continued to tug at him as he reached down for something else. It was a flat fragile image of a family standing beside a vehicle whose make he was sure he had never known yet was familiar in recollecting.

Thomasson shook his head as he let go, and the image floated to the floor. This place wasn't right. The more he looked around, the more familiar things were, and it wasn't just the sense of recognition that scared him but the feelings which played on that recollection and filled him with a sense of joy.

4 | Thomasson's Antiques

Thomasson smelled the rising vapors of his coffee as he peered out the window of his store. How many mornings had gone by since he'd taken off his coat and rolled up his sleeves?

Glancing over, the coat was still where he'd hung it, dusty and floating on a rack which he'd righted and placed by the door. It felt like years, but surely it could have only been a week or two at most.

He'd overcome the initial confusion of his recollections and decided he would continue sifting through the old shop until he understood more of what was happening. To his delight, he'd found a variety of free-standing shelves tucked in the back of the building. Clearing a space for each, he placed them neatly into several rows to create a few comfortably short aisles. Now that he had a place to put things, he began digging through the scattered oddities that littered the floor.

A wonderful variety of foreign things kept him on his knees for many hours as he sifted through each item. The more he looked, the more he felt like smiling behind his Face. Its alabaster features, while pleasant, could never express what he now desired.

It was the simplest things that creased the corners behind his Face. A small wooden box, a few links of fine chain, a hefty metal pen smooth to the touch. They felt familiar, and more than a few times he would hold them to his chest and lightly chuckle. He found a place for each, unable to categorize any one section due to the great diversity of items.

When he'd grown tired, he was happy to find a small living quarter at the side of the building, behind a wooden sliding door. The bed was soft and easy to roll out over the woven floor. Each morning he would rise and return his bed to a small closet, keeping his living space neat and tidy.

Growing hungry, he discovered that a set of meals were delivered each morning at the back door and taken away each evening after he'd set the dishes back outside. Life's needs conformed around him as he worked. If he looked hard enough, he usually found what he needed.

Despite his best efforts, he could never rid the place entirely of its blanket of dust, but the longer he worked with its fine grain between his fingers, the less and less he noticed it. Some things he came to learn just were and that his efforts would be better focused on other endeavors.

So, when he'd concluded with his attempts to clean and place everything in its proper spot, he took a seat behind the counter by the door and waited. Something told him that he should sit there. Sit there and wait for someone like him to stumble by.

5 | The Image

"Aren't you going to take an image, Lucian?" a fellow student asked. Bill turned his head from the view to see that the voice was hidden behind the Face of a childish smile, with large teeth framed between two rosy cheeks. He still was unaccustomed to his new name, even though it had been years.

At the top of the tower, many of Bill's classmates took images for later, some choosing to capture the landscape of the City, others a portrait of the sun. This was the extent of their individuality. Their matching suits and masks left them indiscernible from each other. Yet because they were so close, Bill could clearly see the name of his inquisitor.

"No, I will enjoy it now, and in a few moments, it will be forgotten."

The mask next to him cocked its small head and thin neck. Its lack of understanding begged for a more descriptive answer.

"Why is it that we must remind ourselves in the future that our past was pleasant? Is it so that we will be content, knowing that at one point we lived well? Is this the token we must carry with us, so that the cruelties of the present can be endured without complaint? Are you to be placated with an image, rather than the real thing?"

The mask stared back at him blankly before turning and rejoining the group. Bill watched the child go, knowing that soon he would lose this moment. The sun and City would always be there, but would he ever be here again?

When the chime sounded, he waited a moment longer, watching as the sun set on the horizon. Bill would return home to his new parents, and they would welcome him just as they had their old son. Even though there were many images of the boy throughout the house, there was no lasting memory of him. Only the present image that Bill would show them, night after night.

Act II - Residual

"It was a dream that soothed us and made us whole in the moment, and at the time that was enough, that was living."

6 | THE CAFÉ

Brutus sat at the corner window, sipping a cup of rather old-tasting coffee. The café was quiet, save for the scraping of plates and gentle clicking of the waitress' heels that complimented the silence. Brutus took another sip and set his cup down with care as he noted a tiny chip on the porcelain rim. He rubbed his thumb over its groove absentmindedly.

The chip wasn't the only piece of the café lacking care or attention. Looking around, Brutus' eyes were drawn to a number of imperfections. A speckling of rust dotting the base of a nearby stool. The hint of a stain splashed across the waitress' apron. Scuffs and scratches lightly dusting the smooth tiled floor.

What interested Brutus the most, however, was the window. As he sat in the corner, hands resting loosely around his cup, he peered out through the murky glass of the café. The window had aged with a fine film, and while he might have minded it in any other setting, the slight impairment provided an additional barrier through which Brutus could safely observe the City.

It was from his spot in the corner that Brutus had spent most of the evening just sitting and watching the Faces in the night. Citizens traversed the City, a steady stream of marching steps truncated only by the ebb and flow of rush hour traffic. He spotted no friends or acquaintances traveling together. Life had too many other important things that took up too much important time. Everyone was alone in their journey.

Brutus supposed that many of the people were headed to visit one of the City's social clubs. Until today, Brutus would have been among them. The thought of that obligation made him thankful for the thick pane of glass separating him from those busy streets and all those busy people.

He had awoken that morning as he always did, with noises buzzing in his ears. They followed him until he was floating among the conversations of fellow commuters and navigating the bells and chatter of work. When one noise had ended, he realized another was keen to take its place.

With his colleagues, he had left the office intending to relax at a social club. This was a habit of theirs, as much as it was everyone else's. Though in truth, it was as much a habit as it was a mandate. They would sit, eat, and listen to each other talk. They would talk about a great many things that would soon be forgotten and most likely be repeated.

Finding himself locked in the same routine, Brutus had prepared a rather amusing anecdote about the funny looking egg he had eaten the previous morning. When it came his turn to speak, everyone looked at him, pale white Faces turning in unison from their places around the table. But the words never came.

His pink upper lip twitched as it failed to form the noise of his beginning consonant. He tried re-syncing, making a fastidious yawn behind his Face and bringing it down slowly into a pursed pucker. Gradually his lip quivered and returned to the gentle resting state of his professional smile.

In that quick moment, though, his turn had passed, and the perfunctory story had gone untold. Brutus leaned back in his chair in mild annoyance. He'd have to stop by the cosmetics shop and deal with their incessant upselling, all for a simple recalibration.

Like a clock, Brutus' head ticked from one coworker to the next as they told their stories, and as he did so, he found that he was not so interested in telling his own anymore. This odd interruption had somehow allowed a new thought to creep into his head. *What if everyone had the same glitch, at the same time. Or one after the other. What would be the loss?* What would he hear tonight that he would regret not knowing tomorrow?

So Brutus listened, really listened. He folded his arms and leaned back in his chair as he heard about his coworker misfiling a document he'd worked through lunch to finish. When everyone laughed, Brutus didn't. He found it unfunny and honestly quite sad. The more he listened, the more he actually heard. The more he heard, the more he really understood. All of them were just bouncing from one noise to the next. Each just monotonous enough to blend in with the other, and as that monotony slowly grew, he imagined himself drowning in a sea, surrounded by smiling white Faces. The thought turned so real that Brutus rose to excuse himself and make his escape.

Pushing through the exit, Brutus found himself back on the streets. It was quiet now, save for the soft thudding of his own feet on the pavement. He plodded along until the silence began to weigh on him. In contrast to what had overwhelmed him moments before, this silence now made him feel rather empty. Leaving the club at an off-hour, he had somehow fallen between the cracks of his normal day. It was a time where people wanted to be at home, but obligation called them elsewhere. Any other night, he'd still have hours before he could find himself on this road. The view was more than a little different.

It was the first time he had ever really looked down the path he traversed every day. Signs and lights and doorways stood naked, unblocked by the usual throng of bodies that surrounded them. His usual pace he now found was too quick, and as he slowed, he found the most comfortable pace was not walking at all. So he stopped and took the moment for what it was, an opportunity.

Ahead seemed like an endless street. The farther Brutus looked down the road, the more he tilted his head. Higher and higher until his eyes traced the peaks of the City. He found that looking down the street really wasn't much different than looking up. The thought began to make him dizzy until he heard what seemed like a whisper calling to him. He turned to face it but could find no one there to claim it. Instead, something else entirely stole his attention.

It was a café of all things, marked with an unobtrusive sign. Brutus couldn't pinpoint what made it stand out, just that it seemed out of place, like someone had parted the existing buildings and placed their own creation gently inside.

He found himself drawn to this little thing. First looking left, *empty*, then right, *empty*, he quickly darted across the street. Reaching the sidewalk, he paused to…*admire* what he could now more clearly see. Its eggshell-painted exterior contrasted against the white stone of the buildings around it. A large window cut into the front provided a glimpse of its inner workings. There were booths and stools, customers, and a waitress, with room for more. Looking in at the little scene, he saw pairs of people enjoying their food, drinking their coffee, but nobody saw him, and he wondered at the purpose of the window.

He couldn't stay here forever, though, as much as he'd like. Brutus had to get home. The street was no place to linger. So he nodded his head at the building, his curiosity somewhat satisfied, and as he passed by the door, he snuck one more glance and then came to a stop. There was dirt smudged into the handle. It was an absurd thing to observe, but there it was. How such a thing happened, he didn't know.

He looked around for a moment. The thought of spotting a Cleaner in the distance and flagging them down passed through his mind, but there was no one on the street but him.

Brutus sighed and stepped forward, reaching out, he grabbed the handle with his thumb to polish away the flecks. As he wiped, his hand slipped against the handle, and the door swung open.

"Have a seat wherever you like, I'll be with you in a sec."

"Oh, I was…just cleaning the handle…" Brutus finished in a whisper. He'd never walked into a restaurant he didn't intend to eat at before and wasn't entirely sure what to do. Brutus didn't want to be rude, so he looked around. There was an open seat in the back corner by the window. He slid in and grabbed the menu. A cup of coffee couldn't hurt.

A tiny anomaly had drawn him in, but the worn and lightly blemished interior had welcomed him to stay. Brutus couldn't fathom how the café had escaped the watchful eye of the Cleaners, and for whatever reason it had for continuing to exist, he found that he was grateful.

Turning his attention back to the City, Brutus glanced at the sky. The evening was overcast, a blank canvas of smooth gray kissing the white geometric bones of the City. Rain had started, dampening the streets and sidewalks, calling forth a surge of umbrellas to cover the Faces of the steadily growing crowd. Brutus recognized the commuters who had begun as a trickle and would eventually form a steady column. This was his crowd, and with them came the call to be on his way. His coffee had gone rather cold, and he thought it best to catch the train before the weather station really started to let it pour.

He was paying for his drink when he saw her. Standing across the street, making no attempt to shield herself, a woman waited. Her Face was unlike any other he'd ever seen. Rounded white ears protruded from the top of her head, and her eyes were like golden stars. There was something about her nose that seemed slightly off, and he realized that it was not unlike that of a Mouse. In her hand was a yellow rose that she held close to her chest.

Motionless, she stood in the place that Brutus had been not hours ago, watching people approaching and passing her by. In a lull between pedestrians, the woman suddenly and purposefully extended one of her slender hands and dropped her yellow rose. A man approached and, without breaking his stride, curved ever so gently around the obstruction and continued on down the sidewalk. After a few moments, the Mouse bent down to pick up her flower.

Brutus watched the man who had passed her, wondering about him as he disappeared from sight. He let the strangeness of the encounter settle as he returned his gaze to the woman and was met by those two golden orbs staring back at him. He held his breath as if caught peeping and watched as the Mouse slowly turned and stole away into the night.

7 | PERSPECTIVE

Gabe climbed the final flight of stairs. He'd been doing this all his life. Every high tower, every roof, he'd climbed. Climbed all the way to the top because that's the only place where Gabe could see.

With hands pressed against the glass, he searched with an experienced eye. Towers and more towers were all he saw, with billboards and signs, advertisements, and company logos, but no end. He never saw an ending. No matter where he stood or how high he ascended, he never saw the end, just the City. He was thankful for his Face because it hid the utter disappointment that bordered on despair. The others in the observatory seemed to be there simply to fill space. Few looked out the window, and those who did lingered only a moment before moving on.

He returned his gaze to the infinite cityscape. Like a sedimentary layer, one could see how the City had been built. Skyscrapers straddled ancient homes, and paved pathways wound through the City's structures. Yesterday could be seen in today, and he was tired of the view. Here was as good a place as any, he decided. The road to the end has to start somewhere.

8 | Brutus Heads Home

Brutus' head bobbed in line with everyone else. His Face smiled along with the rest, but beneath it, he curled his lip in confusion. He was having a very strange night, and in all honesty, the reprieve his commute gave him was a welcome one. He had never had occasion to give something so much thought. Now though, his mind swam with curious things.

The closer Brutus got to the train station, the more crowded the sidewalk became, and the more he was forced to stop and start, to slow and augment his pace. The vehicles of the road streaked by with such speed he couldn't tell their make or model. The City was quite large, and they had a lot of ground to cover. Fortunately, Brutus lived and worked near enough to a station that all he had to do was walk.

He heard the train before it came into view. Its rhythmic punctuations were therapeutic to his tired mind. There was some type of tune locked into its arrival that Brutus couldn't quite understand, and the inability of ever knowing was soothing in a way that allowed him to just enjoy it for what it was.

Three more times he heard the train's song, as it ferried away those pieces of the City called people.

There was an abrupt transition from night into a kind of clinical day as Brutus' train arrived, bringing a stark contrast to the monotone City surrounding it. A vessel for advertising as much as it was transportation, the words and shapes blurred by too quickly for him to read and certainly too fast to understand. The metallic supports of the station hummed, and the floor buzzed beneath his feet as Brutus' train crawled to a stop and the doors opened for him to board. It was, as always, on time.

He trundled aboard and wrapped his fingers tightly around the loop above his head. Like most City dwellers, Brutus rarely altered his routine, and so it was that he stood in the same position each day. Though the café had thrown him slightly off and subsequently, everyone behind him. He was now standing one space ahead of his usual spot.

The City stood still and silent, watching with thousands of tiny eyes as the train burrowed through its webbing. The lull of the train's movements put many to sleep, and even as Brutus stood, he felt as though for a moment here and there, that he had dipped gently into that world of dreams. The train hummed as it slowed to a halt. Brutus' body swung gently against its decreasing speed, and he opened his eyes to see that they had come at last to his stop.

He followed as the train emptied, stepped into a new line, and waited to swipe his pass so he could be on his way. Brutus had no view in line but that of the white-tiled wall opposite of the ticket gate. It was a sort of finish line, and though he'd never physically pass through it, the wall was still a comforting reminder to see, and know he was almost there.

Today though, a small group of Cleaners was restoring the wall. One had their wand crackling and hovering gently above the tile as he lowered it from top to bottom, revealing an even whiter and brighter color as it moved over the unseen blemishes of the tiles below. Another walked along the line where the floor and wall met. He shot out little bursts of flame, burning away the dark black goo that had formed in its crevice.

Upon seeing the newly revealed hue, Brutus felt a sense of gratitude towards the Cleaners, that they had made something he enjoyed that much more beautiful. He took a step forward, at this point envious of those who had passed through the gate. They darted off as quickly as they could while still walking, branching left or right to their own individual exits.

A man with an admirable hat and a smart briefcase had just passed through the gate. He was free of the confines of the line, and just as Brutus was taking another step towards that same enviable achievement, the man in the hat collapsed. Briefcase skidding across the smooth floor, hat flying from his head, he embraced the ground like an old friend.

Brutus' lip twitched as his eyes panned from the man to the ticket gate. A noise drew him back. It was a type of cry that muddled into a grunt. There was someone walking away. Their pace was off, and Brutus saw the man on the ground, hand clutched to his smiling Face. As he did so, a high-heeled shoe came and went, plodding over the man's exposed ankle. Brutus watched for many moments as this process repeated itself.

He searched the station to see if any form of help might be coming. Another person approached, staggered over the fallen man, and scuffed their shoe across his back. It seemed no one had noticed him—no one but Brutus, and the Cleaners.

The crackling wand and bursts of flame had stopped, and the tinted masks that hid their Faces slowly turned and stared. There was a hint of movement from the one who had been guiding the flames, but then the man picked himself up, collected his briefcase and hat, and was on his way seemingly unperturbed. The Cleaners watched the man go, and when he was out of sight, they returned to the tiled wall and to the black seam in the floor.

Brutus exited the station without further incident. The air out on the street was cool as it brushed his neck and turned stale once he reached the canal. Looking down at the placid trickle, he remembered when it was a living river running through the City. Couples with pleasant Faces would sit by the stream to eat their lunch. His own parents had brought him out many times as a child to enjoy the water in the fading afternoons. At some point, the City officials had decided to pave the canal. They had been given extra funding to make the City cleaner. One week there was life amongst the water, and the next, there was nothing but smooth concrete lining a dying river.

Brutus passed over the murky waters, breathing in its decay and thought for a fleeting moment that it was a shame the water was still there at all. From there, he wound through the labyrinth of pavement until he found himself bending the last corner before home. Brutus paused for a moment as he reached the cosmetics shop.

The windows were still lit, open late into the night. Women with tight blouses and welcoming Faces busied themselves with customers. In the softly lit display window lay a dozen golden stands propping up a dozen Faces. Staring outside their glassy prison with firefly eyes, they fixed their lingering gaze on passersby. Each Face was roughly the same as the one next to it, with slight variations in the size and degree of expression. The pale alabaster skin that formed the malleable yet hardened shapes complemented the monoliths of the City that surrounded them.

A large screen with an ever-changing background centered itself above the showcase, and scrolling text in bright letters read: "Custom made to fit your individuality! Find the true beauty within yourself at Dorian's Cosmetics!"

Brutus watched the letters play across in a ribbon several times. He repeated the words softly to himself, staring at his reflection and noting that his mouth formed each individual and distinct letter with ease. Whatever had been the issue would be tomorrow's problem to fix.

The automated voice softly sounded over the street speakers and declared the time. It was late. Brutus tore himself away from his reflection and turned to walk down his street, feet intuitively shuffling the same steps home they had made for years.

Through the lobby, a quiet ascent up the elevator, and Brutus came to a halt outside his apartment. A quick jingle at the recognition of his Face, and the door slid open. His wife turned her head towards him from where she sat, sensing his presence but not really seeing him.

Brutus hung his jacket up neatly in the closet. He shrugged his shoes off his feet before walking over to his wife on the couch. Shelby's Face was set in a relaxed smile, eyes pulsed with bursts of white light. She touched the side of her Face, and the light subsided, leaving only two wet sapphires, too perfect to be real.

"How are you? Had a nice day? Anything interesting on tonight?" The routine questions fell off Brutus' tongue with little thought.

He grunted to his wife's responses before heading to the kitchenette dispenser, where he searched through the menu in anticipation. He hadn't put anything inside his stomach but coffee since lunch. He tapped across the image display until his fingers found a relatively nutritious meal and dialed in his order.

"Your meal will be ready in 10 minutes," said the dispenser in uneven tones.

"You haven't eaten yet? It's late, why didn't you have something earlier?" Shelby's voice rose and fell as her questions disappeared, unanswered. Brutus was too lost in his day to respond, and she didn't care enough to ask again.

He ate his meal in relative silence and took a shower before heading to bed. Shelby followed him just a few minutes later, where she dutifully pressed her body against his until he gave in. Their experience was perfunctory, as they stared at each other through pale blank Faces.

Shelby dived thirstily into her pillow as soon as they were finished while Brutus lay awake. He remembered her again before sleep finally began to settle in, the woman with the Mouse's Face. Standing across the café, with her yellow rose. As he stared, her golden eyes slowly grew larger until they merged into one shining light, and he was then taken over by the powerful insisting of his weary body to sleep.

9 | Captivating

"I must ask the stars for their forgiveness, for I often look upon them without their permission," Cynthia said with her neck craned towards the sky. Her off-color orange dress clung to her body like an unwanted piece of lint, stained with the day's meals, while her purse dangled by the tip of her finger.

What should have been her life was no more important in this moment than the trash dusting the streets. So utterly captivated was Cynthia by what she could only describe as distant cities. A comparison she knew was impossible to truly form. What were they, she wondered, and why did they make her feel as she did? A hand gently crept up to her Face. Its smooth surface reflected nothing of what she felt.

There were wide sockets where her eyes should be and a smile that was carved for all to see. This was her Face, a Face she couldn't ever change. A Face that would never reflect who she was. It was in this moment that Cynthia felt something more than she ever had. The longer she stared, the greater her breaths became, and she desperately wished her carved smile would be nothing more than the slack jaw of awe.

Cynthia eventually pulled herself away from the stars, almost refusing to step into the train. The others there paid little attention to her or the strange behavior that led her to look up as the train pulled away, rather than down as all the others did.

10 | THE PEN

A gentle buzzing filled his mind, muted and harsh. The shrill tones grew into a constant and inescapable summons. He pressed a button behind his ear to answer the call. It was a familiar voice, but not a pleasant one.

"Yes—sure—right away—of course," Brutus replied to a string of demands, none of which he fully heard. Some records of something, to be sent to someone for somewhere, in department this or that. He touched his desk screen to wake it up. Tapping here and swiping there, Brutus went about completing the task he was assigned.

His day at work had begun. His time was spent arranging and filing the various documents he received and then reporting back. Unless, of course, he was the one sending the documents. Then it was his turn to wait to hear back that they had been thusly filed correctly. It was not very thrilling.

Brutus, though, had never met anyone who found their work enjoyable or interesting. Almost everything ran by the press of a button or the flick of a switch. It was a City of glorious things, waiting to be given purpose by people like Brutus. What really was left for a man to do but file, and file well. Taking the human touch out of the equation made things simpler in many ways and was certainly more reliable and efficient.

Brutus found himself staring at his desk screen, his work momentarily forgotten as he lost focus. The image on the screen blurred as he took in the glow of the monitor. The monotone light of the screen reminded him of Shelby's eyes before he had left for work that morning. He had risen on the time and lingered in the steam shower all before his wife had even moved from her sunken-in side of the bed. He was just finishing getting dressed when she stumbled out of the bedroom and into the kitchen to dial their breakfast into the menu. They sat across from each other eating, their mouths biting down on thick slices of silence along with machine-made eggs.

After breakfast, his wife migrated to her favorite spot on the sofa. Her eyes flickered on into beads of light as she absorbed her morning shows. The couch had formed to fit his wife, her favorite cushion a plaster mold of her slowly growing figure. He had wished her a good day but was met with no response, only the stare of those brightly glowing sockets.

He could not push her eyes out of his head, and those illuminated beetles had followed him all day, click-clacking their way around and around inside his skull. They haunted him even now, hours after he had seen them last, though he really wasn't sure why they continued to follow him so. Those white, pulsating eyes, always looking thirstily but not really seeing. They were almost old now, technology from some time ago. Those vibrating lights had taken his wife away from him and trapped her in a world of color and endless distractions.

Brutus realized he was still staring at the screen and found that the light made him tired. He pushed himself away from his station and walked down a long row of cubicles identical to his own. One could appreciate the exact symmetry of the floor, as desks stretched out in rows across the expansive room, all uniform, all the same. Pulsating hubs of light with diligently working Faces stationed behind them.

Brutus wove through the endless rows, past their decorative plant, and into the break room. He nodded to a coworker who sat in the corner, watching the news on the wall while eating his lunch. He had chatted with the man about petty things now and then, and racked his mind to remember his name. Brutus looked just above the middle of the man's eyes to bring up his tag. *William, that's right.*

If he had been forced to guess on his own, he would have been wrong. Shrugging it off, Brutus grabbed a cup and poured himself some coffee. He sat on the opposite side of the room and stared intently at the news. Red ribbons slid across the bottom of the wall, containing snippets of information from around the City. Words strung together in an endless stream of vague statements. Above the ribbons of text, a male news anchor with an announcer's Face read from a script.

"—third time this week. And with the growth of many new apartment complexes in the south end, this may be a good time to think about upgrading your home to a luxury more suited for your lifestyle. Featuring a new state-of-the-art activity room in the larger flats, you'll find yourself never needing to upgrade your vision since your own home can build any dream you desire. This new technology gives—"

Brutus found he didn't really care. The news was more like one big commercial anyway. More concerning was the fact that his coffee was weak. Despite constant complaints throughout the office, the coffee was always too weak. He tossed his cup into the incinerator, defeated.

Instead of returning to his desk, he took a quick detour to the bathroom. He probably could have held it, but he wanted to stall his return to work, even if just for a moment longer. He took his time relieving himself, and as he finished up by washing his hands, he examined his reflection in the mirror.

His Face was pasty white, with skillful lines etched in at just the right curves and angles to convey complete apathy through his constant smile. It was a newer upgrade but generic. Simple was better, and generic was easy to maintain and understand. His skin was hard and smooth. His eyes were black and jellied, his rubber lips soft and pink as they set upon each half of his hinged jaw. The Face fit flush with his hairline, allowing for dark strands to fall carelessly over his forehead. As he leaned in closer to the mirror, he could see a few faint scratches on his cheeks and a small chip on his left eyebrow.

"Everything gets a little worn with age, I suppose," he said to his reflection. His rubber lips made barely a ripple as he spoke. The bathroom door swung open in reply as another occupant entered the room. Brutus tore his gaze away from the mirror and left swiftly.

It was early in the evening as Brutus made his way to the social club. It was an easy journey to make. All he had to do was fall into pace with the crowd around him and finally tell his story about that funny looking egg. Striding along in tempo, Brutus let his mind wander while his feet did the work. The sky was a great slab of gray that blended in with the high-rises scraping their way into the clouds. Brutus felt dizzy as he craned his neck to look upwards, trying to discern again where City ended and the sky began.

He was jostled out of his observation as someone walked into him. He stumbled for a moment, the strap of his case sliding from his shoulder. Perplexed by the irregularity, he looked up just in time to see a flutter of color weaving away, a yellow scarf disappearing into a sea of people. The offender had vanished without a word, leaving Brutus as a stone for the river of bodies to part around.

Brutus turned around to collect his fallen case. He slid it back over his shoulder and was about to fall back in line when something caught his eye. Looking the wrong way down a one-way path, he was struck by a strange building nestled in a corner he had never before noticed. Brutus broke away from the crowd with a few hasty apologies and instead navigated against the current and towards the curiosity.

He stood at the entrance of a small shop, wedged in between the crevice of stone giants. Uneven slats of dark wood covered the bones of the structure, while chipped tiles laid across the building's roof like scales. Two sagging windows were set on either side of the entryway, too dimly lit to expose whatever lay inside. Brutus wondered if the structure wouldn't simply collapse on itself if the buildings on either side of it were to suddenly disappear. Large peeling letters on the aged sign in front of the shop read: "Thomasson's Antiques."

It's a marvel the Cleaners have left this place intact. Brutus clicked his tongue and shook his head in wonder. Common sense told him to turn around and leave the anomaly unhindered, and Brutus would have listened, if not for the crinkled Face of an old woman that now peered at him from behind tattered curtains. Before he could turn and pretend he hadn't noticed, the door to the ancient building groaned open, and a wizened hand jutted out to beckon him inside.

A creaking floorboard met his foot with a sigh as Brutus stepped over the threshold. A throat cleared amidst the clutter, and Brutus met the gaze of a bent old man with the wrinkled Face of an ancient woman. It was as if the building had wheezed the old man out from the cracks in the floor. He was the shop in human form, just as tattered and ancient as the building. The old man stepped towards Brutus, his hands resting easily behind his back.

The thought occurred to Brutus to inform the man of his mistake. An error made in the rush of a morning, an absurd mix-up of Faces, but politeness and courtesy stayed his voice.

"Welcome, welcome," the man murmured from behind his grinning Face. Brutus stood fast in the doorway, itching to retreat.

"Come in, come in. I'm Thomasson, please have a look around." The man insisted while inching closer to Brutus. The top of his balding head just reached Brutus' shoulders. He tilted his Face up with a frozen grin. Nodding at the old man, Brutus took another step forward and entered the shop. It took a moment for his jellied eyes to adjust themselves to the dark and cluttered interior. When they did, he saw that the store itself was slowly digesting odds and ends, covered with layers of age, all piled inside the belly of a dying beast.

"What can I do for you? Looking for anything in particular? I'm sure you'll find it here," Thomasson said kindly.

Brutus hesitated. He was not afraid, but unsure. Unsure of how so many absurdities could exist in one single space in time, sewed concurrently into a pattern he didn't understand. There was a betrayal of purpose within these events which he could not quite grasp. He put it aside, but not so far as to let it entirely out of his mind.

Looking around, he saw things made of brass and wood, things with metal innards leaking out onto the shelves. Things carved and drawn by hand and covered in imperfection. Wooden boards with little figures dotting colored squares. Metal shapes for making noise, devices used for keeping time, and tools for unknown purpose. None of these things were uniform. None of these things were new, hardly any of them looked useful, and all of which he was very much unaccustomed to.

Brutus took a few polite and careful steps through the aisles, feeling the presence of the old man behind him. Growths of what must be antiques festered in every visible space. The shelves he traversed were sinking from the weight of the baubles and trinkets they held. Even in the dimly lit shop, Brutus could see dust kissing almost every surface. His head began to feel clouded, and the sense of drowning lapped at the corners of his mind.

After what he felt was an obligatory circuit, Brutus stepped away from the man to take his leave, when the shining glint of cool metal caught his eye. Instead of walking out the door as intended, he walked right past it, drawn towards the mysterious object.

"What is this?" Brutus heard himself ask.

"Why, a pen of course," Thomasson explained patiently.

The cold metal was smooth in Brutus' hand, and he held it there for a long while. He slid his finger down the side of the slender body and dotted it with his fingertips. He could see his small, stretched reflection in the metal, his pale Face, white and smooth as marble. Inexplicably drawn to the object, Brutus took a chance.

"I think I'd like this." Brutus looked up, pen balanced in his fingers.

"Oh yes, that's a great choice," Thomasson said, nodding his approval.

Well-worn hands unlocked themselves from their resting place behind the old man's back and put themselves to work in practiced efficiency. The transaction was completed, and Brutus' shiny new pen was stowed safely into a small plastic bag.

"Thank you so much for stopping in," Thomasson said behind the old woman's smile. "Enjoy your purchase, and come back again."

Brutus tumbled out a hasty goodbye and left the shop feeling on edge like he had just committed a crime, though what it was he could not list or state, just that something felt very wrong about what he'd done. Tucking the little bag containing his purchase securely into his coat pocket, he felt the sudden urge to get off the streets and into the four solid walls of his apartment as quickly as possible.

Still confused from his unusual interaction, Brutus eyed the crowd and waited for a moment when he could slip back into the flow of traffic. Just as an opening appeared and Brutus was about to take a step forward, a white suit emerged, nearly colliding with him.

"Excuse me," Brutus said, mumbling out his apology, embarrassed to have almost caused an inconvenience.

"That's quite alright," the man said as they parted ways.

Now, even more eager to leave this hidden corner of the City, Brutus shuffled back into line. He gently patted the pen in the pocket of his coat, ensuring that it was still there and that the experience had not just been some odd delusion. The entire encounter, so utterly foreign and bizarre, felt unreal to Brutus. Against his better judgement, but brought on by a need to confirm with his eyes what his mind so easily remembered, Brutus chanced a parting glance at the little antique shop in the corner.

It was still there, just as the pen was still in his pocket. Even the man he'd nearly collided with was real. Hands in his pockets, he strolled gently up to the storefront and disappeared inside to what Brutus could barely make out as the beckoning Face of the strange old man. Brutus took note of the long white hair the man in the suite sported, tied back neatly at the base of his neck. In addition to his strange hair, Brutus was struck by the man's pristine white suit, all of which blended into his pale and disimpassioned Face.

It was an unusual look, and Brutus decided that must be the type of people who were drawn to that old shop. A thought, which of course, immediately left Brutus feeling even more uncomfortable, and he found himself glancing over his shoulder the whole way home. Unsure of what he was looking for, only aware of the need to do so. Drinks, coworkers, and obligations completely forgotten.

The strangeness of the unexpected events that had taken place that evening faded quickly once Brutus found himself back on familiar ground. The streets pulsed once more with bright lights, box shop windows, and crowded sidewalks. Brutus welcomed the distraction of the advertisements splashing color around him as he stepped in line with the stream of foot traffic.

As he found his way back to the tired canal, Brutus felt the urge to erase his foolishness. It had to be a violation to own something so old and from such a terribly dusty shop. How easy it would be to hold the little plastic bag over the cloudy waters and just let it fall. How easy to just return home and forget where he had been. Though, after all, it was just a pen, just a trinket. *What harm could it do?* Brutus' hand fell from his coat pocket where his purchase lay untouched. He turned from the canal and continued home.

Following the predictable path, Brutus finally stepped through the front door of his apartment building. With the aid of the humming elevator, he ascended to his floor with ease, and with one final quick glance, shut himself behind the safety of his home.

Though the comfort he had hoped to find inside dwindled. His wife sat in her predictable perch and gave him a little wave of greeting before plunging back into the world behind her eyes. At that moment, Brutus felt utterly alone, and his thoughts ate away greedily at the silence. Too tired to fight it, he plopped down on the couch next to his wife and gave in to ruminating.

In the City everything was new, clean, and purposeful. If something aged or broke, people just put it in the incinerator and ordered a new one. Sometimes, people even pretended something was broken, so they could justify getting something new.

Why would anyone keep such clutter, and why would they wind through the City to purchase something from that beast in the corner, instead of just getting something new from home? Brutus looked around the room and saw nothing that reminded him of the odd items he had seen in Thomasson's shop.

He couldn't make sense of it, but what now troubled him more was the fact that he had bought something from that little shop. He shivered slightly as the thought occurred to him. He could barely fathom what reason the shop had to exist, yet he had purchased an item there, so what did that say about him?

Brutus tried to find the reason why he had found the pen so interesting. *Perhaps it was just a rash decision,* he thought to himself. *I don't know what to do with this thing. I doubt I'll ever really use it.*

Curiosity eroded his thoughts. Throwing out an excuse to get to bed early, Brutus locked himself in the bedroom. Carefully pulling the plastic bag out of his pocket, he dumped the pen onto the bed, almost afraid to touch it. He let it lie there for a moment while he disposed of the evidence, tossing the plastic bag into the bathroom incinerator. He sat on the bed and slowly picked up the silver pen with a shaking hand. He examined it again and pressed down on one end. His curiosity was rewarded with a satisfying *click* as the nib jutted out of the tip.

Click, click, click—

Knock!

"Why is the door locked? I'm coming to bed."

"Sorry!" Brutus jumped at the noise, hastily shoving the pen into the pocket of his coat as he ran to unlock the door before Shelby could knock a second time.

"Didn't realize it locked," he offered up an excuse. Shelby shrugged and went to the bathroom to perform her pre-bedtime rituals. Brutus sat back for a moment and watched as she brushed her hair, reset her Face, and used the bathroom.

There was love there once, but not anymore. Once, maybe, they were happy, though even that he couldn't quite recall. Perhaps they never had been good, but at least the appearance of a normal marriage had hung on the wall. He had long known the truth that lay about him, but hardly had the courage to put words to it. He didn't know the woman with him in the room now. It was only the dangerously strong pattern of routine that kept the two strangers living together.

Brutus' mind continued to race long after the lights had been told to dim. Blurring thoughts danced through his mind as he tried not to think, but to drift away into the darkness of sound slumber. When sleep did eventually take him, it was troubled with twisted Faces peering out of sagging windows and the glimmer of a yellow scarf dancing just out of reach.

11 | BRUTUS GOES BACK TO WORK

"Damn," Brutus said, withdrawing the cup from his mouth. He could feel the hot liquid pooling under his lips. Setting down the cup, Brutus took up his napkin and turned towards the café window. He flexed his jaw to detach the lower seal and lifted his Face up gently to wipe the spilled coffee from his lips.

A Face sealed tight around every contour, except for the lips. There was a small gap where his real lips and the Face's didn't meet, which meant every so often, on occasion when things didn't sync, you could spill just a little bit of something on the inside. Brutus was sure there was a name for that little gap, but at this moment, he simply called it a pain. He dabbed the last bit of coffee away and gently re-sealed his Face, careful to ensure that no one saw.

He really was going to have to stop by Dorian's. This was the second time his mouth had failed to sync. It was just around the corner from his home, but something about that place, even proximity didn't quite excuse. Though they called themselves professionals, it seemed they never had a professional answer to give. It was likely they wouldn't fix, but rather try and replace. He couldn't remember a time when he'd stopped by, even for just a general servicing, and they hadn't tried to up-sell him. As well, if he had to get a replacement, then Shelby would want one too. It probably wasn't even broken but would fix itself in time.

Brutus sighed and stared out the window. Across the street was the spot where he'd stood just days past. What an ordinary and common spot it was, nothing but buildings and shops lined up one after the other. Seemingly solid structure all the way across, blending together at the seams as if they were just pieces of a larger building. He was glad that he had stopped there, at that time, to be able to see this quiet little place where he now sat.

There were a few pedestrians, passersby on their way to work. Their comings and goings reminded him of the Mouse. She had stood just across the street with her yellow rose, and Brutus noticed her absence now as he looked up and down the road from the safety of his booth, unable to spot her. He supposed it made sense though, he had seen her in the evening, and now he was patiently waiting for his eggs at breakfast. Her golden eyes filled his memory, and her strange mask reminded him of Thomasson's. Perhaps she had stopped there as he had and found something quaint to take home.

A dish clattered in front of him, and he looked down to see a plate of eggs staring back. The waitress that had brought them stood at the end of the table. Her apron, a reflection of her surroundings, was spotted with grime and age. Remembering that the last bit of his drink had drained into his Face, he ordered one more thing before she left.

"Coffee."

"What's that? Oh, twenty-two please." Brutus had made it all the way to the office and into the elevator without even really noticing. His mind was preoccupied with rummaging through what he could remember of the past few days, while his fingers traced the cold metal of the pen in his pocket. The woman who had asked him a question shuffled forward to press the appropriate button.

She was one of the regulars that trundled into the elevator with him every day on his way to work. Today though, he observed that she appeared to have squeezed into a dress that was a few sizes too small. *That must be why the elevator feels so cramped today,* he thought. Her Face was tightly formed into a doll-like beauty and set into the usual smile, but on closer inspection, Brutus noticed parts of her chin and neck were leaking from the sides of it.

The elevator stopped at almost every floor, and each time new passengers departed and entered, the woman had to rearrange her bulk to accommodate them. This subsequently was an inconvenience for Brutus, who was forced to move to accommodate her. She reminded him a bit of a sausage he had eaten once that had come with a slice of his morning toast. Thankfully she waddled off at the eighteenth floor for the filing department and left him in peace for the short remainder of his ride.

The workday began with the monthly meeting. Everyone sat at their stations, eyes flickering vibrant green as they all waited for the boss to start. Brutus engaged in the required pleasantries with his neighbors but avoided initiating conversation if he could help it. A beeping sounded in Brutus' ear, and he joined the meeting. He watched as his coworkers' tags slowly faded into line on the peripheries before Shaun crept into view.

Shaun droned on about improvements to be made by the staff, while praising the company's management team. He asked for everyone to come up with some ideas about how to improve work ethic and efficiency. He raised morale by announcing top employee promotions, and then reminded everyone to work harder. Shaun even threw in a windy anecdote about a restaurant he visited with a friend before wrapping up the meeting with words of empty encouragement and a rather heated discussion about what style of shirt could be ordered with the company logo on it. Six minutes passed its scheduled conclusion, the meeting finally ended.

Brutus disengaged and turned back to his work, his jellied eyes pulsating shades of blue in tandem with rows of coworkers on either side. He absentmindedly tapped at his desk screen, trying and failing to work. He thought of the café. Its chipped coffee cups, its stains, and its view.

I could do it again, he thought to himself as he fiddled with the pen in his pocket. *There's no harm in stopping for another quick cup of coffee after work. I might even see her. There's no harm in just looking out a window.*

He ended up convincing himself that he was merely curious. There was nothing wrong with visiting the café on his way home. His coworkers hadn't seemed to miss him. He could stop by for a bit, and if nothing interesting presented itself outside his window, well, that would be it. He would grab his train home, continue with his nightly routine, get some dinner, watch a show, bother his wife, and he would be safe at home in his whitewashed walls, far away from the café.

He would go tonight after work and put his mind at ease. With the decision made, time suddenly danced to a near stop, slowly reaching the peak of the hour before dragging on to the next.

Brutus' anticipation spread like a sickness as he stared into the neon glow of his desk screen. The colors blended and swirled together, forming streets that turned at odd angles and buildings that jutted from the ground like crooked teeth. Brutus found himself standing in those twisted streets, in a blur of light and slabs of stone. He felt the café behind him, knowing it was there even when it wasn't. The Mouse stood across the street, dressed in a light yellow sundress. Brutus stepped forward and followed her into dark spaces.

Through twists and turns and dimly lit halls, he stumbled and ran but was always just out of reach. Her dress twisted around her moving body and grasped at the air with the rustle of freshly fallen leaves. He ran for hours that were only seconds. Then she stopped in the middle of nothing and turned to face him. A jarring brush of white against the dark. She made no noise, but he knew she was laughing at him. He stared into those deep golden eyes and knew she was laughing.

Brutus was pulled from his trance as the desk screen chirped. Its farewell song signaled the time for him to leave. He obeyed without question while his station shut itself down automatically.

As the elevator hummed its way down to the ground floor, Brutus stood in the corner contemplating where his mind had been wandering all day. He supposed that if he did chance to pass the Mouse on the way to the café, and if she were to drop something at his feet, he would have to be polite and pick it back up.

From the office, Brutus took his usual evening route home. The City was alive with people leaving work, and Brutus found himself strolling at a pace that was unusual to him but one he found quite enjoyable. This new pace of course, meant new Faces and, therefore, new sights. He had no idea where they'd come from or where they worked. They were similar enough to his usual crowd, but differed in noticeable ways now that he was paying attention.

Eventually the crowd thinned, peeling away into the various establishments of the City. They would be there for several hours before finally going home, leaving Brutus a relatively empty street to travel on. He passed his usual evening haunt, a quick glance revealing his coworkers already seated inside, drinking and exchanging their usual round of stories. They had left no empty seat for Brutus, and he found he was not upset by his own absence.

Moving past his commitments, the café came into view along the empty street. The Mouse wasn't there, *but oh well. I can still enjoy a cup of coffee, and if she shows up, well…*Brutus crossed the street to head into the café. Along with his coffee, maybe he'd see about grabbing some food. That way, at least Shelby wouldn't question him when he got home.

The door resisted his push, and it was on his third attempt to force it open that he saw a notice stuck onto the glass. It was printed officially and stated, "Closed indefinitely due to irregularity."

Brutus read the sign several times and pressed his nose to the glass, trying to peer past the darkness. He could see nothing of what he'd hoped to experience, simply an impenetrable blackness. Brutus felt a dull pang of disappointment mixed with the stab of loss. He had only just come to know the place, and now it seemed that it was gone forever. Brutus lingered as long as he could, his shallow breath slowly creeping up the darkened glass. It had been a nice reprieve from the routine, a pleasant fiction to linger in during his workday, and now the Cleaners had come and taken it away from him.

Brutus sighed. Pushing himself away from the window, he turned to leave the pleasant memory behind. Colored lights met his eyes, providing them a maze to wander through. He traced the outline of the giants in the sky. Sliding down their smooth exterior, he suddenly found himself frozen. She was there, standing across the street, with her golden eyes boring into him.

Brutus crossed the street as if in a trance. As he approached, her arms dropped to her sides, and out of her porcelain hands, a yellow rose softly fell to the ground. Brutus watched as its petals met the pavement and, without thought, bent to pick it up. He returned the rose to its owner, pressed into those soft hands, and took a step back. The Mouse moved her head, and from behind her strange Face, the sweetest young voice sounded out against the darkening night.

"Interested?" she asked him.

"In…?"

"What do you think?"

"I don't know," Brutus faltered in thought. "I'm sorry, I really don't kno—"

A sharp buzz filled the air, like a mosquito infinitely beating its tiny wings. It was Shelby; of course she was calling him now. The Mouse stared at him, her eyes unknowable.

One step then two, backing up slowly then turning, Brutus gave his back to her and briskly walked away. The persistent buzzing still in his ear, he tried to control his gate as he left the woman and the now-closed café.

The train ride home was a blur of electric blue. The buzzing of Shelby's call had long been replaced by the pounding in his ears. He marched swiftly towards his apartment, feet guided by the rampant beat of his own heart. He slid his hand around the barrel of his pen to click away the sickening feeling that danced between his stomach and his throat.

Click, click, click.

He passed over the canal without even noticing. He tromped past Dorian's Cosmetics without a second thought for his Face, striding in pace to the pen's muffled demands.

Click, click, click.

Finally, Brutus found himself once more outside the door to his apartment, but he hesitated before going in. He didn't know what he had expected from his failed visit to the café, but he felt a small tinge of guilt. His marriage may have burnt out long ago, but Brutus still felt obligated to be honest with Shelby. Opening the door perhaps more forcefully than intended, Brutus stepped into the box that was dubbed home and was greeted by two pulsating white eyes.

Brutus realized by his wife's usual silence that this small deviation in his life had gone unnoticed. He hung up his coat, keyed in some dinner, and settled down on the couch. Only after he had managed to choke down a few bites did the blazing-eyed monster turn towards him and mumble behind frozen lips, "I called you a little while ago. You were supposed to pick up my order this afternoon, did you remember?"

"Oh, I'm sorry. I got tied up at work, completely forgot." Brutus tensed, waiting to be chided. "Sorry," he added again to her silence.

His wife merely shrugged and was then still. Brutus realized that behind her vibrating eyes, he could not even tell if the woman was alive. She could be dead for days, sitting in that same spot behind those white screens, and he wouldn't even notice. The creature next to him let out a small sneeze, proving that she was still very much alive indeed.

12 | Coffee

"Coffee."

"Toast."

"Eggs."

Cynthia filled the orders as they came but couldn't shake the feeling from the other night. Her status in the world had never lent itself to the feeling of emotions. While others might hide it well, Cynthia had never had to try. For her life had been the café. For her, life had been:

"Coffee."

"Toast."

"Eggs."

As she placed plates in front of void-faced masks, she wondered how this could be considered living. How could she have been content with approaching life as she had, watching the news and her shows?

"Coffee," spoke the man in a white shirt. His Face was plainer than hers, and the only thing partially interesting about him was his slightly looser than acceptable tie.

Interesting. She had never cared before if anyone was interesting. She had never really cared about anything at all. Cynthia wondered why she looked and why she didn't just fill the order. It took her a moment to notice, but the man she was staring at, was staring back. Through the black pits that were the eyes of this man's mask, Cynthia felt that she could see his real eyes clearly. Studying her as she studied him, rather than the soulless stare that they all shared. She felt the searching they did up and down her body. For Cynthia, looking at him was as magical as the night she'd spent staring at the stars. This man was as vibrant as those distant lights, and like those lights, she didn't want to leave him behind. Then in an instant, he looked away from her and down at his cup.

"Too much," was all he said, and she looked down at his table. The man's cup had overflowed. The coffee, which she had so meticulously and precisely doled out over the years, now ran freely from its pot, into his cup, over its lip, and onto the table.

Cynthia didn't know what to do, so she turned around and walked into the kitchen. Deep breaths filled her lungs as the uncertainty of her actions raced through her mind. The pot was still in her hand, the dregs of her failure slowly dripping onto the floor. Her lifeless smile betrayed the terror Cynthia felt but hid her behavior from the cooks who looked on, waiting for her to deliver an order.

"Eggs," she said.

It was a lie…the word echoed in her head. *Eggs,* it was her calming mantra, *eggs,* she'd made an order that no one had requested, *eggs,* she didn't even like them, *eggs,* the man with the coffee!

Cynthia grabbed a rag and walked briskly to the front of the café. The man was gone and with him his searching eyes, but he'd left her the coffee and his payment. Cynthia bent over the table, rubbing the almost dried spill around. Stains streaked across the flaking green surface, and as she leaned over to reach, her dress slid gently up her leg. Turning to correct the shifting fabric, Cynthia noticed her reflection in the chrome of the stool and noticed the curve of her body. It gave her a moment of pause. Had she always looked this way? Was that what he had noticed? She glanced at the other customers to see if she had drawn anyone's attention, but all they ever wanted was:

"Coffee."

"Toast."

"Eggs."

Her legs were wet now as Cynthia moved back from the table. They had sopped up a spot that her rag had missed. Cynthia smiled behind her mask and moved back to the kitchen. She tossed the rag onto the counter, ignoring the stare of the cooks as they waited for another order, and instead walked to the back of the café. There, in the semi-lit rear of the building, the door to the alley lay unused, except on the occasion to deposit the day's trash. Its color was faded, its hinges battered, a neglected and forgotten thing. But it was so much more than that, just as Cynthia was so much more than a Face.

Grabbing her mask, she peeled it off and turned it around. Its fake smile worked its fake charm on her, convincing her that it reflected a sense of what people thought was friendly. It reflected what people didn't realize, was a slave.

Letting it drop from her hand, Cynthia pushed open the door. She kept her eyes closed. She wanted to see this new world, she wanted to live her new life. As the air hit her face, Cynthia breathed deep. It didn't matter that the air carried the rancid rotting whiff of trash. It didn't matter that the sun on her face stung. What mattered was that she was free. Cynthia opened her eyes, ready to greet her new world, ready to see life!

The Cleaner was the first and the last thing she saw as she burned as bright as the stars.

13 | THE CLUB

Work flew by Brutus as if he was in a blur. Pale Faces spoke at him in an unintelligible language. His hands pushing this button, punching that screen, and filing, filing, filing documents away without a detailed thought in his mind. It was as if he inhabited two separate worlds at once, his physical body performing his daily routine in an almost automated manner while his mind raced with possibilities.

As Brutus tried to focus on his work, it became harder to push the woman with the rose and the café out of his mind. What was usually the dull drone of his thoughts providing background commentary to the events around him, was today alive with images; images of the Mouse, and not just her Face but everything underneath her mask and clothes as well. Then there was the café.

He wanted to be there now, smelling old coffee and scratching at stains on the countertop, not endlessly tapping his desk screen. He wanted to look out the window and watch the people passing in the night. What a shame it was gone forever.

The blackness of that lost view filled his mind until the electric bells were ringing, signaling the end of the workday, and calling him back from the depth of his thoughts. Brutus found he could not recall a single task he had performed, but he didn't care. He was going back to her, tonight.

To ensure his plans would not go astray, he reached up to the dial behind his left ear and muted his calls. There would be no notifications and no distractions. Turning the silence on brought a shiver down Brutus' spine and evoked feelings he didn't understand. The gentle jostling of the crowd on either side slowly rocked him back into a state of comfort, ease, and familiarity.

When his destination came into view, Brutus peeled off from the other commuters, feet tracing familiar steps. He felt the need to recreate what had been so perfect, and so wasted the night before. He crossed the street early, each step taking him both farther away and yet closer to his desire. Seeing her from across the street, he would walk to her, entranced by those golden eyes, giving her time once again to drop the rose she would surely carry. This time, he would bend down to pick it up, and there would be no call to stop him from what came next. He kept his head down as he walked. He didn't want to see her a moment before he was ready, a moment before it was perfect.

While the crowd slipped away into its nightly haunts, Brutus followed his feet, step after step, line after line in the path until finally, he was standing with his back to the dark shell of his once-beloved café. His lips twitched behind his Face as he lifted his head, and then his heart stopped. She wasn't there.

Streetlights flickered on in tandem as the sun set, and the City was cast into a dusky glow. Brutus felt himself retreating into his old self as disappointment crept in and choked all other senses. *I should have known better. It's not like I would have had the courage to go through with it anyway. What a complete waste of a day,* he thought to himself as he shuffled across the street over to the spot where she had dropped her yellow rose just days ago. Fingers slid over the metal pen in his pocket as he tried to find some comfort to hold on to.

Brutus examined the slab of sidewalk where the Mouse had stood, perhaps in some way trying to find the outline of the footprints that she might have somehow left behind. Nothing but smooth pavement, polished to a hygienic finish. Following some odd instinctual urge, Brutus turned around to face the café and did his best to imitate the Mouse he had seen from across the window. Shifting to the left, and then a little bit more to the right, Brutus felt that he found the spot in which she had actually stood, and tried to derive some type of comfort from it.

He had suffered the loss of two new things and felt cheated from what could have been. Pleasant memories that never were, painfully relinquished as he stared across the empty street into the black void of the café's window. For a moment in his mind, he thought he could see himself there in that booth, sitting with the Mouse, enjoying a simple cup of coffee in a heavily chipped mug.

Heaving out a heavy sigh, the warm breath of his body chilled into a light vapor and dissipated into the night air, carrying away those happy thoughts. It was time he got home, he had lingered long enough. No amount of time would give him what he wanted. Turning to leave, a great and vast emptiness jumped out at Brutus, and for a moment, he lost his footing and felt as though he was falling.

Brutus, like all people, had found a sense of security in knowing that something permanent and substantial was behind him, or around him for that matter. It was for this reason that Brutus found it so startling when he turned to leave and realized that rather than having his back to a grand building—which he was sure had run the length of the street—there was now a rather long and obvious alley.

Brutus' Face showed nothing of the confusion that hid beneath it but simply smiled for him into that empty place. Taking a step back, Brutus looked down each end of the walkway and saw that it was, as he expected, a continuation of building after building. Except for this, this alley in front of him.

It was half as wide as the café and seemed to run a significant length back. With the illumination of the streetlights, it seemed a rather obvious gap now that Brutus was aware of it. He battled with confusion as he tried to reconcile the scene with what he remembered. He was sure it had not been there the first time he had gone to the café, and possibly not the second. It must have been new, as of this day, but still, there were questions and gaps that left Brutus feeling uncomfortable.

As Brutus took an exploratory step forward into the alley, his shoe struck something solid. Looking down, he found a lip of stone that stretched from one building to the next, across the entryway of the alley. It was a perplexing piece of uselessness, and it captured Brutus' attention.

That mild aberrant barrier drew Brutus in, and compelled him to go further. Its long, simple shape rose no higher than Brutus' shin and was an easy thing to cross. Though as he lifted his foot, there was an odd sense of foreboding about stepping on the thing, and so, carefully, he made sure that each foot went up and over, and made no contact with it.

There was no light here, and all he could see was owed to the glow of the street that had managed to bend its illumination into the gap. While the alley was dark and unknown, Brutus found a similar sense of welcome that he had derived from the café. Unhurriedly he strolled down the impossible alleyway, running his hand gently against the wall that encased it. The texture of the siding intrigued him as it turned from smooth to rough under his palm. He took a moment to step back and examine the wall of the alley.

The shadow of symmetrical patterns that could only have been derived from structure lined the wall. Tracing the outline with his eyes, his fingers motioned in the air beside them. Brutus found that these lines met to create the imprint of something distinctly edificial. He turned to perform the same observations on the opposite wall, finding that the same series echoed across to the other side. Now he was sure of it, there had been a building here. The question was, though, *when had it left?*

It was as if the bones of the building had been projected onto the wall, a silhouette of a thing no longer there to cast a shadow. A thought crossed Brutus' mind, and after mulling it over for a brief moment, he extended his hand and turned the knob of a door that was no longer there. Brutus then filled his time entering and exiting rooms, imagining what was there and what purpose it had served. He navigated his way through the winding maze he had created until he had explored every last room, and decided to leave out the back door.

Locking it firmly behind him, Brutus left his imagination and suddenly found himself again in the dark alley. Realizing that while the pastime had been amusing, he probably should be returning home. The thought to unlock the imaginary door and pass through the building once more to reach the street had crossed his mind, but his practical nature returned to overrule the idea. He had just extended his foot to begin the process of returning home when a faint thumping sound brushed the corners of his mind.

Stopping in place, Brutus did his best to focus on the noise. It was an odd instinct that froze him in place, like prey hearing the subtle sounds of a predator, knowing with all possibility that at any moment, something could be coming for them. Craning his neck, Brutus pivoted his head, leaning and turning until the noise became louder.

Deeper into the alley, a faint light glowed, and from it, the gentle thumping drifted through the air and into Brutus' ears. Like the building that should have been behind him, the light ahead, he was sure, hadn't been there before.

The first thought that crossed his mind was, *when had it arrived,* before an entirely more concerning thought approached, *why?*

Frozen, Brutus watched, wary of the danger the light could possibly bring. Even his breathing slowed as his ears strained to listen. Minutes passed, and the light and sound neither approached nor strayed but stayed fixed in place in the darkness of the alley.

Brutus' body relaxed as nothing happened, and he felt rather silly for having been concerned. Whatever it was, it was no harm to him. Without the threat of danger, curiosity crept its way in. Brutus' feet started moving before he did, and through the darkness of the alley, Brutus moved towards that perverse star. With every step, the thumping grew louder, and the dot of light grew brighter, and in what seemed like no time at all, Brutus found himself facing a rather large cat.

Its ears and whiskers were outlined in bright neon lights, but the black painted cat underneath was still visible. The sign was surprisingly large and not at all what he imagined he'd find here in the darkness of the alley.

An advertisement perhaps, but for what though? The thought brought Brutus closer. Beneath this sign was a simple, uninviting door with no windows and modest printed lettering secured above the entryway that read: "Anhedonia".

The muted thumping was a rhythmic beat, still muffled, though, from what Brutus could tell, by the confines of the place called Anhedonia. It was stronger now, and he found he could almost physically feel what could only be music coming from inside.

A familiar hand gripped the handle to the door and gave way to its insistence, while familiar feet guided Brutus in. Deep throbbing music met his ears and vibrated his very core, weaving around Brutus to create the illusion that he had stepped into the dark beating heart of the City itself.

He descended poorly lit stairs until he entered into a great atrium of colored lights, pounding music, and people. It was crowded with a sea of alabaster Faces and glowing eyes of blue, green, and red, pulsating in rhythm to beating sound. Brutus' attention was stolen by the mass of bodies gathered, swaying and bobbing as they moved to the music.

They were unlike any of the people he passed on his daily commute. Instead of pressed suits in dark tones, they wore exposed collarbones, ankles, and thighs, seemingly dressed more in their own skins than any clothing he was accustomed to. Others gathered along the outskirts in small booths and dark corners, drinking heavily and laughing loudly. A brightly lit bar across the way beckoned a steady stream of thirsty patrons.

Seeing people interacting with each other and ordering drinks, he reasoned that he must have wandered his way into some sort of social club, though it was a bizarre version of the clubs he was used to. The music never seemed to end but simply twisted itself from one pounding beat to the next, and Brutus found he couldn't hear his mind well enough to find his thoughts.

A series of half-formed ideas bubbled and popped as they surfaced between fleeting moments of changing beats. *Maybe it's…I wonder…Must be a…* Through the incessant interruptions, he noticed a woman swaying gently at the edge of the crowd, a little apart from the rest. *I'll just ask her what this place is,* he thought, and as Brutus approached with his hand extended in greeting, the woman's eyes met his.

"Excuse me, I'm—" but before he could form his question, the woman's hand closed around his and pulled. It was a mistake to have ever come off the stairs, Brutus realized, as he was swept into the churn of dancing bodies.

He gasped as hot flesh pressed against him. The smell of perspiration and warm musk permeated the filter at his nostrils. Fingers grazed his body, and Brutus struggled to understand what was happening as the crowd pressed in harder around him. He was lost and suddenly found it impossible to breathe. He craned his neck above the crowd for air, but lights strobed his vision, and he closed his eyes in pain. Losing his footing, he felt for a moment that he floated, carried away in the current. A type of panic infected Brutus, and he found his heart racing as he struggled through the throng of bodies.

Finally, he pulled himself up to the bar exhausted, as if he had just swum against the current of a great river and almost drowned getting to the other side. He sat down hard on the padded stool, watching the purple glow of the neon-lit bar as it reflected in shining surfaces while he caught his breath.

The beating of his heart matched pace with the music pumping wildly in his ears. He flinched as phantom fingers brushed against his body and turned to see no one close enough to touch him. Brutus shifted in his seat so he could see the crowd, haunted by the feeling that they might drag him from his stool and back into the undertow of Faces.

The need for a drink to calm his nerves struck Brutus, and he motioned meekly at the server, but no sign of recognition or acknowledgment flickered behind the electrifying violet eyes. Brutus sighed and resigned himself to waiting his turn. He was not eager to fight his way out of the nightmare he had wandered into and was resolved that he might be stuck on his little rock at sea for some time.

Shrugging his jacket off his shoulders, movement caught his eye. Beyond the convulsing crowd, a stage jutted out from the darkness. Figures stood on the raised platform, with very little covering their bodies. They moved to the synthesized melody in a very different way than the crowd. Gyrating their hips, bobbing their heads, moving their hands across their exposed skin and over each other, all with Faces of frozen ecstasy and glowing yellow eyes. He had seen his wife nude hundreds of times before, but he had never seen anything quite like this. Brutus watched the dancers in fascination and found himself lost in the movement of their bodies and the sweat beading on their skin, changing hues of neon blue, green, and pink as the lighting faded in and out.

"Corporeal the form of desire is," a voice sounded softly in his ear.

A startled Brutus almost toppled off his stool as he wrenched his head away from the dancers. The owner of that softly assailing voice was seated next to him, wearing a well-fitted white suit that caught the changing hues of light refracting throughout the club. His thin-fingered hand tucked a strand of long white hair back into place before nonchalantly scratching his chin. It took Brutus too long to comprehend what he was looking at before it dawned on him that the man was wearing only half of a Face, with the raw flesh of his cheeks, lips, and chin fully exposed.

A chill pinched the back of Brutus' knees and ran down his legs, as if he had just seen something terrifying and disgusting. The fleshy lips moved again, fluid and full. Brutus could feel hot breath on his neck and could smell a faint trickle of whiskey, and seeing its source turned the experience from benign to nauseating. Swallowing the revulsion building in him, he was grateful that this stranger was not afforded any glimpse of what lay behind Brutus' own Face.

"Uh, I'm sorry, what was that?" Brutus asked. There was a twitch that formed into the hint of a smile, and moved again. Brutus couldn't help but stare in wonder at the complexity of motion in the exposed lips.

"They are mesmerizing, aren't they, Brutus, my dancers?" He leaned closer now so Brutus could hear him. His hand lightly brushing Brutus' shoulder before trailing back to his glass. In one swift and hideous movement, the man brought the glass to his mouth, formed his lips around the rim, and drained the liquid. Brutus shuddered at the soft, smacking sound. Finding the need to look at something else, Brutus focused on finding the man's tag, but was puzzled when only emptiness stared back.

"Yes, they're…nice," Brutus responded lamely. He flicked his eyes around the room, hoping to find a closer exit to plan his escape.

"A man could get lost in here if he's not careful. I try not to let that happen. Too much of a good thing spoils the pleasure," the mouth spoke at him and broke into a wide smile. Brutus stood up at the sight of the neat rows of teeth shining emerald in the fluorescent light.

"Yes, you're quite right. And I'm afraid I better get going now anyway," Brutus mumbled awkwardly as he tugged at his jacket.

The stranger watched with an expression of mild amusement while Brutus fumbled around with his coat, which had become snared on some unseen snag. With an audible rip, the jacket came free, and Brutus hastened to don it before turning to leave somewhat rudely. He froze when he felt a light touch on the crook of his arm, and a soft voice whispered once more in his ear.

"If you found some enjoyment in my club, then might I recommend you give this a try, next time you are feeling adventurous." The stranger pushed a folded slip of paper into the palm of Brutus' hand. Smiling, he turned and disappeared into the crowd.

Brutus slammed the door behind him and ran down the dark alleyway. He swallowed his heart back into his chest and bent over to breathe in the City around him. It was dark outside, late into the cycle of night, and well past due when Brutus should be getting home. Without a glance back down that dark alley, where the perverse star and silhouettes of missing things lay, Brutus picked himself up and walked briskly home.

Only after preparing himself for bed and settling in for the night did Brutus remember the folded slip of paper in his now slightly ripped jacket. Double checking that his snoring wife was fast asleep, Brutus unfolded the note delicately. It read in lilting, hand-scrawled letters:

4726 Chadwick Lane. Ask for Groves. Lucian sent you.

Brutus tucked the note back into his jacket pocket, rolled over, and fell almost immediately into an exhausted sleep.

14 | IRREALITY

The chance adventure of last night had taken a lot out of Brutus but had filled the void that had been growing since the absence of the café. He spent the rest of the week sticking to his routine and trying to get back on track, though he hadn't found it in himself to rejoin his coworkers for their nightly socials. Somehow knowing the experience could be nothing like the club diminished any desire to meet with them.

It was that strange experience at the club in the alleyway that played across his thoughts while his hands performed their work. He kept the folded note he'd received tight in his pocket, next to the pen. It was a simple pleasure to have evidence of his secret expedition, and for the time being, that was enough. He felt a slight flutter of dimmed excitement every time his hand grazed his pocket or brushed over the note. He had completely memorized every word, and it gave him satisfaction to know that at any moment he wanted, he could act on those instructions and perhaps, discover something new.

He also found himself fixated on the stranger he now knew as Lucian. Brutus was unsure if he should be afraid of the man or flat-out disgusted by him. He kept hearing that smacking sound in his head and was having trouble getting over the softness of his lips. Brutus felt himself questioning whether he hadn't just been in the company of a madman or some escaped lunatic. *After all, normal people don't just go around exposing themselves in public like that,* Brutus thought while clicking his pen absentmindedly.

Brutus' direct line buzzed as Shaun's name and icon appeared on the screen. He sucked in his breath and let the line ring until the last possible second before answering it.

"This is Brutus."

"Hi, it's Shaun," the voice whined over the phone.

As if I don't know who's calling, Brutus thought to himself.

"Hello Shaun, what can I do for you today?" He was thankful for the auto-tonation his Face provided to cover up his inappropriate inflections. He held his breath, waiting for his boss to speak and hoping the request would be minimal this late in the afternoon.

"Do you have a minute to stop by?"

"Sure. I'll be right there." What Brutus really meant was, *no. I don't have a minute. I'm trying to get my work done in peace, so I can get out of here and rest before I have to come back and do it all over again.*

Sighing, Brutus locked his workstation and headed to the end of the hall towards Shaun's office, passing others in their cubicles with their heads down working. Some had photos on their desks, others had custom mugs or drawings from their children, but nothing that really told Brutus much about who they were. They all looked like carbon copies, busying themselves away for eight hours a day so they could go home, tune out to their favorite shows, kiss their loved ones goodnight, and then turn around to do it all over again.

Brutus knocked when he got to Shaun's office, even though the glass partitions clearly showed his approach. His knock was met with a raised hand. Shaun had taken another call during Brutus' journey down the hallway. Ever important and always busy was Shaun.

After waiting patiently for a minute, he hung up the phone and waved Brutus inside. Shaun didn't apologize for the wait but simply got down to business. *Why should he? After all, when you're busy and important, it's expected that others wait for you.*

"Have a seat." Shaun motioned to the empty chair across his desk, and Brutus sat. Leaning back casually, Shaun took a sip of coffee from the mug in his hands.

"I wanted to ask you about that budgetary summary you sent me. I don't understand why it takes so long to get those reports, and I want to see that process sped up. Can you think of a way we could do that?"

Brutus shifted in his seat. "Uh, I'm not really sure, to be honest, I pull those reports as soon as they're ready in the system. I'm not sure I can go any faster than that."

"Well, Brutus, we all wear many hats in this office. I know you have a lot of other duties to take care of, but I was hoping we could speed up that reporting process so that you could start tackling the referral project we discussed. Maybe you've taken on more than you can handle though?" Shaun's Face was set in a safe smile.

Brutus felt heat start to spread up the back of his neck in embarrassment, with just a touch of anger. He hadn't volunteered to take on more work, he had been "volunteered" by others.

"I may be a little burnt out, to be honest," Brutus said, opening up to his boss more than he expected. "I think I just need some more time to get caught up before I can start any new projects."

Shaun sat up and fixated his pulsating white eyes on Brutus. "I am a little disappointed at that, Brutus. You aren't really being a team player. We have to work together, that's what makes this floor so successful. Everyone works hard, and sometimes you've got to do more than your share.

"And for that matter, I haven't seen you out with us at any of the socials for weeks now. I'm just not sure what you expect if you put so little effort into your work and your coworkers? I'm beginning to think that maybe you're just not a good fit for the culture of our organization."

Brutus sat frozen to his chair and stared back at Shaun in silence. He didn't want to play games, he didn't want to spend time with people he didn't like, he just wanted to keep his head down and do his job so he could leave. *Why would I want to be a team player, when it means turning into an empty suit like you?*

After a moment's pause, Shaun continued, "I don't understand why you don't want to be part of the team. Just…try to put some more effort into your work, okay? See what you can do about speeding up those reports, and find some time to get started on the referral project."

Brutus nodded a promise to do better. He politely told Shaun to, "Have a great weekend," and excused himself.

"You can close the door," Shaun's voice whined out a final command, and as Brutus left, he shut the door behind him.

As he plodded back to his desk, less motivated than ever to sit down and get to work, Brutus felt Lucian's note in his pocket, and his heart skipped a beat. Tonight, he knew exactly what he would be doing.

Nervous was the only word Brutus knew to describe how he felt, but it didn't entirely cover it. There was something more palpable hiding beneath, *fear perhaps?* He could have easily looked up the address ahead of time to prepare himself for what to expect at the listed destination, but every time he came close to unveiling it, he had to stop himself. He wasn't sure what made him more uncomfortable, the idea of knowing what the address led to or the thought that he would be too scared to actually go if he knew what was waiting for him.

Brutus arrived and found himself wishing the journey had been longer. It was easy enough to find but also easy enough to miss if you weren't looking for it. The building was smooth and blended into the symmetry of the City around it. As Brutus approached the entrance, something caught the corner of his eye. It was a doorknob, resting at the level that all doorknobs do, except as Brutus noticed, it lacked the one essential thing that made it useful, a door. Instead, this doorknob rested in a flat wall of smooth stone, unabashedly displaying its uselessness to anyone who chanced to walk by.

Secretly relieved for the excuse to delay his entry into the unknown just a little bit longer, Brutus stepped to the side to examine the object. It shouldn't have been allowed to exist, and yet by some oversight, it remained. It must have been an old entryway or some type of bizarre amusement. Whatever it had been, it was most certainly a peculiarity now.

Brutus grasped the doorknob. To his surprise, it actually turned, and Brutus almost let loose a chuckle. He spent a few more seconds turning the doorknob to nowhere back and forth while bystanders passed, too preoccupied with their own journey to notice. After one last turn, Brutus swallowed down his mild amusement. For some reason, he felt compelled to pat the smooth concrete of the wall, as if to thank it for its time. His nerves quelled for the moment, he walked around the corner and found the building's proper entrance.

Almost immediately, Brutus identified where Lucian had sent him. The shop was nothing more than a facility for recreational Irreality, an activity that Brutus was fairly well acquainted with. They were short-lived and shallow experiences, but they gave Brutus something to talk about with everyone else. When in doubt, defaulting to a discussion with your peers about what you got up to in Irreality over the weekend was a safe bet.

Inside the shop was not much different than any other box store Brutus had ever visited, and he began to doubt that this experience would leave him with anything new. The interior was smooth and sterile, full of cookie-cutter furniture, all accented in grey steel, and warm lighting spilled across the lobby. Several brightly lit and colorful kiosks stood in a row by the entrance with the words "Self Service Irreality" dancing on the wall above them. Brutus was drawn to them initially and browsed through their featured selections.

They were listed in different experience categories and sorted by price. Today's specials included several classics that Brutus was familiar with: Empty Commuter Train, Virtual Shopping Boutique, and Apartment Upgrade Tour were some of his favorites among the listed. Brutus spent a few minutes monotonously tapping through the Irreality choices, but nothing stood out to him. Then he remembered the rest of Lucian's note, and the clear and straightforward instructions soothed the uncertainty of his current situation.

Brutus tapped out of the kiosk and turned to the lobby counter. A woman stood motionless behind the front desk. He assumed she had been there the entire time, watching him aimlessly navigating the choices. There was something about her that was entirely forgettable. Brutus had the strange thought that if he turned away, he would forget she had even been there at all. As he approached the counter, the woman stood fixed in place, unmoving. Her lips were set in the usual polished smile that rested on the Face of most City-dwellers.

"Hello, and welcome! How can I help you today?" a soft and pleasant voice bubbled out.

"Hi there, uh, I'm good, thanks," Brutus replied gracelessly.

There was a pause of pressing silence. Turning slightly towards him, her soft voice piped up again.

"Thank you for visiting us. What can I help you with today?"

"Well, actually, I'm here to see…uh, Groves?" Brutus felt embarrassed even asking the question. The woman behind the counter moved again, ever so slightly, folding her hands in front of her. "Lucian sent me?" Brutus added quickly, beginning to think that somehow he had misinterpreted the note, perhaps coming to the wrong address altogether.

To his surprise, the woman relaxed and, without missing a beat, nodded and motioned for Brutus to follow. She ran her hand across a door at the back of the shop, and it slid open at her touch to reveal a staircase descending out of sight.

"Enjoy your time with us today." The woman ushered him forward.

Brutus made to return her politeness with a thank you but found the door shutting behind him with a soft click.

"Thank you," Brutus said anyway to the door.

He hesitated at the top of the stairs. There was an obviously marked exit button on the door behind him. With just a quick push, he could be out of the shop and on his way home. It was all so far removed from his usual route there was no reason he would ever have to pass by here again. Yet, the woman behind the counter was so polite, he felt it would be worse for him to risk the embarrassment of leaving right after she took the trouble to help him. Brutus' feet shuffled forward, and he began his descent.

Brutus entered the underground level expecting to be met with some unknown menace. Instead, he found himself in a mirrored copy of the room he had just left, complete with an attendant standing behind the counter. Brutus had to check behind him to confirm that the dark stairway was indeed there, and he had not somehow turned himself about and ended up exactly where he started.

Taking a moment to look around the room, Brutus found his initial assessment was not entirely accurate. Other than a near-identical layout and furnishing, the only variation to the row of kiosks on this floor was the signage dancing across the wall. Brutus read "Self-service OB" and felt his stomach immediately jump into his throat.

Where Irreality was almost guaranteed to come up daily in conversation, OB was something different. It was something he had only heard whispers and rumors about. He froze in place, not even knowing where to start. The same creeping feeling he had experienced when he had bought his pen from the old man washed over him.

"Hi there, welcome! What can I help you with today?" The voice was deep and lilting, his Face a replica of the smile he had met upstairs.

"I…I'm here to see Groves. Lucian sent me," Brutus repeated, feeling just as awkward. The Face across the counter stared back at him for a moment and then came out from behind the desk and guided him towards the row of kiosks.

"It sounds like this may be your first visit here," the attendant said. "If you are familiar with our Irreality system, the kiosk interface over here is exactly the same. It's just the selections that are varied."

He guided Brutus a few feet over to the nearest kiosk, tapped it on, and then stepped back so that Brutus could take his place.

"Take your time in making a selection, and let me know if there is anything I can help you with." The man took his leave and settled back into his perch behind the counter.

Brutus turned his attention to the brightly lit screen and felt the breath catch in his chest as he sorted through the options. Almost every category stirred up thoughts that Brutus found himself uncomfortable having. The quiet of the room bore down until all he could hear was the beating of his own heart as his fingers slipped across the screen. Finally, Brutus double-tapped an image, confirming his selection. The kiosk chirped in tonal recognition.

"Great choice," the man behind the counter said. "Please connect using the first door on your left." He motioned, and a partition slid open.

Rather than following into the open door, Brutus approached the counter in one last attempt to stall whatever experience lay ahead.

"I'm sorry, but what is this?"

"Well, sir, your selection—"

"No no, I mean, this place? It's…irregular."

"Ah, yes, I see." The attendant nodded in understanding. "We find that sometimes what our customers need is something a little more personal, but we understand that it's not for everyone, which is why we're off the main showroom."

Brutus bobbed his head in a false understanding of the attendant's words as another question formed, "Why OB though?"

"Well, we like to think that we, in our service, help our customers 'Obtain' a sense of 'Balance' in their lives, thus, OB."

Brutus nodded again to the simple and somewhat more understandable answer. He tapped the counter and thanked the man for his clarifications.

"Enjoy your session, sir."

Brutus entered the room. It was decorated to match with a simple grey cushioned chair encased in smooth, sterile walls. Brutus sat himself down. The partition closed with a soft hiss, and instructions danced themselves across the blank wall. He slid a compartment open on the side of his chair and used the cables that extended from it to connect into the OB he had selected.

His eyes pulsated with light as the room around him slowly faded away. A few moments of darkness consumed Brutus before a new world materialized around him. He was back where he was just this afternoon, surrounded by the walls of his boss's office, the glass door to his back. Brutus marveled at the details of Shaun sitting before him, leaning casually back in his chair and sipping coffee from the same mug he always had glued to his hand. Looking out across the office, his eyes met with a blur of carbon-copied desks and workers. As it had been this afternoon, all the heads were bent, glowing eyes fixated on their work. He could not see the end of the hall where his own cubicle lay.

"...I just don't understand why you don't want to be part of the team." Brutus turned around at the bleating sound of Shaun's voice.

"Just, try to put some more effort into your work, okay? See what you can do about speeding up those reports, and find some time to get started on the referral project."

Brutus nodded at Shaun and found himself again promising that he would do better. He made to excuse himself, wondering why he had chosen this experience.

"You can close the door," Shaun tossed the words into the air as Brutus made to leave.

Brutus paused, hand resting on the handle. *'You can close the door?' Can I Shaun, can I really?* Brutus felt the annoyance of this afternoon wiggle its way back into his belly. Annoyance tumbled into a long, stewing anger that had been set to a simmer for years. His hand closed firmly around the handle, shaking slightly.

"No." Brutus' tone pierced through any regulators housed in his Face. He turned on his heel without another look towards Shaun and walked out of his office, leaving the door very much, ajar.

15 | PEREGRINATION

He had traveled for days following the sun as it set. Each sunset, he would climb, climb as he always had, and look upon the City. It never changed, and as night fell, he would descend to the streets below.

Living off convenience store food, he had been well fed for the first few days of his journey, but as he reached farther out, fewer and fewer people inhabited the spaces around him. At some point, the people had disappeared altogether. The shops and buildings were still there, the train still ran on time, but the streets were empty, and as Gabe inspected the buildings, so were they. At first, the people had just disappeared, but he could still find food in the shops. At one point, he'd even seen a man stocking a corner convenience store. But now, everything was empty.

As the sun rose again, he picked himself up from the sidewalk he'd chosen for his evening slumber. He'd begun his journey by obeying the common practices. He'd waited for traffic to halt before crossing and walked only on the designated strips. Now though, he walked the massive streets starved of nourishment and social interaction. All his life he'd spent looking out, and never appreciated what was around him. He missed the warm bodies as they passed him on the cold days and the unintelligible conversations of those around him on his morning commute. He missed the news. He missed being talked at.

16 | Brutus Goes Back to the Club

Brutus was a changed man. The fact that he had stood up to his boss, even in a virtual scenario, had bolstered his confidence. He busied himself with his weekend chores in an almost jovial fashion. Even his wife noticed a small change in him, which she responded to by flatly asking him to, "Calm down." Brutus, of course, acquiesced and continued his weekend routine in a more muffled frivolity.

"No," he told the self-cleaning sink as it hissed soap and steam in his Face.

"No," he whispered to the dispenser as it went about crafting his meals.

"Nope," he hummed in the elevator as it scuttled its way down.

Brutus' routine persisted into the workweek as usual, though the tune of *no* continued to flit about his head. The City certainly hadn't changed. The commute was packed with the same crowd, the train ran at the same time, and work provided no surprises. Yet, Brutus himself felt different. He felt empowered.

No, he thought, as he ran an errand for his coworker.

No, he sang in his head as he made a fresh pot of coffee for his department.

Absolutely not, his mind chanted as Brutus complied with another assigned daily task. It was his new mantra, and he marched to the tune of *no, no, nope,* up and down the halls of his office all week while he went about his day, completing his duties and making obligatory small talk.

After work, he went straight home each night. With the café still closed, he really had nowhere else to go. He didn't feel the need to revisit Irreality, not yet at least, and venturing back to Lucian's club never crossed his mind. He fell easily back into what was safe and familiar and embraced it with the soft song of *no* incessantly traipsing about his head. The Mouse had faded to only a shadow of a thought, slowly eroding away with the rinse and repeat of each passing day.

Only a week had passed since Brutus' experience with Irreality, but it felt like the passing of an age. Brutus was mulling over this very thought as he waited at the signal with the rest of the pedestrians, patiently watching the traffic whiz by in blurs of blue and yellow light. The vehicles fell into a sequential halt as the light changed, their shiny carapaces reflecting brightly despite the thick gray skies.

The signal chirped pleasantly, telling the foot traffic it was their turn to cross the black sea of asphalt. Brutus' feet moved automatically to heed the command. It was while he was crossing the street that he felt a hand move through the crook of his arm. Startled, he looked down, only to find that he was being pulled from the crosswalk.

"Let's go this way, shall we?" the familiar voice of the social club owner echoed from an unfamiliar Face.

"Lucian?"

"Who else would I be?"

This was a very good question because when Brutus looked over, he did not see the half-Face which had so dismayed him before. Instead, it was a Face like any other, rather generic like his own, but concerning still was his lack of a tag. *What is it with these people and not wearing their own Face?* Chilling bumps ran up his arm at the thought.

Brutus complied, though, with the gentle pressure on his arm, guiding him to turn away from the daily commute and wander off course. The two figures walked briskly for a few minutes in silence, Brutus with his broad shoulders and dark suit paired next to the thin, tall man dressed in white. They looked like two of the mismatched wooden figures he had seen in the old antique shop. He wondered what Thomasson would think if he saw them walking together now and without any patterned squares to guide them.

"Where are we going?" Brutus ventured with hesitation. It felt almost rude to ask.

"Oh, just around the block." Lucian gestured in an erratic spiral, pointing at nothing in particular.

The pair walked on together in a few moments of heavy silence that Brutus was keenly aware of. A smattering of conversational topics rolled around in his mind.

"Do you think it's going to rain?" Brutus blurted out.

"No," Lucian replied simply. Silence slithered back, only abated for the briefest of moments. The pair made it to the street corner and hooked a left. Glancing over at the figure striding beside him, Brutus chided himself. *A man like that doesn't care about weather patterns. Be interesting.*

"I don't think I've ever taken this route before."

"I didn't think so," Lucian's reply was pointed but not unkind.

Brutus began to feel embarrassed, and the need to apologize for his lack of articulation was the only other thing that came to mind.

"Sorry," Brutus mumbled. "I just…I think I've run out of things to say," he finished rather bluntly.

"Haven't seen you at my place for a time, Brutus." Lucian glossed over the failed conversation without missing a beat. "You really should stop by again."

"Yeah, sure. I just haven't had the time."

"Hmmm," Lucian hummed his reply. "Not a problem. Anhedonia will still be there when you are ready. I wonder, has time hindered you from visiting the address I gave you?"

"No, actually." Brutus felt cornered. "I managed to stop by last week."

"Did you enjoy yourself?"

"I did…actually." Brutus felt the back of his neck flush. Lucian did not press him on his experience but simply gave him a small nod of approval.

The two rounded another corner. Brutus could see the familiar sight of the dancing streetlights and his twice-daily crosswalk waiting for him in the distance.

"Thank you for the walk, Brutus," Lucian said softly. "I do hope you'll consider stopping by my club again soon. I would enjoy seeing you there."

"Yeah, thank you. Maybe I'll stop by tonight," Brutus said noncommittally. "Have a good—" but Lucian was gone before he could finish.

Brutus found himself drifting among a group of strange Faces he'd never seen before but who all looked stale and familiar. The chirp of the crosswalk fluttered into the air and pushed the crowd forward. A ball of ice plopped into his stomach. He was going to be late for work!

The flow of traffic plodded along at the usual pace, but as efficient as the City moved, it could not make up for lost time. Brutus made his way across the street almost at a run and stumbled into his office at ten past the hour. He could feel the glances of his coworkers upon him as he hurried to his desk, but none of them stopped their routine to pay him any notice. Setting down his briefcase and tapping on his desk screen, Brutus felt another presence move up behind him. It was Shaun.

"Brutus, you're late," the voice wheezed out from behind him. He froze, then turned slowly to face his boss.

"Yep," Brutus agreed, and waited for the world to end.

Shaun stood fixed in place for what felt like hours before he turned and strode away. Coffee cup in hand, the boss of the floor lumbered across the hall and into the break room. The call of coffee in the early morning may have been the only thing that saved Brutus from an untimely end. He quietly turned back around in his chair, coaxed his desk screen back to life, and went about his day.

The journey home at day's end passed quickly and without surprises. As he walked shoulder to shoulder with the evening commuters, Brutus found himself daydreaming about sitting in the corner of the café, looking out his window. He could almost see the table, the speckled window, the stained sill, and he felt a detached sadness for what he would never have again. But in the corner of that loss, there was something gained, something new. The steady beat of passing traffic hummed beneath his feet, and Brutus felt his body tingle with anticipation. It was simple, all he had to do was turn left down the alleyway rather than continue home.

Brutus didn't even bother to tell his wife he would be late. He doubted that she cared much either way, and as he turned down the alley, the City was warm, and the air felt heavy. Dark, thick clouds draped over the concrete forest, the weather station gearing up for another round of cleansing rains. Brutus chided himself for not reading the weather updates and forgetting his umbrella. But the rain had barely even begun to spatter across the ground by the time Brutus found himself once more in front of Lucian's club.

The glinting yellow eyes of the illuminated cat on the worn sign stared past him as he approached, as if watching something down the alleyway behind him. Brutus hesitated for a moment, feeling overwhelmed, feeling watched. The alley was quiet, save for the soft pattering of rain just beginning to fall. Brutus followed the gaze of the cat and felt the blackness pressing in from the path behind him. The hairs on his neck stood up, and a shiver ran from his shoulders to his groin. Faced with the unknown chill in the darkening night, Brutus chose the now more familiar and crept past the watchful cat.

Jarring tonal melodies pulsed around him as a different kind of darkness enveloped him once more. Rather than being frightened as he had on his first visit, Brutus felt almost excited this time. Now knowing what to expect, he could take in the details that had darted over his head as he had drowned during his previous visit.

Squinting through the dimly lit interior, Brutus noticed the wallpaper peeling at the edges, its pattern unfamiliar and faded. His polished shoes slipped over uneven flooring, created from years of grime and forgotten nights. *Another relic of the past hiding from the Cleaners, another treasure for Thomasson,* Brutus thought to himself, his inner voice almost yelling over the bass vibrating up his spine.

This time an experienced traveler, Brutus was able to navigate through the club with a more practiced grace. He sidled around the edges, stepping daintily over finished bottles, errant feet, and spilled drinks. Plopping himself down on a stool in front of the bar, Brutus breathed a sigh of relief.

He may have been acquainted with the pulsating war raging on inside the club, but the experience was still draining none-the-less. Celebrating a small victory, Brutus ordered himself a drink and waited as the bartender took his time in providing it. Sipping the cool spirits and enjoying the sweetness rolling over his tongue, he wondered why the owner hadn't turned to automation to serve the libationary needs of his clientele. Although, Brutus found he did enjoy the antiquated personal touch, like the waitress in the café.

He sat at the bar as time ticked onward, watching the patrons around him talk, drink, and dance. Thumbing the perspiration on his glass, he found himself wondering where the social club's owner was and what he was doing. Although there was no promise of him being there in the first place, Brutus felt a stirring of disappointment as the hour lengthened, and the man he still knew nothing about was nowhere to be seen.

Tossing back the rest of his drink, Brutus picked up the jacket he had laid neatly across the stool next to him and made to leave, but not before that familiar voice brushed across his cheek like an evening breeze.

"I'm glad you decided to come back," the fleshy jaw barely moved as it spoke, "but I see you're already on your way out." Brutus again found himself staring at the exposed nakedness of it, less with horror tonight and more with fascination. It was truly mesmerizing to watch. He nodded at the mouth's observation and stood transfixed.

"Yeah, I was. Just stopped by for a bit," Brutus pulled himself out of his stupor to spit forth an answer from behind frozen, polished lips.

"Can I interest you in another drink?" Lucian asked, and without waiting for a reply, he motioned to the bartender. Service was much faster for the club owner. Two glowing glasses of neon spirits chinked onto the counter. Lucian slid one over with a delicately gloved hand, and Brutus took a seat once more, laying his jacket down across his lap.

"Thanks." He took a sip of his drink in a display of gratitude. It was warm and bitter but oddly satisfying. Lucian pulled up a stool beside him and took a long draught, his bare lips glowing violet from the reflection of the backlit bar. Brutus resisted the urge to shudder as he watched them wrap around the rim and suck down the liquid within. A thought popped into Brutus' mind, one that he normally would have ignored if his senses had not been altered by drink and decor.

"I wonder if I might ask," Brutus began. Lucian stretched the creature on his face into a broad smile and nodded.

"Of course."

"Your Face…why remove just the lower half. Why not the eyes?"

"Because eyes can lie, my dear Brutus," Lucian answered without pause, "and the mouth is a luxury of truth. You can't hide a smile or straighten out a frown. Whereas the eyes can hide so very much." The pulsating black orbs crackling in Lucian's sockets seemed to move, ever so slightly, as if to accentuate the truth of his words.

Brutus thought on this a moment without really understanding what the mouth had just told him. He scanned the room, avoiding Lucian's gaze. *Had it really been just this morning that the two of them had taken their little detour together?*

"I'm sorry, did you say something?"

"I didn't say anything Brutus," Lucian responded.

"Huh." Brutus shrugged and continued, "I'm surprised there are so many people here, it's not an easy place to find." He found himself almost yelling so that Lucian could hear him, yet when Lucian replied, it seemed without effort.

"People have a knack for sniffing out what they're not intended to."

"Uh-huh…'Anhedonia'…it's catchy. Did you come up with the name?" Brutus, shouting again.

"I named it after someone very dear to me." Lucian raised his drink to his lips once more and drained the glass, letting out a satisfying smack. "And now our time begins to hollow. Brutus, you should enjoy yourself a little bit more tonight."

Extending a hand, Lucian motioned to the throng of bodies covering the dance floor.

"Oh no, I can't do that." Brutus almost laughed aloud at the absurdity of the suggestion, and for the second time that night, readied himself to leave. It was then he caught a glimpse of something yellow fluttering in the crowd. It was there and then lost again, weaving in and out of existence between a mass of flesh.

"No? I think you can." Lucian's soft voice barely registered in Brutus' head as he left the bar behind, his jacket forgotten, keeping his stool warm.

There it was again, the flash of yellow in the dark, and this time he saw who it was connected to. It was a tight, form-fitting dress with a long ribbon threaded up the back. Pale skin shone with sweat as the woman moved in sequence to the deep, throbbing beats. She had the Face of a Mouse, alabaster shining brightly in fluorescent lighting, her mouth formed into a coy grin.

Moving without thinking, Brutus stepped into the sea of dancing bodies, navigating the human currents as if in a dream until he found his own body pressed up against the warm skin of the woman in yellow. She stood almost a head shorter than him. Her small frame was pushed up against his repeatedly as the crowd thrust them together. Brutus caught her scent as her hair brushed against his sensors. It brought on memories of something old, yet familiar and comforting. For the first time in a long while, or perhaps the very first time at all, Brutus felt the crook of his lips stretch behind his mask, and he smiled.

They danced well into the night and well past any expectations. At some unspoken hour, the music stopped and with it the dancing. The club's patrons slowly dispersed out into the world and back onto the streets from which they had come. Back to the City, back to the ordinary. It was as if he had been woken from a dream, and he suddenly felt very foolish and found that his feet hurt very much. The Mouse, momentarily forgotten, slipped away and vanished out of sight. Brutus searched through the fading crowd, hoping to catch just one last glimpse, but no trace of her could be found.

17 | A Side of Carrots

When Julia's family died, she grieved for them in the same way others before her had. She collected their belongings, moving from room to room, tidying and dusting away the evidence. Shirts and pants she folded neatly into little squares, stacking one upon the other. She did, however, become quite anxious when trying to place their shoes neatly and orderly inside one of the bereavement boxes she'd been provided. Had one pair been but an inch longer or shorter, they would have stacked most assuredly. In the end, she was left with a chaotic interior.

When at last her work had been somewhat confined within six rectangular boxes, she placed them neatly outside in two stacks of three. Within a matter of hours, the evidence of her family had been wiped away, almost as efficiently as if performed by a Cleaner. By the time she sat down for her evening meal, she had quite forgotten about the hardships of her day. Yet somewhere, unbeknownst to Julia, an error had occurred.

Julia's meal had consisted of a lean steak, a side of carrots, and a scoop of peas. She'd eaten quietly and alone, neither enjoying nor disliking her meal. So when she was finished, and her plate was clear, she leaned over and let it fall into the incinerator. Removing herself from the kitchen, she put on her nightgown and made herself comfortable in the sitting room. Tuning in to her favorite channel, she watched and listened for several hours until it was time for sleep.

As she turned off the lights throughout the house, Julia's eye caught the sight of two lean steaks, two sides of carrots, and two scoops of peas. To say that Julia was surprised would be a lie.

From an early age, she had been taught to clear her plate and that the dispenser would give her no more, or no less than what she needed. Sitting down, Julia went through her mealtime ritual again and again, until both plates had been cleared. Leaning over, she tossed them both in the incinerator and removed herself to bed.

In the morning, Julia went through her usual grooming routine. She washed her Face thoroughly to remove daily grime and dried it thoroughly with a freshly cleaned towel that had been delivered that morning. When her Face was immaculate, she slipped it over her head and secured it snugly into place.

Stepping into the kitchen, Julia sat down for her morning meal. The sensor in her chair triggered the table's lift, and it began to grow wider as her chair slid back to accommodate for the expanding mass. The fins on the edge of the table slowly turned as a new center appeared, carrying with it her breakfast and finally coming to a stop as the pieces locked together. She finished the food on her plate, then the food on the plate of another, and then another. Collecting up the dishes, she placed them into the incinerator and began her journey to work.

From her home, work was ten miles, but with the train, walking was kept to a minimum. Every day she met the same people in front of the same elevator. They exchanged their pleasantries, discussed their morning meals, the weather, and how efficiently the train had continued to run. When the box finally descended from its heights, Julia and the gathered group would all squeeze in and begin their day of work. Each taking turn to clock in as the elevator rose to Julia's floor.

Again and again, Julia repeated these rituals morning and night, eating the meals for three, never realizing the error as she had always trusted her home to feed her what was needed. As time passed, Julia's towels began arriving in larger sizes. Her clothes were automatically tailored to fit her growing body, and towards the end, Julia had to stop by Dorian's to exchange her Face for one slightly wider. To Julia, this was all a part of daily life. Her gradual change in size was so nuanced and catered that Julia didn't even realize that every day, fewer and fewer of her co-workers would ride the elevator with her as they rose to their place of work.

Though one Tuesday morning, Julia did not rise as usual, she did not go through her regular grooming routine, she did not wash her Face as she often thoroughly had. The grime of the previous day would remain as her towel hung unused, now several sizes larger. The sensor in her chair did not trigger with her growing weight, and the table did not expand with her three-course breakfast. The incinerator did not glow to life as it consumed the porcelain.

Her ten miles went untraveled, and pleasantries were never again exchanged, and as the box descended, her co-workers stepped greedily through, not realizing that there was now space aplenty. Her absence went unnoticed and uncared for by all, all but one.

18 | Brutus Finds a New Routine

Brutus awoke feeling refreshed, energized, and different. The last few weeks had seen a change in him. He arose not to the monotone jangle of his alarm, but to the soft sound of rain tapping on the windows of his apartment. The City rained at least several times a week to wash the streets clean, yet Brutus could not recall the last time he recognized the sound of falling water. Rusty and unused beneath the shell of the Face he wore, Brutus managed a simple smile.

His wife lay still, her side rising and falling in the steady rhythm of deepest sleep. Brutus had risen early, wide awake even though he had barely slept after arriving home late from his now nightly visits. He crossed over to the double windows opposite the bed and looked at the scene. All apartments in the City came standard with a phase-glass window where stock imagery replaced the transparency. Brutus suddenly realized that neither he nor his wife had ever thought to change the view.

The windows currently displayed a swift sunrise with fingers of light painting streaks of gold and purple hues over a polished white city. It was the same view that greeted him every morning, but today Brutus could see more. He heard the rain bouncing off the exterior panes, but the skies were clear and cloudless.

Reaching up, he tapped the window and pressed his thumb against the glass until the imagery faded. The sunset and marbled City were replaced with dull gray skies and heavily falling rain. Line after line of windows stretched out of view—a thousand other buildings just like his, with windows just like this one. Brutus noticed with an odd pang that all of them were powered on, all of them shutting out the real view in favor of the factory settings. Brutus turned to ready himself for the day, leaving his own window powered down.

Everything in his apartment seemed new and fresh to him, almost as if he had another's perspective. Brutus took his time getting ready, letting the warm jets of water rinse the sweat from his body, feeling his hair as he combed it back over his head. For breakfast, he overrode his usual order of a high protein meal and keyed in pancakes instead. The syrup was hot, the sticky residue lingered on his rubber lips, and Brutus licked them clean, savoring the sweetness.

He threw the plates into the kitchen incinerator before tying up his polished shoes, grabbing his umbrella, and heading out for the day. Brutus had not felt so cheerful in a long while. He might have even whistled, if he knew how. As his hand brushed the door, he heard movement in the room behind him and turned to see his wife shambling out to her spot on the sofa.

"Good morning dear," Brutus' pleasant intonation was genuine today, but the sentiment was not returned. She sat silently, nested in her usual spot, eyes pulsating in radiant electric colors. As he turned to leave, he had an idea.

Brutus retraced his steps backward near the sofa. He stopped, walked back over to the door, and stopped. He repeated this process again, this time stomping his feet as loud as he could. He reached the door, slid it wide open, and waited for it to shut. Still, the creature had not moved. He called her name. She twitched maybe, but did not turn that hideous head around. He moved forward and tripped.

Looking down, Brutus found the assailant to be one of his wife's shoes feigning innocence as it lay like a wounded animal in the middle of the floor. He picked up her shoe, a pink strappy thing with a heel almost as long as his hand. He had no idea when she had purchased it and had no memory of her wearing it, at least not around him. He took aim. *This should get her attention,* Brutus mused to himself and hurled the shoe across the room at his wife's head. It had been ages since Brutus had thrown anything, and he missed.

The pink stiletto sailed past the creature on the couch and landed with a soft thud on the floor. Brutus watched as his wife turned her head slightly as the shoe passed her field of vision and shifted herself deeper into her nesting place without a word. Brutus turned and left for work. His wife had never been much of a morning person.

The newness he felt did not fade as he had expected it to but hung like a shadow in the air around him. It was the little things that popped out at him. Little things, simple things, like a tear in the jacket of the woman ahead of him in line, or the shape of a crack in the sidewalk.

He entered his office building as if it was the first time he had stepped through those towering front doors. He marveled as his fingers brushed the panel on the wall and as the elevator scuttled down to greet him. Brutus stepped into its great silver belly and selected his floor. He noted the extra room in the elevator offhandedly before realizing that the Sausage-lady wasn't present.

He tried to enjoy the extra space provided by the absence of her bulk, but instead found that others had replaced her. It was a feeling as short-lived as the journey and forgotten not but a few seconds after he stepped out the elevator and into the busy yet unchanging office floor.

Even his work interested him now. He found himself watching his coworkers at their identical cubicles. Number Six would get up at five past the hour, every hour, almost like clockwork to fill her cup of coffee. Number Twelve had an odd habit of jittering his right leg up and down while he sat. Number Twenty-seven sneezed at least three times before lunch. And if he looked close enough, Brutus could even find imperfection in the office interior itself. One corner had a crack that looked like the outline of the City river, and just to the left of the breakroom, there was a stain nestled into the pepper gray carpet.

Brutus supposed that his newfound awareness of the world stemmed from his visits to Lucian's social club. Every evening, his new convention was to take a left turn down the alley on the way home and pay a visit to the club, which is where he found himself today after work, sitting in his usual spot at the bar, drinking in the nightly scene.

The music thudded in his head, drowning out thought while otherworldly lighting highlighted angles, shapes, and curves. He could never tell if it was the same patrons that visited the social club night after night, or newcomers wandering in off the streets just as lost and confused as he was on that first night. The Faces were always the same, and the stream of bodies never failed to bubble forth out onto the dance floor.

On most nights, Brutus joined in. On some nights, he just watched. He had yet to see the Mouse again, though sometimes he thought he saw a glimmer of her yellow dress in the corner of his eye.

Sometimes Lucian was there when he visited, and sometimes he wasn't.

Over time, Brutus began to consider Lucian a friend, and the stiffness of their conversations broke into easier rhythms. Brutus found that the two of them could chatter away an evening discussing not much of anything at all. It was these nights, where he sat with the half-masked man and talked into the early hours, that Brutus felt most alive, and it was on such a night that Brutus found himself seated on his stool, talking with his friend once more.

"I wanted to thank you," Brutus said as he swallowed his drink. "I never would have come back here if you hadn't taken the time to invite me. This place…I really needed it."

"Not at all Brutus, not at all," Lucian replied. "It is always my pleasure to provide respite." He leaned back in his seat and tucked a strand of long white hair behind his ear. "I wonder, though, if you would permit me another suggestion?"

Brutus leaned forward to catch Lucian's words before they faded into the empty spaces. "Of course."

"Meet me tomorrow outside of your work in the morning. I have something to show you."

Lucian had guided him to Irreality, had made Anhedonia a second home for him. What more could he possibly have to introduce him to? Brutus did not hesitate in his decision to find out and nodded his compliance at once.

"Sure. I'll see you tomorrow then." Brutus readied himself to leave, feeling the closure in the conversation.

"Excellent. I'll see you tomorrow, first thing." Extending a gloved hand for a parting shake as was his custom, Brutus grabbed it before departing. His head was spinning with anticipation for tomorrow, and what it could possibly be that Lucian wanted to show him.

19 | Brutus Goes on a Fieldtrip

He barely slept at all that night, lying awake until the early morning hours. Brutus rose hastily, dressed, and left, all before his other half had even stirred. The crowd could not have moved more slowly, while the traffic lights seemed to stretch their boundaries. Even the train sped along at what to Brutus felt like a lumbering pace.

Finally, he reached the front of his office building. Instead of entering, he stepped to the side and waited. Brutus did his best to ignore the subtle glances of those headed in to start their work as they saw an anomaly standing awkwardly aside.

The streets slowed down and emptied as rush hour dwindled. Brutus checked his watch and saw that he was officially late now for the start of the day. Nerves started to grow, and an uneasiness overtook him as the empty, quiet streets bore down around him. The City watched him now through narrow-eyed streetlamps and squinting windows. He caught his breath as he saw a man stroll casually around the corner. The Face he did not recognize, but the steady gait and long white hair gave him away. *Saved!* Brutus thought, though he wasn't entirely convinced that he was. Today officially marked his second tardiness, and he was sure that was not something to be overlooked.

"Good morning," Lucian said cheerfully from behind a rather subdued looking Face.

"Hi," said Brutus, relieved. "I was beginning to think you might not show up."

"I always keep my word," Lucian replied coolly, and Brutus sensed that he might have taken offense.

"Sorry, just a little nervous, I guess. I'm…late for work again."

Lucian said nothing in reply but motioned for Brutus to follow him, and so he did. Taking him around the block and down an unnamed street,

Lucian finally stopped and stepped behind a public incinerator. Brutus noted that the path they had taken dead-ended with a wall blocking any further travel. Sticking out of it was a brass rail, poised at an angle as if it used to accompany a set of stairs that no longer existed. Brutus was once more reminded of Thomasson's Antiques and contemplated for a moment the increasing number of erratic patch jobs left over by the Cleaners. *Are they losing their touch, or am I just now looking for it?*

"Put this on." Lucian's command cut through his thoughts and drew him out of his contemplation. Brutus stepped back in horror as he saw what was held out for him. He stumbled and fell on his backside with a sharp pain shooting up through his wrists as they broke his fall.

"I can't do that!" Brutus gasped, pointing at the hollow Face in Lucian's hand. For Lucian, a back-alley club owner, to show up in another man's Face was unnerving at best, but not really anyone else's business. For Brutus, though, a respectable salaryman, the thought was incomprehensible. He got to his feet, shaking.

"No. I'm sorry, and I'm really late. I need to get back to work."

Brutus walked briskly past Lucian, taking careful pains to avoid his gaze. He was both angry and afraid, his ears flushing bright red in betrayal of what his Face hid so well.

"I'm sorry to hear that," Lucian said softly as Brutus passed.

Disappointment dripped from his voice. Brutus paused at the edge of the street, the trail of Lucian's sentiment demanding a reply. He suddenly felt awash with embarrassment for letting his companion down. Brutus dialed up the time. It was twenty minutes past the hour. Facing his boss now seemed just as impossible. He turned back, hesitating.

"Look, I just—I don't really—is it safe?"

"It's just for the day. We're going on a little trip," Lucian answered without addressing any of his concerns. Brutus could feel the seconds pass by as his perception of time slowed in opposition to the frightful beating of his heart.

"I don't know…" Brutus trailed off in an incoherent jumble of worry, which Lucian promptly interrupted by guiding the empty Face into his hands. Brutus closed his mouth immediately, shutting off a steady stream of excuses. A knot formed in his chest as he held the mask. It was shapeless in his fingers, a dead white fish with humanoid features carved into its belly. The mask squirmed as his hands shook, catching the light, making it come to life. Startled, Brutus dropped it. The Face landed with a soft smack on the ground, its malleable contours spreading like a freshly cracked egg.

If Lucian was annoyed with Brutus, he voiced none of it. Instead, his white-clad form glided forward to calmly bend and pick up the fallen Face. He dusted it off with a few quick swipes from his softly gloved hands and passed it again to Brutus.

"Let's try not to drop it this time, shall we?" Lucian said. "You can have some privacy if you like, now go and change." He motioned to the bulky form of the street incinerator bulging out from the side of the wall. Brutus complied and stepped behind it, hiding himself from the view of Lucian and any unwelcome passersby.

He had never been so nervous in his life. The last time Brutus had removed his Face was two years ago, when he had done a full upgrade. It was a relatively quick process and in a sterile and socially acceptable environment. *Plus, my upgrade was brand new. Who knows where this has been, or for that matter, how Lucian got it?* But Brutus didn't want to think about that, one thing at a time. With sweaty shaking hands, he disconnected and unfastened his own Face and stowed it safely in his briefcase.

The fetid stench of the City immediately assaulted his unfiltered nose, making him gag. It smelled of soured and spoiled food. He held back vomit in a series of deep, dry coughs as the rotten sweetness overwhelmed him. The cold air stung his cheeks, and the unshaded brightness in the sky forced him to squint his eyes. Fumbling with the used Face, his focus now was plunging back into a safe, sterile environment. At this point, he didn't care where it came from.

He tugged the new Face down over his own in a rush that left his hair tousled and his eyes slightly askew, but he could breathe clean filtered air again. Inhaling deeply, Brutus filled his lungs several times before running the regular calibrations, which auto-formed it to the soft and unique contours of his face. A quick message popped up before his glowing sapphire eyes, welcoming back the true owner of such a fine Face.

"You are 'Mark' today." Lucian cast a strong arm around Brutus' shoulders, guiding him back onto the streets.

The two walked in silence for a time while Brutus tried to get used to his new mask. The settings were configured for the previous owner and not very user-friendly to change. Finally, they slowed to a stop in front of a large office building.

"Your job awaits," Lucian said with a glint of light coursing through his beetle-black eyes.

"You're kidding. After all that?" Annoyance was beginning to outweigh Brutus' unease. "We're just back to where we started."

"Look again," Lucian requested. At his behest, Brutus examined the building more closely. At first glance, it was almost identical to his office. However, upon a more detailed once-over, he found the directory display to list a completely different organization. He looked back over his shoulder to see Lucian sitting patiently on a bench nearby.

"I still don't think I understand. Why are we here? Why this?" Brutus raised his hand in a circular motion, indicating to Mark's Face resting on his.

"You're here to go to work, Brutus," Lucian replied in even tones, "and I believe you are almost late for your shift. Off you go." The thought of being tardy for a third time, coupled with his complete lack of comprehension, jump-started Brutus into a trot. He hastily made for the front door, which unlocked with ease at his touch. He turned around as the glass doors closed gently behind him and noticed that Lucian had not followed him into the office building. Instead, he could see a white figure strolling away and disappearing as he was swallowed into the teeth of the City.

Brutus stood in the doorway of the familiar yet foreign building like a lost child, frozen in fear and uncertainty. He could just as easily have left, striding out of those clean glass doors in front of him, and followed Lucian into the distance. Yet, something inside of him stirred. Curiosity, perhaps? After all, there was no going back to his own workplace today, the time for that had long passed. Brutus marveled at the outline of the double doors, trying his hardest to understand what made them any different than the doors he passed through twice a day at his own place of work.

A rustling noise behind him drew his attention, and Brutus turned to see a Cleaner waving her electric wand over a patch in the wall until it slowly melded into conformity. The figure in the white jumpsuit slowly turned its cyclopean eye towards him, as if trying to see through the Face he now wore.

That's my cue, Brutus, who was now Mark, thought to himself. He gave a cheerful nod to the Cleaner and walked briskly down the hall in the opposite direction. It was then Brutus realized that he had no idea where Mark was supposed to go. Stepping into the elevator, he picked a floor at random and got out when the electric bell chirped dismissively.

Brutus immediately did a double-take. It was as if he had walked into his own office floor. The same desks lined the room, the same colors dulled the walls. There was even a large office at the back, past all the cubicles, where a man sat with a chiseled work-Face who looked remarkably like Shaun. Brutus would have been convinced that he had indeed simply circled back to his own place of work, had there not been someone else in his seat.

No one looked up from their desks as Brutus took a few steps forward. His hand gripped the pen in his pocket with a sweaty palm as he nervously clicked the nib in and out while he walked. If the workers had heard his approach, they didn't show it but busily kept their heads down and stayed focused on the task at hand. Phones buzzed like bees, and fingers typed and tapped at screens like the feet of tiny spiders padding across glass.

Brutus walked softly down the repeating rows of cubicles until he got to the same spot that would have been his own station, Number Twenty-Nine. The man who sat in front of him now was almost identical to Brutus. Neatly pressed grey suit, medium build, identical model of Face. He could have been convinced that he was looking at a mirror image, if not for the neatly combed sandy hair that juxtaposed Brutus' own dark brown waves.

Number Twenty-Nine turned around abruptly, as if he could feel Brutus' stare.

"Mark, what are you doing?" The sandy-haired Brutus stared at him as he spoke in flat tones.

Brutus waited calmly for Mark to respond.

"Mark?"

"Oh, I…uh…" Brutus then remembered he was indeed Mark for the day, and was expected to respond. "I just got turned around."

"Well, Number Eleven is right over there, so…" The man paused after speaking. His tonal adjustment hid the annoyances in his voice that his posture and cadence did not.

"Right. Sorry. It's early," Brutus mumbled excuses as he hurried down the aisle and over towards the empty desk. He sat down with a sigh, and the desk screen fluttered to life, activated by his very presence. Tapping it fully awake, Brutus began looking through the network, convinced that he would have to fake it for the day to make it through. He was surprised to see the same applications on Mark's display that he worked with so readily at his own desk. Tapping here and swiping there, Brutus quickly got the hang of Mark's work and was reviewing procedures and filing documents with ease. Sure, they had a different company logo in the corner, but they were all the same, more or less. A beeping melody sounded in his ear, piping through Mark's network.

"Hello, this is Brutus. How may I help you?"

"Who?"

"Ah-hmmm. Sorry. Mark. This is Mark. How may I help you?"

"Hi Mark. We need you to file the review of Certification BZ-12. Can you then approve its transfer and get it sent on to accounts payable?"

"Sure thing, thanks." And Brutus closed the call.

*Cert BZ-12, Cert BZ-12…*he chanted to himself as he sorted through electronic files, finally finding the proper document. And so it went until Mark's turn for a lunch break came.

Brutus screen-locked his desk and made his way to the break room. Even this looked similar to where he ate lunch every day, though the furnishings were a deeper gray and set about in a different pattern. Grabbing his allotted lunch from the meal-generating kitchenette dispenser, Brutus took a seat at one of the tables and watched Mark's coworkers come and go.

They are all the same, he thought to himself. They could all be transplanted into his own office, and no one would know the difference. Men in dark suits, women in pencil skirts and blouses, their hair colored varied from black to dark brown, to sandy brown, and most were cut into one of three variations in style. No one wore a pop of color, and as he listened in to all the buzzing conversation, he found that no one said much of anything at all. Taking a bite of his sandwich, Brutus chewed slowly, so the munching didn't block out his hearing.

"—and Jeanette says she's trying a new diet, lost eight pounds in a week!"

"I just upgraded to a higher resolution of sensory enhancements, everything looks so real now, almost like—"

"—found it on the streets, and of course I told him we couldn't keep—"

"—got one of those wristbands that monitors your sleep cycle and puts you back into deep sleep automatically once it senses—"

"—it's a subscription manager, see it takes all of your services into a bundle and handles them automatically—"

A dozen conversations that Brutus had heard before and was sure he would hear again. It was fascinating to him, as he sat in the corner watching and listening, but also disheartening.

I am no different than anyone else, he mused as he bit into a waxy red apple. *There must be a dozen carbon copies of me out there, all repeating the same day and the same events over and over again. And for what? To make just enough money to keep a roof over our heads and to buy the latest upgrades when they come out.*

Brutus wiped his lips and cleared the table of any crumbs that had escaped. Balling up the wrapper that had encased his lunch, he tossed it into the break room incinerator. He left the room without anyone engaging him in conversation and headed for the bathroom, as was his habit. He took his time relieving himself in the shining white porcelain and then wandered over to the restroom sink. Straightening up as he washed his hands, he caught his reflection in the mirror. Brutus faced his glassy doppelganger straight on.

Mark very well could have been Brutus all along. They shared the same make and model, the same pale white skin and rubbery pink lips. Brutus brushed his dark, unkempt hair out of his eyes and felt as if he was watching a stranger move his body for him.

As the sculpted Face stared back at him, he felt the smallest pang of unease as he realized he could hardly remember what his real face looked like underneath. He smudged the glass with his finger and, lowering his voice to a careful whisper, asked of himself, "I wonder…if someday I'll ever see what's behi—"

The door opened as two office workers came in, chatting about the weather pattern for the week. Brutus stepped away from the mirror and slipped out as the door closed behind him.

The second half of the day was slow torture. Whatever amusement Brutus had found in the absurdity of the morning had vanished. Each call he took, each form he filed, each button he tapped sent a pang of frustration and annoyance through his bones. When the bells rang, signaling the end of the day, Brutus shut down his desk screen and was the first out the door. He heard his temporary coworkers call out behind him as he rushed past them.

"Mark, are you joining us—"

"Hey Mark, where are you—"

"—Mark, meet us at the social—"

But Brutus continued past them without acknowledgement.

He felt his skin begin to crawl and tingle beneath Mark's Face. He wanted to reach up and claw it off, rip it away, and hurl it across the floor. The glass double doors of the building swung wide, allowing him to exit. Brutus began to scratch at the Face like a mad man. He had to get free, had to shed Mark's skin.

"Brutus?" the familiar voice calmed him almost immediately. "Over here." Lucian had been waiting for him outside of the office building. He was sitting on a concrete bench, ankles crossed. Upon Brutus' approach, he rose and met him halfway.

"How was your day as Mark?"

"I need to get this off. I can't breathe." Brutus began to feel frantic again.

"Then take it off," Lucian told him calmly.

Brutus looked around and squatted behind the bench that Lucian had been resting on just a moment ago. There was no time for back alleys, no time to be more discrete. With a few quick taps, he disconnected the interface and slid the Face easily off of his own.

The inside was moist with perspiration. Brutus dried himself with his tie, his skin feeling extra sensitive to the touch of the raw materials. As quickly as he could, he fished his own Face back out of his briefcase. He was relieved as it fell gracefully into place. A few quick calibrations and it reformed to fit his unique contours.

Almost immediately, Brutus felt like himself again. His custom settings kicked in and cooled his cheeks to just the right temperature. His sensory filters let in just the right amount of smells and sounds. He looked down and realized he was still clutching Mark's Face in his left hand and tossed it aside, eager to rid himself of even the memory of it. It landed softly on the seat of the bench where it lay pale and fleshy, like a dead creature spat up from the City sewers.

Lucian strode over to the bench and gently scooped up the Face, placing it securely in his coat pocket.

"I believe the owner might wish this to be returned," he said simply. Brutus had the sudden urge to ask just exactly who Mark was and how Lucian had come by his mask in the first place, but decided against it.

"I don't ever want to do that again," Brutus exclaimed, feeling the need to explain himself and his actions.

"I thought you would find it interesting, living a day in another man's skin," Lucian replied.

"We're all the same. Anyone can do what I do," Brutus told his white-clad companion in a shaking voice. "There's nothing new here, nothing special. There's no reason for me to even exist."

"The same could be said for any one of us," Lucian replied, the wind catching and fanning out his long white hair.

20 | NOSTALGIA

Unwilling to face his boss after skipping work the previous day, Brutus made up a fantastic lie and dialed in sick for the second day in a row. It was the first time he had ever done that in the seven years he had worked for his current employer. Regardless of what the outcome would be, Brutus really could care less at the moment. Where life had seemed so refreshing and vibrant just the day before, everything around him now felt pointless and monotonous.

Life had lost its shine for Brutus. A candle that burned brightly on a short fuse, its glow had dwindled and burnt itself out in a puff of smoke. Brutus had seen through the facade. He had seen what all the promises amounted to. It all boiled down to everyone running through the same pointless motions, day after day. With each goal that was met, another formed, just slightly out of reach, and so the repetition could continue.

We are very good at creating our own problems, Brutus thought as he ran his fingers over his metallic pen. He used to believe that his work had purpose, that he was part of a bigger whole. Even when the days dragged on, he could usually find some simple solace in the repetition of tasks and getting things done. But what was it he did, really? File electronic documents, send out messages, follow procedures, all to support some imaginary system created by the thoughts of men that trapped him within it. Perhaps he should find comfort in the fact that he was not alone, that dozens of others were out there right now, living his same life. Rinse, wash, repeat. Rinse, wash, repeat.

He balanced the pen on his fingers, the silver barrel reflecting the lighting in the apartment. The living room wall flicked on with the afternoon news, which was mainly composed of thinly veiled advertisements in the guise of objective facts. He watched as two small children stared into a cleanly lit window, examining the newest upgrade for their Faces. A large logo landed on his living room wall, supporting the manufacturer who was supposedly sponsoring the current news segment. Brutus waved his hand in the air, and the scene dimmed and faded away. He'd seen enough consumerism for the day.

The only real thing Brutus had to cling to was his pen, which he clicked to life over and over again. After listening to the *click-click* of the pen for several hours while he brooded in his living room, Brutus finally stopped to examine the exposed nib. He had carried it around with him for weeks, completely forgetting what the tool was intended for. The urge overcame him to see what would come out of the tip if he pressed it to the proper application.

He began looking for something to write on. His wife had gone out with her girlfriends for lunch, so Brutus found himself unhindered in his search from room to room and drawer to drawer. He found electronic pads, plastic menus, glossy advertising postcards, but no notepad, nothing to write on was to be found. Brutus could not say that he was overly surprised as there were more convenient mediums than paper, but he had expected to find a sheet of something regardless.

He clicked his pen once more in irritation, and the dullness of his situation closed in around him. Examining the gold that gilded the pen's accents, Brutus thought of the old man who had so graciously sold it to him. He would have paper on hand, Brutus was sure of it.

With no work to go to and the club closed until dusk settled in, Brutus would travel back to Thomasson's and buy some paper so he could see what would worm its way out of the tip of his pen. Leaving the apartment in disarray from his fervent crusade for paper, Brutus put on his hat and coat, and set out into the City.

It took him most of the day to navigate back to the old man's shop. Popping down the wrong streets and backtracking down unknown alleyways, Brutus found himself lost in an architectural maze. Yet he continued to trust his gut and follow his feet, and after many wrong turns, he finally made the right one and found himself once more standing in front of the old shop.

Through the sunlight breaking in between the gaps of the buildings around it, Brutus saw a fine and steady stream of dust dancing through the air, stemming from the mouth of the shop. It was a living creature, wheezing and coughing up time itself.

The street was dark and empty. Suspicious of the silence, Brutus traversed the path ahead at a quickened pace. The interior was dim as he peered inside, and his heart fell as he suspected it was closed. He had taken too long to find it. Yet as he turned away, he heard a disturbance and looked to see the old man with the wrinkled woman's Face in the doorway, beckoning him inside.

The front door closed behind him with a soft thud and shook loose a small shower of dust. Contrary to the anxiety he had felt during his first visit, today Brutus felt like coming home after a long absence.

"Thank you for letting me in so late," Brutus told the shopkeeper. Thomasson nodded his head, his old woman's eyes fixed in a crinkle with a kind, unwavering smile.

"It's good to see you again. Visitors here are infrequent, as you by now know. It is a pleasure to keep my door open, and a lamp lit for you."

Brutus nodded and started looking around.

"Is there anything you're looking for?" the old man asked.

"Well, actually, do you have any paper or something to write on?"

The old man nodded and told Brutus to wait a moment while he shuffled towards the back of the shop with hands behind his back, disappearing between an old bookcase and a sagging shelf.

Brutus watched Thomasson vanish into the dust and took the opportunity to look around the shop. The moribund attitude he had been carrying around with him all day melted away, allowing curiosity to grow in its place.

He walked slowly, weaving his way through shelves and cabinets of all shapes and sizes. The interior seemed to be the living opposite of the white marbled City that surrounded it. Instead of carefully sized structures and geometric perfection, the old antique store seemed to pride itself on inconsistencies. No two furnishings were alike, and no rhyme or reason could be found for any of the displays. Even though the inside was crammed full of man-made objects, it seemed like a structure that had grown organically and continued to shift and change even as Brutus wandered about inside.

The dirty floorboards bent and groaned under his weight as he waded through the shop. Brutus busied himself, examining the oddities displayed on the crooked shelves littered around him. He flipped through some old leather bound tomes and marveled at a pocket-sized analog clock with intricate engravings. Each item left a silhouette in the dust, a clear guide for Brutus to follow as he put them back into place. He handled each piece with care and thorough inspection, as if he were an archaeologist discovering a lost civilization.

A small hand painted feline figurine with uneven eyes. A well-worn toolkit with wood-handled instruments. Bowls and cups of various colored glass. Folding fans with strange writing splashed across the fabric. Brass hollowed instruments with rusted keys. Bell-shaped lamps without wires attached. Canvases filled with bright, nonsensical colors. There were hundreds of items hidden among the shelves. Brutus could spend weeks in this shop and hardly discover half of it. As he sifted through an old wooden box with a broken hinge containing small glass orbs, a large book fell from its perch and landed at Brutus' feet.

The hard smack of the object startled him, and he hastily bent to pick it up. The book was leather bound in a rich chocolate brown cover that was peeling at the corners. Intrigued, Brutus opened it. He had to adjust to keep loose yellowed pages from spilling out onto the floor. Instead of blocks of text as Brutus was expecting, he found pictures stuck to each page. Spotting a spindly stool in the corner, Brutus sat himself down and inspected the book.

The images were static and lay flat on the page. Cut into little rectangles, they were yellowed with age and monotone. There was no depth to them in field of view, but they captured strange scenes that Brutus could not relate to. Four characters seemed to be the focus of the book, a family with two children. From time to time, all four appeared grouped in various positions at strange locations, looking at Brutus and smiling. The rest of the images seemed to depict the family's day-to-day life and interactions. Objects and strange landscapes Brutus had never seen before popped up in many of the photos. Fascinated, he slowly flipped through the pages, devouring the imagery of each.

One photo in particular caught his eye. It was the portrait of a younger woman with long, straight dark hair. The image's quality was poor, and the lighting fell across the woman in a way that blurred out the details of her features. Brutus leaned in close. He could barely see the contours of the woman's face. It was a blank slate, an empty silhouette staring back at him, no fixed smile, no resting eyes, nothing. Brutus stared at the face without a Face and tried to picture what it should have looked like. The photo fell from the page as he brushed it with his finger, the adhesive failing after many years. It was just then that he heard the footsteps of the old shopkeeper padding up behind him. Brutus hastily closed the book, slipped the loose image back between the pages, and returned it to its resting place.

"I think I have something of interest for you here," the shopkeeper's voice rustled from behind the old woman's Face. He held a notebook in his hands, bound in a thick black cover. "It's missing the majority of its pages from previous use, but there should be enough to get you started."

"Thanks," Brutus said as he took the book from Thomasson's curled and cracking hands. He flipped it open to see creamy white pages lined in blue. On the inside cover of the book was a small inscription faded with age that read:

> *To my dearest Adaline,*
> *May you always find inspiration in the world around you.*
> *Happy Birthday! Love, Dad*

Brutus felt his eyes sting as he read. He paused for a moment, blinking until the pain went away.

"This is perfect, I'll take it," Brutus said after composing himself and followed Thomasson as he shuffled back to the front of the store. Thanking him, Brutus took one last look around the old antique shop. Time had kept him away before, but now that he had time, he felt he wasn't quite ready to leave yet. *Why shouldn't I stay just a little bit longer?*

"You know it's funny, I've been seeing a lot of things around town that remind me of you," Brutus said.

Thomasson cocked his head and thought for a moment before answering, "Thank you. It's good to be remembered."

The answer confused Brutus, largely because of Thomasson's sincerity. He had paid him no compliment, offered him no service, and yet the old man was grateful. Brutus scratched the back of his head, now feeling somewhat awkward to continue.

"Well, they're quite useless things, to be honest. Leftover doorknobs, forgotten curbs, railings without stairs…things the Cleaners have somehow missed. Whenever I see them, it reminds me of when things weren't…all the same, much like your shop here."

Brutus paused for a moment, hoping he hadn't offended the old man, but Thomasson slowly bobbed his head forwards and backward, letting Brutus know that he was listening. For once in all the City, the smile on a Face seemed genuine.

"When I see these unusual things, when I'm here in your shop, it somehow feels comforting, like I'm coming home to a place I haven't been in years… but," Brutus continued, "looking at all these old and forgotten things, what's their use, really? Is there a point to leaving any of it behind?"

He hoped he wasn't rude in asking but figured if anyone might know, Thomasson would.

"Old things can bring a happiness and a comfort to many that can't be replaced by the new," the old man replied wisely. "It's not their physical function that matters, but the memory of their purpose."

"I don't know, I find looking ahead to be more, inspiring than focusing on the past," Brutus replied somewhat arrogantly.

"Isn't that just another type of nostalgia?" Thomasson paused. "You're looking forward to something you've already done and remembering the joy of that experience. Even if it was something new, the anticipation you have for it is precipitated by your past, measuring both joy and displeasure as possible outcomes. The past plays a larger role than you give it credit for, and if you think planning for the future is what you've been learning with the half-Face, then I think there's still more for you to understand."

Brutus stalled as he mulled the words over. He thought back on the curious things he'd increasingly come across in the City, and wondered at the idea that they'd ceased to serve a physical purpose and were now only a memory. But then, would that make their purpose different for each passerby who happened to notice them? Had the Cleaners seen it the same way he had, or had it been more about efficiency and cost? So many greater lengths had been taken to change the City, why had they been left behind? With honesty he couldn't bear to share with Thomasson, Brutus wasn't quite sure he understood.

"Hmmm, it is getting very late, isn't it?"

The old man's words interrupted Brutus' contemplation.

"Of course. Thank you for the notepad, Thomasson. Have a pleasant evening, I hope I'll see you again soon."

"Yes, please come back again, anytime," the voice followed him outside, and an old woman's Face watched from the store window as he left, a twinkle glinting in the shopkeeper's eye.

Soon after arriving home that night, Brutus mumbled some excuse to his wife about needing to use the restroom and locked the door tightly behind him. Sitting there, over the cold seat, Brutus opened the notebook and let it fall onto his lap. It was well worn, used and Brutus stared into the aged pages for a long time, long enough for his vision to blur around the edges and the restroom to start spinning.

As he sat, his pen stayed tightly clutched in his left hand as he stroked the barrel. At long last, Brutus clicked the nib into action and lined the tip up with the page. Using a grand sweeping gesture like a painter about to set out to work on his canvas, Brutus raised his hand into the air and brought it down swiftly towards the page, but stopped short as if met by some invisible barrier. Thinking for a moment, hand raised to chin, Brutus shifted on the toilet seat and turned the notebook just a bit to the left before readying himself for a second try. Working up his courage again, Brutus gave the pen another flourish and went about trying to mark the blank page but stopped short of making any actual lines. Again, and again, and again he tried.

Click, click, click.

But Brutus could not bring himself to leave even the smallest of impressions or the tiniest of dots. He sat in the bathroom for most of the night, trying yet failing every time he attempted to use his pen for its intended purpose. His experiment was brutally interrupted by a sharp knocking on the door as Shelby came to claim her allotted evening restroom time.

"Just a second!" Brutus hollered over the droll hum of a bathroom fan. He waved his hand in the air to flush the toilet in support of his deception.

"Just hurry up!" Shelby quipped back at him.

Tucking the notebook in the back of his pants and pulling his shirt down over it, Brutus opened the door to an inpatient Shelby who rushed by him without a word. Exhausted, Brutus went straight to bed without even taking off his clothes and fell asleep almost as soon as his head hit the pillow.

The next day, Brutus braved his way to work. Armed with his pen in his left pocket and his notebook in the right, he boarded the train in the early morning rush. For some reason, his visit to Thomasson's had given Brutus the courage to face going back to work. Never having been absent in such a fashion before, he didn't know what to expect, and yet the weight of the notebook in his pocket gave him a certain tenacity he was unaccustomed to. So what if he hadn't been able to actually bring himself to use it yet? Just having it in his pocket was enough.

Entering the double doors and making his way up to his office cubicle, Brutus was keenly aware of the similarities to his day as Mark. This regrettably confirmed his supposition that his work was but a mirror image of the man with whom he had shared a Face for a day.

Ignoring the fact that he should have checked in with Shaun first, Brutus bee-lined for his cubicle. Stretching his back, he sat down as if nothing unusual had occurred. The light above his desk screen flickered on, marking his presence.

When the first hour passed, and Brutus remained undisturbed, he began to celebrate, thinking that he had gotten away with it. Fifteen minutes later, though, a shadow loomed over him as it approached from behind. Brutus swallowed hard and kept his head down until he heard the simpering of Shaun's voice.

"Brutus, can you join me for a few?"

"Yes, of course," Brutus replied without turning around. He felt the presence of Shaun lessen as the soft thudding of footsteps receded. Brutus followed Shaun once more down the rows of identical cubicles and into his office. Shaun motioned for Brutus to sit while he remained standing behind his desk. Brutus sat.

"You've been out for two entire workdays," Shaun said, matter of fact.

"Yes, sorry. I was…not feeling my best."

"So it must be something pretty bad." Shaun allowed no air of suspicion to creep past his tonal filters.

"Personal reasons, mainly," Brutus mumbled.

"Marriage trouble?" Shaun asked.

"Y-yes. I'm—we're having a rough time." It wasn't entirely untruthful.

"It's important to keep them separate, work and personal life," Shaun spouted forth his commentary as if it were some profound and life-altering revelation. "I'm going to mark these instances of absence in your records Brutus, so just make sure it doesn't happen again."

Shaun continued to lecture Brutus on the importance of teamwork, work culture, and personal engagement. Brutus found himself nodding silently to everything his boss said without really listening until finally, Shaun moved to open the door and usher Brutus out.

"Have a good day, Brutus."

"You too sir, thank you."

Keeping his head down, Brutus shuffled back to his desk, clenching his hand around the pen in his pocket. Breathing deeply, Brutus sat down and tried his best to get back to work. His hands went through the motions required to perform the tasks at hand, but his mind raced. He could not rid his thoughts of the imagery of Shaun standing behind his desk, lecturing him about his performance. Shaun's words rang in his head until they mixed with the clang of the bell, signaling the day's end.

Brutus tidied up his workstation, double-checked that everything was in order, and readied himself to leave. He tapped the notebook and pen on his way out, reassuring himself that they had not, in fact, climbed out of his pockets and were still where he had put them. He then headed out of the office, ducking invitations for after-work socialization, and made his way to Lucian's club.

21 | THE EDGE

Gabe had stopped looking ahead. The road, like the City, had no end. It just simply was. Instead, he looked at his feet as he walked, struggling to put one foot in front of the other. As Gabe had run out of food, his mind had ceased to keep track of time, and he was without any form of comparison. All he knew was that when he put one foot in front of the other, the lines on the road moved behind him.

This was his only comfort as he wandered on his quest. Though suddenly and without warning, the lines stopped, and so did his feet. Finding the strength, Gabe looked up. In front of him, he saw the withered corpse of a man. Its ivory visage had been stained by the passage of time, its clothing, which had once been a pressed shirt and tie, was now worn thin by the friction of use. Gabe felt a pity he did not understand at first but was compelled to reach out. He wanted to touch this poor person because he knew their pain.

Their hands met in the space between, and Gabe was surprised. Its hand didn't feel like flesh, it felt cold and without texture. His eyes trailed up at the gentle ripples that emanated from where their two hands met, stretching past themselves over the buildings in front of them and into the dull gray sky where it was impossible to tell where the City ended, and the sky began.

It was a reflection, there was nothing ahead of him that was not already behind him. It was then that Gabe recognized the man in the mask. In the middle of the street, at the far reach of the City, he had found himself. He had found the edge.

It was then that, for the first time in his life, he looked back.

22 | A Choice for Brutus

The streetlamps flickered on as evening fell, and Brutus made his way to Anhedonia. He was almost bursting with excitement as he traversed the crowd. The last few days had been more intense than anything Brutus had experienced recently, and all he wanted to do now was sit back with a drink and talk to Lucian about it.

His companion did not make him wait long. Brutus had only sat at the bar for a few minutes, nursing his drink, when Lucian sat down softly beside him. His exposed jawline was set into an amused grin, lips parting briefly to place his order.

"Good to see you, Brutus."

Brutus returned the greeting in fashion, wondering again at his strange Face-changing friend. Emboldened by recent events, today Brutus had nerve enough to ask.

"Where do you even get these," Brutus motioned with the open palm of his hand, "all the different Faces you wear? I mean, they would each have to be registered and the expense…"

"People are more often willing to part with what's important to them than you'd think," Lucian answered candidly.

"Wait—what? So how do you do it, get them to give them up? Do you steal them, did I…" Brutus lowered his voice to a harsh whisper, "did I wear a stolen Face!?"

"Your panic does wonders for your rationale," Lucian laughed, before smoothly folding into a different topic to ask Brutus how his day had been after returning to his own place of work.

It was not long before the two were engaged in fluid conversation, and Brutus found himself erupting in an excited bout of uncharacteristic storytelling. When he told Lucian that he had taken a second day off in a row, he beamed inwardly when Lucian congratulated him on his audacity. After that, Lucian listened quietly and without interjection. His soft, curled smile stayed fixed in place as if he was wearing a Face. Every so often, he sipped his drink and licked his lips before his lower half fell back into the same position.

When Brutus started telling Lucian about his return visit to Thomasson's Antiques, Lucian drained his glass and set it down with more force than needed. If Brutus had been more observant and not so caught up in recounting his tale of adventure, he would have noticed that from this point, Lucian's smile had slipped away.

"—and then I came back here!" Brutus finished detailing recent events and ended by taking a swig of his own drink that he had neglected until now. He slurped down the sweet liquid and thirstily waited for Lucian to speak. But Lucian did not answer right away.

Instead, he raised a gloved hand to his face and stroked his chin. When he did speak, his exposed jaw did nothing to hide his frustration. "And you thought it was a good idea, to visit that old man's nostalgia shop?"

"Well, yeah, I—"

"Brutus, let me be very clear. There is nothing for you there. I thought you would understand that by now. I know that man, and I know that shop. Don't let yourself be tricked by his foolishness."

"But I didn't—it's not—"

"Whatever experience you think you had there, you'd do well to forget it, along with the old man. Drowning in his own sentimentality, holding on to the long past, never looking forward, all the while offering platitudes to anyone dumb enough to listen." Brutus had never seen Lucian speak so forcefully, words almost spitting from his lips.

"It was just a—"

"It wasn't anything. That old man will choke on his oddities until they consume him, and the Cleaners will be there to ease the mess. That's it. There is no future in holding on to the past."

Even though the social club was alive with the buzz of conversation and deafening melodies, Brutus heard nothing but a sharp ringing in his ears. He sat quietly, trying to swallow down the lump in his throat. He hid his right hand in his pocket, clutching the notebook close to him as if Lucian could see the object through his coat and might rip it from his fingers.

"You want to see something real? Come with me."

Brutus got the feeling that Lucian's request was not optional. He got to his feet quickly to follow the white-clad figure as he glided across the room. Just before exiting the club, Lucian reached into his pocket and elegantly slid into place his lower jaw in one fluid movement.

It was a curious thing, as all things about Lucian were. Aside from the cracks which noticeably ran across his Face from where the two halves met, was the smile. It was, as best as Brutus could put it, a crooked thing. On the right side was a somewhat overly accentuated grin, bordering on manic, where the left side was a sharply curved frown. Both styles were unusual in their extremes, but together, absolutely unique.

The air was warm and heavy as the City settled in for the night. Blackness painted the sky and crept into the cracks and corners, only to be kept at bay by the sentinel lamps that lit the streets. The pair traversed in silence. Brutus thought twice about asking where they were going. Through the City, they wound their path, Lucian making each turn with purpose and certainty, almost as if guided by an invisible string.

As Brutus turned another corner to round another City block, he caught himself and almost tripped to avoid crashing into his guide, who had come to a complete and sudden halt. Recovering, Brutus looked up to see a large factory, glowing with green and orange lights and humming with purpose.

A large, illuminated monument sign nestled at the factory's feet identified their destination as an automated food processing plant. It looked almost identical to any other workshop that Brutus had ever come across. The only difference was denoted by the signage out front. By the shape of the caricature smiling in the illuminated logo, it seemed this specific factory was in charge of producing the City's bread products.

"Let's take a look inside, shall we?" Lucian whispered into the air, motioning for Brutus to follow him. After a moment's pause, he stepped forward and followed through the gates and up the ramp that led to the entrance.

We won't be allowed in, not at this hour, and not without proper identification for the doors. Brutus secretly hoped he was right, that the field trip would be canceled, and he could just go home and rest. To his disappointment, a blue light flickered on as they approached, and the automatic doors slid open in a wide welcome. Without missing a beat, Lucian stepped through the entrance as if he was a long expected guest. The factory lobby came to life slowly as they entered. There was no receptionist, no front desk, and no workers.

"Where is everyone?" Brutus asked as he looked around.

"All of the City's factories are fully automated. No need for people to waste their time pressing buttons or worrying about repetitive tasks. This is what progress makes possible." Without waiting for reply or further inquiry, Lucian left the lobby, making his way toward Wing E, and Brutus sped up to match his gate.

They walked through sleek metal halls and down tubes of grated steel. Doors and lights and wires and buttons littered the factory on every level. They passed enclosed halls with no apparent purpose. They saw dials and knobs in a rainbow of illuminated colors, turning and depressing themselves in practiced rhymes. Whirring and whispering and clanking could be heard from all angles and at all sides, as if the factory itself were a living creature, with metal gears for joints and organs made of plastic tubing.

As they wound themselves through the plant, Brutus thought of his own job and his own repetitious performance. He wondered how it was that his position even existed. How long would it be before the City transformed his office into a similar automated wonder? He could picture the long rows of cubicles and desk screens tapping themselves to life with no workers sitting behind them.

As they wandered through the halls of the living factory, they finally found their way to the center. A small room with ceiling to floor windows on all sides looked out over the facility's pumping heart. Veins of tubing sprang out of the flooring in corded bundles. Buzzing machines fluttered about, their proboscises injecting viscous fluids of various colors into unknown ports. Brutus was keenly aware of the noises coming from the heart. An incessant angry hum that rose and fell, followed every so often by the *whoosh, whoosh, whoosh* of the pneumatic chutes ferrying finished paste out into the City's kitchens, ready to be synthesized into any number of assorted bread products. Brutus observed the inner workings for some time, mesmerized by the precise repetition.

The entire factory seemed to work fluidly as one moving piece, though Brutus had his reservations. "If no one works here, what happens if something breaks or goes wrong?"

"It doesn't," Lucian replied. "The City has faith in that simple truth."

"But how is it maintained?" Brutus asked. "Who oils the cogs, who monitors the production?"

"It's all automated, Brutus. It is a self-sufficient marvel. The City has invested a great deal in automating the droll needs of its citizenship so that attention can be given to more important matters."

Lucian, who had been staring at the heart of the factory alongside Brutus, now turned to face him.

"I wonder though," Lucian continued, his odd smile cast upon his lips, "what do you think would happen if someone were to flip that little switch?"

Brutus turned to meet Lucian's gaze and then followed the finger of his gloved hand to see a small switch, glowing orange, on the nearby wall. There were dozens of buttons, knobs, and dials clicking and whirring about, but this switch alone looked unique. Brutus turned back to Lucian, smiling under his Face softly at the joke.

"Wouldn't that be something?" Brutus answered dismissively.

"It certainly would. I think you should try it." Lucian was serious.

"No, I couldn't. Who knows what that would do?"

"Precisely, who knows? You should find out."

Brutus stared at Lucian awkwardly, not sure how to respond. He chuckled softly and shook his head, then stood scratching the back of his neck to fill the silence.

"It is a simple thing to take risk, to take action," Lucian continued, his voice so soft it almost crooned, "as easy really, as a flip of a switch. Most people go their whole lives without taking action. Pity…"

The disappointment from Lucian's voice hit Brutus like a brick. It would be easy, just a quick flick, and probably nothing at all would happen. *Even if it did,* Brutus reasoned with himself, *the factory was made for this. It will right itself in no time.* He turned from Lucian and stepped over to the switch. It glowed at him with a pulsating orange light. Brutus raised his hand until his fingers just barely brushed the switch, then let them fall short.

"No," he shook his head and shrugged. "Better not."

"Well, that's that then," Lucian said, the frown of his smile more apparent as he turned and made to leave. "You can close the door."

Brutus stood frozen, his ears ringing as he stared at the now empty room, void of Lucian's presence, the door hanging ajar. He could hear soft footsteps retreating into the distance.

Without thinking, Brutus turned in a blur and forcefully flicked down the switch in one fluid movement. The glowing orange dimmed, and the whirring in the room turned into a gentle whine, and then a simper until silence finally fell. Brutus looked out into the heart, startled. The whooshing tubes and stirring electric insects were still and unmoving. In a slow but determined pattern, the lighting began to switch off square by square, one click at a time. In horror, Brutus turned back to the switch and flipped it up and down again in panic. The room grew dimmer still, the switch flopping up and down, dead.

Brutus turned on his heel and made for the door, lights flickering off in sequence behind him. Working himself up to a sprint, he navigated back through the metallic halls and empty rooms. Silence and darkness followed behind him, nipping at his heels. Darting into the lobby, Brutus' heart plunged as darkness set in completely and overtook him. He was trapped. He would die in here, drowning in silence and blackout. He looked around in terror, feeling his way around the room, bumping into corners. He fell to the floor and curled himself into a ball, his eyes stinging and wet behind his Face.

"Brutus?" His name rustled through the air. Looking up from the floor, he saw Lucian's Face smiling at him, framed in the doorway. A white gloved hand extended towards him, as another held open the sliding front doors, now dead in their tracks. "It's okay. Shall we go?"

Reaching out of the darkness, Brutus clasped the hand extended towards him and was pulled onto his feet. His legs wobbled as if made from the same jellied substance he had watched just moments before being pumped through the factory's now lifeless heart. Shaking, he managed to follow Lucian out of the plant and down the ramp. Looking behind him as they made their way back onto the streets, Brutus' eyes reflected no light and no color. The food processing plant was quiet, a husk of metal, a bulky black shape now barely visible in the night. The signage illuminated nothing. Brutus tore his eyes away from the sight of death and turned to follow Lucian. The pair walked on in silence as the minutes passed.

"Let's get something to eat," Lucian suggested finally. Brutus agreed with a nod but remained silent as they continued, their footsteps hollow echoes bouncing off the concrete body of the City.

The marbled slabs around them transformed from blank blocks of stone into leisure centers. Lucian led Brutus to a small restaurant stall at a nearby street corner. A low bar with black padded stools waited for them under a jutting overhang. The eatery was empty. Lucian walked in, ducking slightly under the eaves, and made his way to an illuminated menu displaying several variations of noodle bowls. Tapping twice on the house special,

Lucian then waited for his order to be spat out. Two large bowls, steaming with hot broth, rolled out onto the countertop.

"My treat," Lucian said to Brutus as he picked up one of the hot bowls and handed it to him.

"Thank you." Brutus grabbed the bowl with both hands and made his way to one of the empty stools. He poked at the noodles floating around the broth, finding that he was not very hungry. Despite the inherent mess that the meal should have left behind, his companion managed to consume his with a certain amount of tact and grace, somehow leaving his white suit immaculately clean. Aside from the slurping of noodles out of broth, the two shared the meal together in silence.

As Lucian sipped the last bit of broth from his bowl, a soft drizzle began to spatter across the overhang. Brutus readied himself to leave, but Lucian insisted they stay until Brutus ate his fill. Not wanting to be rude, Brutus focused on forcing down a few more bites of food.

The anxiety that still overwhelmed him after the factory tour made the noodles sit like worms in his stomach. The rain on the eves sped up its pattern, turning into a heavy downpour. Lucian let out a soft chuckle beside him as Brutus tried to down another mouthful. He would have felt self-conscious, embarrassed even, had he not noticed that Lucian was paying him no attention at all.

"Why do people run from the rain?" Lucian asked with a wide, sweeping gesture. "Look how they cower beneath the eaves and gutters of the world."

Brutus looked out across the square to see pale Faces scurrying away from open spaces, desperately trying to find shelter from the downpour.

"People don't like to get wet," He said before taking another bite.

"No matter what you do, you're going to get wet," Lucian leaned forward and, with a sly smile, pointed a finger back at himself, gently tapping the side of his nose, "and that's why I've learned not to mind the rain."

Brutus responded by wiping up the droplets of spilled broth in front of him and dabbing his shirt before getting up to dump his bowl and utensils into the incinerator. He returned to Lucian, and the pair readied themselves to leave.

Brutus hesitated before stepping out from the eaves and into the deluge, moving forward and then stepping back in an erratic motion. It had been a very long day, and Brutus felt as if his mind was a pile of wet paste, sloshing around inside the casing of his head. He turned to the silver-haired man standing next to him, waiting for a cue. Lucian laughed and clapped a hand on Brutus' shoulder.

"Live in the moment, Brutus, it's all we've got," and with that, Lucian stepped out from the protective overhang into the street and began to walk. His white suit turned dark gray as it soaked through.

Well, at least I'm close to home, Brutus thought to himself before he plunged out from dry safety. His feet splashed in the rivers forming on the hard asphalt. It only took seconds before he was soaked to the bone. Dress socks sodden, he could feel the water squelching between his toes. The shock of the cool water lasted just moments before his body heat warmed it to a more pleasant temperature.

"Wait up!" Brutus quickened his pace to catch up.

"I'll walk you home," Lucian said as he fell back, allowing Brutus to lead the way.

"Thanks."

Brutus looked around to get his bearings and led the journey home. He and Lucian kept up a steady banter of shallow conversation on the way back to the apartment. Rain continued to fall in heavy sheets, scaring away all traces of life, except the two of them plodding along in the dark.

"This is it," Brutus said at last as he slowed to a stop.

He watched Lucian's Face as he tilted his head up to try and see the top of the towering apartment complex. Droplets pooled in the creases of his jawline and ran like rivers, dripping down his chin.

"See you around, Brutus." Lucian nodded his goodbye before turning to walk back down the street they had just come from, presumably to return to his haunt at the club.

Brutus entered the ground floor lobby dripping from head to toe, water audibly sloshing around inside his polished shoes. Ignoring the lingering stares and not-so-subtle glances, Brutus made his way up the elevator and sighed as he closed his apartment door behind him. His wife, sitting predictably in her usual spot, gave him a half-hearted wave as he entered but said nothing about the state he was in. Brutus dripped his away across the living room and into the bedroom. There he stripped down and began ringing out his soggy clothes. Picking up his coat to do the same, he sucked in his breath as his hands ran through the pockets.

His notebook was a wet mass of pages.

He stared at it for a long while, mourning the state of it. Suddenly, the bedroom door opened behind him. In a flash of instinct, Brutus hurled the book away from him and watched as it slid under the bed.

"What are you doing?" His wife's voice cut dryly through the air. Brutus looked up at her without moving and caught himself in the bedroom mirror. He was crouched on his haunches, sopping wet, and completely nude aside from the placid smile etched on his pale white mask. Brutus couldn't help himself. After all he had been through today and the absurdity of his current position, he tilted his head back and let out a loud bark of a laugh.

"Brutus, wha—" His wife started to say, but was cut off by the continued laughter that bubbled out of his Face.

Startled by the strangeness of the noise and the obscenity of what crouched before her, Shelby jumped back in alarm. It was the fastest Brutus had ever seen his wife move, and that doubled him over even more. Shaking in silent, gleeful sobs, Brutus didn't even notice his wife backpedal and exit the bedroom as quickly as possible.

He lay there sprawled out on the cold, wet floor, shaking into the early hours of the morning, until he finally drifted off to sleep. It was a deep and troubled sleep, filled with large, shapeless mouths filled with factory teeth and rain that filled up the streets until he drowned in it.

In the now sunken City, all he could see was murky darkness, and all he could hear were low, chattering whispers. As he continued to sink and suck water into his lungs, little orbs of light fell around him, illuminating the waters in dimly lit spheres. It was in these spheres that he could see oddities from the old man's shop sinking with him, sifting down into the deep ghostly lighting.

As Brutus landed at the bottom of the pit in which he had been sinking, he saw a lone mask without an owner floating gracefully down beside him, like a petal falling to the ground from a great height. The hollowed eyes bore down on him as he drifted off into another long-forgotten dream.

23 | Devious

Brutus awoke with an aching pain in his neck and a stiffness in his back. He rolled over with a groan as his tailbone dug into the hard floor. He pushed himself up onto all fours before sitting back on his heels. *I spent all night like this?* he thought as he examined his nude form.

A rustling caught his ear as it became apparent that his wife had come to bed sometime after he had passed out on the floor. *She would have had to walk right over me to get to her side.* Brutus found he was not surprised in the least bit at her callousness.

Picking himself up along with the damp clothes that still lay strewn about, Brutus rose as silently as he could to avoid waking the bulky shape in his bed. He tossed his bundled wet clothes into the washer and then turned to examine Shelby.

Her head was barely visible over the bedding, electric beetle eyes flickering dimly as they tracked her sleep cycle. He knew that behind that Face, soft musical notes lulled her to sleep. The same electric melodies would rouse her in a few hours with a gradual crescendo. Then her sensors would immediately switch on to her favorite reality entertainment cycle while she got up to eat and dress and then predictably watch a few hours of shopping.

Shelby was always finding new things to buy and cling to, new things to try and fill some wide, aching hole that Brutus himself could no longer compete with. He wondered when the last time was that she had listened to real silence, and had to suppress the urge to power off the auditory frequencies pumping through her second by second. With a shrug, Brutus turned to take a hot steam shower to clear his head.

Pulling on fresh dry clothes and transferring his pen to his new coat pocket, Brutus did his best to tame his unruly black hair as it cascaded over his forehead. He then sat down for a quick breakfast before work.

"Toast and eggs," Brutus told the kitchenette dispenser as he scrolled through the morning news.

Da-derr.

Brutus looked up at the noise as the menu flashed red.

"Toast and eggs, I said."

Da-derr.

"Alright, what's the matter?" Brutus got up to reset the menu screen and then manually typed in his breakfast order.

Da-derr.

Brutus swore. He looked at the screen and this time read the error message in its entirety:

ERROR 6088: Invalid nutriment available for product 0307

Brutus skimmed through the menu to see multiple items flagged with the same red error code. It took little investigatory effort for him to quickly see that all the menu options with any sort of related bread products were affected. A chill ran down his spine as he re-submitted his order for just eggs. *No, it couldn't have been…*

Sitting down with his plate, Brutus tapped on the morning news and threw it onto the wall. He watched as the daily weather-station report announced clear skies for the day, and he swallowed down his last bite of egg as the briefest of ribbons danced across the bottom of the City's newsreel: "City-wide bread shortage today as automated production factory is slated to go back online after sudden shutdown."

And that was it. A brief and drifting notification that cut in before the day's advertisements began. Brutus' shock slowly transformed into a dull sense of excitement. *He* had done that.

He had done something that had affected the entire City, and by something so simple as flicking a switch. Brutus left for work, light on his feet while attempting a breathy whistle.

He watched as the commuters ahead of him lined up to cross the street. They waited for the tonal birds to chirp and the green pedestrian lights to flash, welcoming them to traverse a few at a time.

Brutus stepped up, waited for the birds to sing their songs amid the flashing lights, then moved with the next crowd. As he crossed, watching his shoes padding forward, he had an idea. Instead of continuing straight across the sidewalk and into the office building, Brutus stepped aside and waited.

As the next rush of commuters made their way across the dark, still river of asphalt, Brutus moved in closer to the street pole. Hidden in the camouflage of dark suits and white shirts, Brutus examined the backing of the automated creature and found he could pry it open just enough to see the wires inside that made it tick.

Quick as a cat, he reached a few fingers inside and gave a sharp tug. The brightly chirping bird wore down into a halting warble as Brutus turned in guilty glee and escaped into his office building.

As the elevator scuttled him up to his floor, Brutus could see the street from the windows he passed. A dam had started to form at the crossing, cresting and breaking as more and more black-suited bodies lined up to crash against the imaginary obstacle. Brutus saw what his handiwork had done.

The crosswalk stood silently in a blank stare, no bird to chirp them across the streets, and no flashing light to signal their turn. Unable to cross, a stream of never-ending commuters piled up on the sidewalk behind them. The crowd quickly bulked up in such a fashion that he could see it pouring into alleys and stretching far down the sidewalk on either side. A black and white peppered river, bursting at the seams, flowing into every outlet it could find as the dam in front shuddered to brace itself against the force building behind it.

Traffic whizzed by at extraordinary speeds, no signals to slow down. Brutus wondered what would happen if the crowd broke the dam and burst forward into the streets, unable to hold itself back. What would happen if fast speeding blocks of metal met with the river of bodies now pooling up in force?

Brutus watched in utter fascination at the scene unfolding below him until the elevator reached its destination and spit him out on his floor. Brutus stepped out and immediately ran to the nearest window to continue his observations of the chaos clambering onto the streets. He was met with disappointment. From his vantage point now, he was too high to see the crossing or the waves of commuters crashing against the streets. With a sigh, Brutus went to his seat and got on with his day.

It was quiet at the office. Brutus had never had such an undisturbed workday. No calls, no interruptions. He went about his work with ease and efficiency, catching up on projects and even getting a little ahead. When lunch bells jingled on his desk screen, Brutus locked his workstation and headed to the break room.

As he pulled his daily allotted meal out of the workplace dispenser, Brutus sat down by himself. It seemed odd that no one else had joined him, as he knew at least a dozen others had the same staggered break. Brutus munched on his sandwich—a thick slab of ham and lettuce, no bread—enjoying the stillness of the room. He finished up and went back to his desk, noticing rows of empty cubicles on either side.

"Well, this is a bit strange indeed," Brutus mused to himself as he looked around. The office floor was vacant, save for a few early shift workers dotting the professional landscape. Instead of sitting down at his desk, Brutus walked the identical aisles, greeting the sparse smattering of coworkers he passed. He had never traversed the entirety of the office floor before. As he circled around, he noticed the light in Shaun's office was off, and his chair was vacant. He, too, had disappeared for the day. With a soft smile, Brutus headed straight there. Gently brushing the handle, he was surprised as it fell open to his touch.

"No," Brutus told the empty office, his voice echoing softly.

"Nope!" Brutus pointed his finger at the vacant leather chair behind the desk.

Brimming with excitement, Brutus stepped further inside. He froze like a cornered criminal when Shaun's automated light sensors turned on. After taking the time to ensure no one had noticed his presence, he chuckled softly and relaxed. Not quite sure what his plan was, Brutus took his time looking around Shaun's office. It was clean, dull, and sterile. The only bit of humanity about it was the series of obligatory wholesome family imagery floating around on his desk screen. Brutus watched the images fade in and out for a few minutes. Shaun only talked about his family if the conversation benefited him, as if his young wife and child were well-earned commodities.

Brutus bent forward, shaking his head, and tapped Shaun's desk screen to life. He could not enter his bosses' network without his credentials. He could, however, change the base display settings as a guest user, and Brutus did just that. Overriding the imagery of Shaun's family, he blanked out the display, setting it to the formless gray of factory default. He then moved the perfectly aligned desk chair ten inches to the left. Pleased with his antics, Brutus turned to leave the office. Just for good measure, he grabbed a handful of overpriced sweets from the translucent dish behind Shaun's desk. He then departed from Shaun's office, leaving the door wide open.

Brutus spent the rest of his workday wandering around, slowly savoring the sweets he had stolen and leaving a trail of wrappers behind him. He had never explored his workplace so thoroughly before and found himself fascinated by all that he didn't know. Winding his way through the labyrinth of cubicles, sucking on sweets, he made little adjustments to any desk with an absent body.

For station Number 45, he tilted the screen at an obtuse angle. At Number 79, he raised the desk chair up just a hair past its customized setting. At Number 113, he lowered the chair by an inch. And at stations Number 156 and 158, he switched their chairs out entirely. When he had finally made his rounds, Brutus returned to the break room and made an extra strong cup of coffee before unplugging the machine and dropping the cord down behind the cabinets. It was the best day at work that Brutus had ever had.

When the workday was done, Brutus tipped his imaginary hat to the office and cheerfully made his way to the ground floor. The streets outside had righted themselves in the time he had left them, but the flow of traffic seemed off, like a syncopated rhythm unable to find its way back on track.

The club loomed in his mind as he made his way towards it. Had it been just yesterday that he had visited Anhedonia and been met with Lucian's frustration? Before he knew it, he was there once more, diving into the darkness and floating on rising hypnotic melodies. As his eyes adjusted their settings to the lighting, Brutus was surprised to see Lucian sitting at the bar, already sipping on amber liquids. He made his way over to his friend, and tonight it was Brutus who led the greeting.

"Good evening," Brutus spoke with excitement hidden behind his motionless Face.

"Good evening, Brutus," Lucian spoke in turn, offering a visible smile. "How are things today?"

"Today…" Brutus breathed in the stale air and sweat lingering in the club, "…today, I'm doing great."

And Brutus began to recount his misadventures. Lucian's smile did not waver this time as Brutus spoke.

"Brutus, I think you deserve to treat yourself," Lucian said, laying a gentle hand on his forearm. "There's someone here tonight I think you'll enjoy."

Brutus followed Lucian's gaze and immediately caught the glint of yellow sequins on the dance floor. He stirred, noticeably intrigued. All he could muster in reply was a weak smile that remained hidden behind his mask.

"Go on then," Lucian offered his permission.

"Thanks…"

Brutus didn't need telling twice. He practically jumped from the stool to chase after threads of yellow weaving in and out of writhing bodies.

"And Brutus?" Lucian called. "Whatever happens, it's on the house tonight." He gave him a smirk and a nod, raising his glass towards Brutus before downing the rest.

Brutus barely heard Lucian's words as he charged forward onto the open floor. He was emboldened by recent events and very nearly carefree. It took some time for him to work his way into the crowd, all the while following the glimmers of yellow. Finally, as he neared the center, he saw her. She danced with passion and purpose, swinging every curve of her body into motion. Brutus approached, bumping up against her as the crowd jostled them together.

"Hi!" He shouted over the noise. "I've seen you before, I'm Brutus!"

"Hi." The Mouse's voice was muffled and gentle.

Her round white ears jerked up and down as she dipped her head in tune with the music. Before any further introductions could be shouted, she spun away from Brutus and moved her body into him. His breath stuck in his throat as her yellow dress caught in the lighting, and her soft skin pressed into him.

Not sure how to react, he threw his hands up and waved them around a bit while trying to match her movements. In a fluid motion, the Mouse turned again, this time to face Brutus. The coy smile stitched into the Face she wore stayed transfixed as she reached up and grabbed his wrists, slowly bringing them down to her level. Brutus continued to stomp his feet back and forth, too lost in her presence to find his coordination. He thought he heard laughter coming from the Mouse as she shook her head at him. Embarrassed, Brutus slowed to a stop and mumbled an apology.

"Shush," she said, "just relax and follow my lead."

Brutus tried to calm down and loosen his body. She ran her hands over his own and gently pulled them towards her. She moved in perfect timing with the pulsating music as she touched his hands to her chest, running them down over her breasts, her waist, her thighs, and finally pulled him in to clasp her lower back. She leaned in close to him now, her wrists resting loosely on his shoulders, her ears brushing his Face.

"Just let yourself go," she whispered. Drunken with the proximity of her touch, he swayed in tune with her body as it pressed against him and tried not to shuffle his feet. This was so much more than he had expected. As one seemingly unending song rolled into another, the Mouse tilted her nose closer to his ear.

"I have a spot for us, if you want to take this somewhere else."

"Sure," Brutus spoke without thinking and followed behind her blindly as she led him out of the crowd and across the room by his wrist. They passed the bar, which was now void of Lucian, and headed for a darkened hallway that Brutus had never before noticed in all his nights here. They passed down the hall and up some stairs. It was quieter back here, the noise of the social club muted but still vibrating through the walls in dulled tones.

"Where are we?" Brutus asked aloud. The Mouse did not answer, nor did she slow her pace as they passed rows of closed doors until finally, she stopped outside of number nine. Brutus stood behind her as she touched her thumb to the brass handle and heard a faint jingle of recognition as the automated door slid open.

He followed her inside to a dimly lit room with minimal furnishings. Aside from a small table, chair, and an open steam shower, there was a large double bed. There were no windows in the room. Instead, the wall across from the bed was embedded with a large image screen, which rested with soft gray wisps of smoke dancing across it. As Brutus stepped into the room and the door suctioned closed behind him, the image screen flickered to life, and ribbons of color rippled across, synchronizing with the gentle and inviting music that began to pipe in around them.

Oh… Brutus suddenly put two and two together.

"Listen, I don't know if we're on the same page here," Brutus said aloud as he backed towards the exit.

"I think we are," the Mouse spoke, her voice gentle and soft, "you just don't know it yet."

As she approached him, she slowly slipped out of her yellow dress. She kicked it aside as it fell to the ground and continued to saunter towards him. Brutus was surprised to see that she had been dancing so close to him all night, with nothing underneath. Her form was flawless.

Frozen by the door, his breath turned ragged. He could feel the heat of her body as she approached him, and he remained immobile while her slender fingers undid his tie and slid off his coat.

"Loosen up," her whisper tickled his ear as she slowly unbuttoned his shirt.

His heart was thumping so fast he was surprised she made no mention of it as she ran her fingers across his chest. Her small hands trailed down until they reached his waist, where they grabbed hold of his belt. The Mouse walked backwards, guiding him over to the bed. Brutus followed obediently, completely lost in her golden eyes and smooth skin.

With practiced movements, she quickly unfastened his belt, unbuttoned his pants, and slid everything down to the ground. Brutus felt like he was somewhere else, someone else, watching the scene unfold. His mind sputtered and tried to click back on in a wave of protest that couldn't quite break the surface. With a forceful yet gentle push, Brutus fell back onto the bedding, and in one swift motion, the Mouse slid herself onto his lap.

Brutus let out a low moan that was both fear and pleasure mixed together. It had been a long time since anyone had shown him any interest in this way, a long time since a warm body had feverishly pushed its way onto his. Brutus' senses were overcome with pure ecstasy as all other thoughts and cares were pushed aside while he lived purely and solely in the moment. The two coiled together in an endless embrace. Sweat dripped from both their bodies and mingled as they moved together as one until Brutus could no longer hold himself back.

He looked to see golden eyes staring at him over the stitched grin of the Mouse's Face. She giggled, rolling herself off of Brutus, and picked up her dress from the floor before going to use the toilet.

"You can use the shower to rinse off," she called from behind the opaque curtain.

Brutus' head throbbed as the room spun around him. He lay there on the bed, sprawled as he tried to catch his breath.

"That was..." Brutus swallowed, trying to find the words. "Thank you."

The Mouse made no reply except to flush the toilet.

"The room is yours for about ten more minutes," she said as she grabbed a glass of water and sat down in one of the chairs, still nude down to her heels. She crossed her legs as she leaned back, stretching her neck from side to side.

Brutus pulled himself up into a sitting position and bent down to grab his clothes where they lay strewn about. Covering himself with his bundled trousers in a delayed bout of modesty, he shuffled past the Mouse and into the steam shower. He rinsed quickly and thoroughly, his mind racing.

It's like I'm standing in a dream, he thought with a dazed smile.

"Did you say something?" Brutus peeked his head out from the curtains, taking care to cover himself.

"I didn't say anything."

Brutus shrugged and dressed in silence.

The Mouse sat still, watching him. Brutus walked over to her as he adjusted his tie and held out his hand.

"Umm…thanks again. Do I, owe you anything?" His hand trembled slightly. The Mouse set her glass down on the table and grabbed his hand. Instead of shaking it, she used it to pull herself up out of her chair.

"No, it's all taken care of, this time."

The stitched smile never wavered. Brutus lingered, looking into the shimmer of her eyes, past her naked body, wanting to see more. He reached up, placing a hand on either side of her Face, caressing her soft white cheeks. He closed his fingers and gently started pulling upwards. Her hands immediately closed around his wrists, squeezing tightly.

"No," the Mouse said forcefully.

"I want to see," Brutus whispered, almost pleading.

"No."

Brutus released his grip and let her pull his hands away. He shook his head, feeling foolish.

"I'm sorry, I—"

"Your time is up, you need to go," she said softly, not meeting his gaze.

"I'm sorry," Brutus said again.

He opened the door and left without turning back.

It was later than usual as Brutus made his way out of the club and onto the streets. He knew that he should feel guilty for what he had done, but he found that, at least for the moment, he just felt sleepy and content. He strolled through the streets, observing the small cracks in the sidewalk and patterns cast by the glowing eyes of the streetlamps.

As he neared his apartment, he heard a commotion and stopped to look. A flurry of shadows tore down the length of a nearby alley in a frenzy before they screeched suddenly to a halt. From where he stood on the street, Brutus could just make out the shadows of four school-age children bending over something small and dark.

The youths bounded back and forth as if trying to block the escape of a small, scurrying creature. One of the figures bent forward with sudden force, and Brutus heard the scared yowl of a cat calling out into the night. Again and again, the figure struck down at the ground, launching the others into a flurry of motion as they scuffed their shoes against the pavement, and then they were still.

The excitement that had suddenly overcome them burned out quickly, and the four youths turned away in detachment. Brutus watched as they drew closer, four pale Faces shining in the night with mild-mannered smiles set perpetually upon their jaws. They passed without a word and set off into the night.

Peering down the alley, Brutus saw a small shadow at its end, lying motionless. Still trying to understand what he just saw, Brutus walked nervously towards the dark lump but kept his eyes fixed straight ahead. He reached the end and was halted with a bricked-up wall. Mustering his courage, Brutus knelt to inspect the ground.

"Wait, what?" Brutus asked aloud. Instead of the small, crushed bundle of fur he had expected to find, he was met with a nub protruding oddly from the ground. An old telephone pole cut down ages ago, its dying roots left intact as the City grew around it.

Cat must've gotten away… Brutus sighed in relief. He gave the protrusion a playful kick before turning away to make the final leg of his journey, exhausted from the day's events.

"Are you tired at the end of the day? A little soggy in the thinking department? Staggering home after a satisfying and productive day of work? What's the last thing you want to do at the end of the day?"

A string of halfhearted ideas played out for Shelby as she watched the advertisement. *Have sex with my husband,* she scoffed out loud, bouncing slightly in her indented throne. The springs within the frame wheezed their discontent at her jostling.

"I'll tell you what it is, it's emptying your pockets. I know, I know, you're saying to yourself, 'Well Steve, I do that every day, it's just something that has to happen.' Well, I agree with you there, but we here think that there's a quick and easy way we can change your life.

"It's called *Pocket-In-A-Pocket,* the new revolutionary way to help start and end your day right. Rather than fiddling with all that change or having to re-sort your tram and passing cards..."

Shelby nodded as the man in her lens spilled his copious amounts of change and slipped while trying to pull his cards out of his normal pockets, sending them everywhere. *I could use one of those.*

"...Pocket-In-A-Pocket makes moving your life around easier. It's so simple, just take the diligently and thoroughly designed pocket and load it up like any of your regular pockets. Then insert your Pocket-In-A-Pocket into your old, boring pocket, and off you go. Then at the end of the day, pop out your Pocket-In-A-Pocket and set them down anywhere. On your nightstand, kitchen counter, coffee table, heck even leave it in your old pants pockets! Next day, get dressed, grab your Pocket-In-A-Pocket, and off you go again. It's that simple.

"Therapeutic Value Channel only sells quality purchases for a quality feeling. That's why we give it our 'V for Value' stamp of approval. We wouldn't sell these if they weren't great, and if you act now, you can get your second Pocket-In-A-Pocket for the same price. That's right, your second Pocket-In-A-Pocket is the same price as the first. What a deal!"

Shelby didn't wait for the advertisement to end. She blinked twice and placed her order for the two Pocket-In-A-Pockets. Her billing information had already been saved as a 'V-alue' customer, and before the advertisement had finished, her transaction was completed.

Her Face smiled for her as she blinked through to another category. Facial accessories were her favorite, and she patiently waited while her eyes tuned in to see what was for sale.

"Rose-colored lenses are the newest and best way to see the City—"

Shelby sighed as she blinked out of the category. She already had those, and they weren't that great. It was time to scan through the channels, a habit that took hours to find anything interesting.

Really, I can't believe there isn't anything new. Her eyes flicked rapidly, sorting through selections by category, release time, best value, classics, and even a few "coming soons".

There were hundreds of selections, but she'd already seen them, and Brutus never caught her hints about upgrading. Linda, her neighbor, was on a premium pass, and Shelby couldn't shut her up about all the things and places she'd seen in her eyes. Even through the walls, Shelby could hear her cackling as she enjoyed her premium account.

Shelby coughed, forgetting to breathe for a moment. It really was ludicrous that she was expected to do everything. It was hard enough trying to find quality entertainment.

"Hello Shelby," the morose voice of her dense husband Brutus grated at her ears. "Watch anything good?"

"Hmm," she wheezed out from her place on the sofa. *'Watch anything good?' No, no I haven't you cheap bastard!*

"Have you, had a nice day?"

"Suppose." *Spare me your insistent driveling, you thick-browed knuckle dragging buffoon.*

"That's good, how about I come and sit with you and we can tune in together on something?"

"Uggh!" she exhaled in annoyance. *Ah, just go away! I don't want to hear your breathing in my ear over the channel.*

To her delight, she heard the bedroom door slide open and then close.

25 | UNFORTUNATE

Brutus lay awake all night, playing his encounter with the Mouse over and over again, savoring every detail as his wife weighed down the bed beside him. By morning, he arose wide awake, despite not grabbing even a moment of sleep. He greedily wolfed down his usual of eggs and toast—it seemed the production factory had been reset—and headed to work as if nothing in the world had changed. He even gave his wife a shock by crossing the living room floor and brushing her cheek with his cold, rubbery lips.

He chuckled to himself at the memory of her jolting forward, startled by his touch. *If she only knew.* Brutus shook his head, separating out his life into neat little compartments.

By the time he arrived at work, his thoughts had drifted back to the Mouse once more. He hardly noticed Shaun asking who had been in his office during the road closure yesterday, threatening to take punitive measures to find the mysterious assailant. Instead, Brutus ran his tongue over his lips as he recalled every curve of the Mouse's body.

Tonight wouldn't be too soon to go back, would it? But Brutus wasn't really asking himself. The screen flashed red then orange as he absentmindedly tapped the wrong command over and over again. Finally, the machine shut itself off and rebooted in self-defense. Shaken out of his daydreaming fugue by the sudden blackness, Brutus decided to take a break and headed for the restroom.

He could hear his coworkers murmuring as he passed. A mutter here, a reply to follow, a sound over there. *Do they usually talk this much, isn't the office normally quieter?* The voices filled his ears with their unsettled buzzing, muddling his brain. *What are they all talking about?* Brutus picked up his pace. *Are they talking about me? Do they know about me...what I did?*

By the time he reached his destination, a mild panic had settled in. He shut the bathroom door and pressed his weight against it as if to shield himself from his coworkers and their judgement. *They must know something, they're all talking about me...*

His vision blurred slightly, and his head spun, just as it had in the Mouse's room. Brushing against the wall for support, Brutus made his way to the sink, his ears ringing sharply. Pushing his palms down on either side of the porcelain, Brutus bent over and began breathing deeply. He looked up to see his pale white Face glaring back at him, and his vision stuttered.

He saw the wrinkled Face of the old woman with knowing eyes dissolve into the skewed grin of Lucian, and the reflection laughed at him. He gave his Face a panicked tap as his vision distorted again before settling back into place. His alabaster visage was there, but there was something keenly real about it. Glowering back at him as the lips actively folded into a scowl, its brow furrowed into an impossible configuration. There was something of truth in the reflection of that untruthful Face, a ripple of an echo from something far away, and fear entered Brutus' heart at what that could possibly be.

He slowed his ragged breathing to regain some sense of calm. He brought his thoughts back to the Mouse, and the idea of seeing her again helped to steady his mind. Pulling back his sleeves, he washed his hands thoroughly with ice-cold water until the ringing in his ears subsided. He dried his hands methodically and left to return to his desk, the scowling Face watching him as he went. This time the office floor was silent, and no voices escorted him back to his seat.

Brutus did not find comfort in the silence, and the end of the day could not come quickly enough. The one thing that filled the silence and kept his unease at bay was the thought of the Mouse. He could see her clearly in his head, but he needed to see her again in person, he needed to be close to her.

When, at long last, the day came to an end, and Brutus was released from his sterile prison, he couldn't push through the crowds fast enough. Each twinkling streetlamp and glaring headlight on his journey was the flicker of her golden eyes just out of reach.

I'm on my way, he said to each golden shimmer.

When he finally reached the club, Brutus shoved the door wide and traversed the club with purpose. Time passed, and Brutus sat, waiting. No

Lucian came to provide him company. No Mouse on the dance floor. *Had last night even happened?* His head spun as he tried to remember the details and will them into reality once more.

He drummed his fingers across the countertop as he ordered another drink. The bartender handed it to him with an exaggerated and unwavering smile. He sipped his drink through pliable lips, and his mind continued to spin with doubt and confusion.

Where was Lucian to bring him clarity when he needed it most? Instead, he was guided to the pen in his pocket, clicking it frantically as he turned back to scan for the Mouse once more. What he saw instead made him choke as he sucked in his drink, gasping between strangled coughs.

Shaun walked in from the back door and looked around. To his horror, he started to make his way towards where Brutus sat.

He did his best to get his hacking under control, bits of liquid spewing from his mouth. Not knowing what else to do, he got up in a panic to try to run and hide among the crowd.

"Hey! No drinks on the dance floor," the bartender reprimanded him sternly with his smiling Face.

"Oh, sorry," Brutus choked out. He tensed as he looked to see Shaun just seconds away from him. His hands acted before his brain could approve, and he let his drink fall from his loosened grip, wincing as it shattered on the ground.

"Careful!" the bartender counseled politely overhead as Brutus bent down to pick up the broken pieces. Shiny brown shoes strode past him, just inches away from his fingers as he picked at slivers of broken glass. Brutus paused, crouching under the bar, and watched the backside of Shaun move away. Relief washed over him like a hot steam shower.

Then a very different feeling flooded Brutus to the core as he watched Shaun approach the dark hallway in the corner of the social club. A young woman with a Mouse's head and a skin-tight yellow dress appeared and grasped Shaun's hand, leading him into the darkness.

"You alright down there?" The bartender leaned over the counter.

Brutus picked himself up slowly and laid the shards of glass he had gathered down on the countertop with a clatter.

"Sorry for the mess," Brutus mumbled, not looking at the bartender, eyes transfixed on the dark corner, hoping she would return alone. The black and empty hallway sucked him in, dimming all other sensations around him.

"It's alright, I hope you didn't hurt yourself." The fake concern in the bartender's words cut into Brutus.

"Wha—no, no I'm fine. Thanks." Brutus said without turning to acknowledge the man.

He felt the club closing in on him, making it hard to breathe. He needed to get out. Stumbling from the bar and navigating through the crowd, he managed to finally escape back into the darkening alley.

The cool night air nipped at his heels as he ran down the alley, his eyes stinging as grey clouds gathered above him, ready to burst at the seams. Choking back a sob, Brutus fingered his pocket for his pen and began to click it in repetition as he made the journey home.

He entered the apartment, feeling Shelby's presence in her usual haunt without even looking at her. Marching into the bedroom, Brutus closed the door behind him and shakily lowered himself onto the bed where he sat in silence.

Click, click, click.

"You're fine, you're just fine," Brutus said to himself. He ran his fingers over the smooth barrel of his pen with his hands in his lap.

Click, click, click.

"It's no big deal, not really. You're overreacting my friend," Brutus told himself. He cocked his head and chuckled at himself behind immobile lips.

"Am I, though?" Brutus' tone suddenly turned cold.

"You fool, you're just the same to her as everyone else."

The pen glimmered as he twirled it around, catching the harsh bathroom light.

Click, click, click.

Brutus clicked the pen slowly, in and out, in and out. He thought of the Mouse, and he tried to focus on the night he had her all to himself. Brutus was again overcome with the urge to put pen to paper and see what might work its way out.

Reaching into his coat pocket, he felt a sudden pang in his chest as he found it missing but quickly remembered tossing the sodden notebook under the bed after the night at the factory. Bending down on all fours, he groped beneath the bed frame until his hand closed on what he sought. He was relieved to see that the journal had dried out for the most part and showed little signs of damage aside from a few more exaggerated wrinkles in the already warped pages.

Brutus clicked the pen one more time until the shining nib protruded from the barrel. *Click.*

He hesitated for a moment before bringing it down to the page in one swift motion and pressed firmly as he drug the pen across paper in a series of lines. He stopped, raised the pen up in the air, and saw that nothing was there but indents cutting across the page.

"What?!" Brutus asked the notebook. "Why don't you work?"

He met pen to paper a second time, pressing harder but producing the same results. He held up the pen and examined it closely. He tried again, scribbling in mad circles, around and around and around, tearing the paper into ribbons. The pages remained blank. The shapes he had cut into the notebook were open mouths, laughing at him in mockery.

Brutus cursed aloud as he flung the notebook across the room. It hit the wall harmlessly and landed with a thud on the ground, splayed open and torn like the garbage it was.

He marched over, picked it up, and walked into the bathroom, where he tossed it into the lavatory incinerator. Watching the dull glow blaze to life, he smiled to himself as the book writhed and melted into a pile of ash, the handwritten inscription on the inside cover distorted in the flames.

Brutus winced and shrunk into himself as from the corner of his eye, he noticed a reflection. The better part of himself told him to walk away and leave, but everything else commanded him to look.

There were no scowling Faces or fever dreamed illusions, just a pathetic, worn, smiling fool. A pitiful and contemptuous thing. He walked over to the bathroom mirror and stared down the stranger, cocking his head at the serene smile. Reaching up, he touched the cheeks and caressed the hollows of the eyes, black and blue and white pulsating eyes of the unfamiliar. Eyes that saw nothing beyond what they were allowed.

Brutus reached his fingers to the seams behind its ears and applied pressure until he felt a release. Then, with calm and steady hands, he pulled off the Face and let it land limply in the sink.

It had been many, many years since Brutus had examined his real face. First, it was from the inconvenience of it, then out of the habit of covering it, and eventually out of fear of what had become the unknown. Built-in moisturizing creams and skincare automation had kept his face clean and rejuvenated even as it lay unused behind layered protection. Yet not even the highest priced model with the best add-ons could buff out the stain that neglect had left on Brutus.

His eyes were dull, yellowed, and peppered with red spider web veins as they sat back in dark, sunken sockets. His forehead creased in a resting frown. Wrinkles cut into his mouth and jaw from practiced indifference. His cheeks were hollow, and his skin as pale as the mask he had worn for so many years. Brutus used his newly found skills to crack a rusty smile and found himself terrified by the ghoul he now saw grinning back at him. He stood for a moment, examining the face, untidy black hair falling across his brow.

Brutus unhinged his jaw and smacked his lips as he opened and closed his mouth to make a series of smacking and popping sounds. He bared his teeth. He wrinkled his nose. He wiggled his eyebrows. He sucked in air and puffed out his cheeks. He moved every muscle in his face, and still, he did not recognize the person staring back at him, nor did he recognize the limp mask lying in the sink. Running his hands through his hair, down the contours of his visage, Brutus pinched both of his lips and landed an open palm against his cheek with a loud slap.

"How can this be me?" Brutus muttered to himself over and over again until he let out one final laugh from that dark and monstrous maw. He then gathered his coat and readied himself to leave, his hand automatically caressing the silver pen. His Face entirely forgotten.

He moved across the room and paused as he reached the door. He turned to see his wife sitting alone, staring dead ahead.

"I'm going out, again," Brutus announced to the room.

Shelby didn't move. She did not turn her head, make a sound, or even shrug in acknowledgement. She did not see the quivering smile on his face or his nostrils fluttering as they sucked in air. He stood there for a moment more, almost wishing she would stop him.

Shelby did not move.

"And fuck you, too," Brutus muttered as the door closed tightly behind him and headed out into the night, his mind a-buzz with a stream of incoherent thought.

26 | CHECKS AND BALANCES

The timing of her death would have been better served at a later date, but even if she had been alive, it would be safe to assume that Shelby wouldn't have turned around to look at Brutus anyway.

As the door slammed shut behind her husband, Shelby slid loosely from her favorite corner of the couch and fell forward, her lens cracking on the glass coffee table before she landed heavily on the ground with a thud.

The seal on her Face slipping ever so slightly as the sound of the shopping channel played into the room for no one to hear. In her unending pursuit for the bigger and better, she'd forgone the simplest of luxuries.

She'd forgotten how to breathe.

27 | A Simple Thought of Sanity

The City was quiet and empty. Brutus wandered through the streets, almost drunkenly swaying as he took in the world through unfiltered eyes. The cool night air kissed his face as he walked, a sensation unknown, making his lip curl and his nose wrinkle at the tingle of it. Brutus brushed his hand across the cold, scratchy surface of the many buildings he passed, all almost identical in shape, form, and purpose.

With each corner he rounded, he braced himself for meeting an unexpected bystander, feeling like a monster let loose in the City. Yet time and time again, Brutus turned to meet no one. He felt naked and exposed, yet oddly free. There was a certain thrill in taking such a risk and exposing himself to the City that always grew but never changed.

He hummed a faltering tune to hear his own voice and drank in the stench of the canal through unhindered nasal passages. The empty silence of the streets started to steer Brutus' mind into doubt. He felt a need to find someone, to hear them call out to him to confirm his existence, yet still, no one appeared.

Weaving through the City, Brutus finally found himself standing once more in front of Anhedonia, almost as if something had been guiding him in his wanderings. His body had brought him here, and so he decided to listen to it.

Without giving it a second thought, he pushed forward through the doors and entered the club. The scene was familiar at first, which brought him comfort, but only for a short while. Almost instantly, he sensed a change in the atmosphere. Pale masks were drawn to him, watching with an unwavering gaze as he walked through the club. He could almost hear their whispered murmurs over the pounding music still piping through. Hands lifted and pointed as he passed, and bodies recoiled as he approached.

There it was, the recognition he'd been looking for. He sucked in air through gritted teeth and felt himself empowered.

He wasn't the Face, he was Brutus.

The patrons stepped aside to give him an unusually wide berth, and he made it to the bar with ease. The same bartender who had served him earlier in the day was still there, busy with other customers. Brutus calmly waited until it was his turn to speak.

"Is Lucian here?" He asked.

The man jerked as he turned to see Brutus. He drew his hands close to his body instinctively and stood, staring at the exposed face. The feelings of horror and disgust the bartender must have felt remained well hidden behind his transfixed smile, yet his silent recoil betrayed him.

Brutus pursed his lips, waiting for a response, and reached up to scratch the crook of his eye. Sucking in air with impatience, Brutus tried again.

"Where's Lucian?" He said, leaning forward and raising his voice. Perhaps the man behind the counter simply hadn't heard him. The spell broke slightly, just enough for the bartender to respond.

"He-he's not here…" The man behind the counter could not control the shaking in his voice as his synthesizer tried to steady his words.

"Of course he isn't."

Brutus bit his lip in annoyance and turned to leave.

No one was dancing, no one was drinking. They huddled in groups, staring and whispering about Brutus. Even through the music, he could hear what they were saying—talk of calling the Cleaners, plots of betraying their fellow patron. Brutus' eye twitched at the thought of their joined collusion. They were all of them against him.

The urge to shout at them and berate them for their betrayal sprung up in Brutus' throat. To tell them how false they were and that even here in this little corner, they were no truer versions of themselves than when they were sitting at work, when they were riding the train, when they were pretending to live.

Faces streamed out of the exit, and Brutus' thoughts were lost as he caught sight of Shaun, his whimpering Face slipping away.

You're not being a team player by leaving early, Shaun.

The thought seemed to give his legs speed and purpose, and as recognition set in, he was pushing his way through the crowd, up the stairs, and back outside. Cold air brushed his face painfully as he tailed Shaun, keeping pace behind him. A chill ran through his bones, and he stuffed his hands in his pockets to warm them. Fingers brushing the familiar barrel of his pen once more, Brutus palmed it firmly.

Click, click, click.

Shaun walked as if pulled on a string, stiff and without falter. Brutus tagged behind softly, scrutinizing Shaun's backside as he walked. His eyes narrowed as he followed his boss, his upper lip curling into a sneer. There was a sense of satisfaction in knowing that he was the monster in the dark, following the unsuspecting traveler.

Brutus caught sight of his face reflected back at him in a passing window and was surprised again at the sense of the unfamiliar. It was then he realized that the stranger staring back at him wasn't Brutus, not really. He'd been mistaken before at the club. Brutus lay back home, slumped over in the sink. The face looking at him now, well, that wasn't Brutus anymore, and that was a good thing. He smiled at his new reflection and decided that he would give Shaun a good scare.

After all, he wouldn't see *Brutus* jumping out at him.

He quickened his pace, slowly closing the distance between himself and Shaun, a monster, taboo and unrecognizable. Shaun turned and had just taken a few steps down the next alleyway when Brutus caught up to him. Be it the patter of his feet closing in or the ragged and unfiltered breathing, Shaun must have heard a presence behind him and so, turned to greet it.

Brutus pounced. Springing forward with a yowl, he shoved Shaun in the chest, staggering him backward. Shaun's Face remained unchanged in its apathetic countenance, but Brutus heard him gasp in shock. That little gasp, that audible sound of weakness, coming from the man that Brutus had taken orders from for so many years, was extremely satisfying.

A patch of redness caught Brutus' eye. It was small but growing in stark contrast against Shaun's white pressed shirt. Confused, Brutus looked down at his own hands and realized that he still clutched the metallic pen. A tiny speck of blood clung to the exposed nib.

Shaun stumbled backward a few feet, unaware of the small puncture in his chest, black jellied eyes focused solely on the terror of the exposed expression in front of him.

Brutus looked around and was relieved to see the alley was still devoid of passersby. As he turned his focus back to Shaun, he noticed a window, and for a moment, panic caught him as he was sure he would see a Face peering back at him, watching his every move. But Brutus saw no Face. In fact, he saw no windows at all. Just two shutters fixed to the side of a concrete wall, framed and bricked up beneath. It was well maintained but useless as it clung to its host.

Seeing the impossible window, Brutus couldn't contain himself and let out a giggle into the air. He'd have to remember to tell Thomasson.

That unearthly sound mixed with the raw, fleshy face was enough for Shaun to recover from Brutus' initial assault. He turned to run, scrabbling in fear and fighting with unused emotions.

The giggle died in Brutus' throat as he lunged forward, triggered by Shaun's sudden movement. Shaun was taller and stronger than Brutus, but he was also slow and unpracticed. Brutus leapt at Shaun, tackling him to the ground hard. He fought back, but Brutus came at him in a frenzy.

"Stop, stop!" Shaun pleaded.

"No." The word tumbled from Brutus as a whisper, barely audible even to himself, before it gathered into a roar.

"No, no, NO!"

Pen held firmly in his grip, Brutus brought his arm down again, and again, and again, thrusting the pen into the soft pieces of Shaun's body. Coin-sized patterns of blood now dotted Shaun all over his chest as Brutus stabbed him repeatedly. Shaun's struggle slowed, his arms falling limply to his sides.

Brutus finally jammed the pen with all his might through the base of the man's jaw, finding a new home in the fleshy inkwell that was Shaun's soft palate. Shaun seized as warm, dark liquid flowed thickly from his neck and trickled down his body. His hands rose briefly to grasp at the foreign object before falling loosely onto his breast.

Brutus stood over Shaun and watched as the blood boiled out of him in gentle waves before slowing into a stagnant pool as Shaun finally lay still.

A flicker of light caught the corner of Brutus' eye, and he turned to see a pale white smiling Face staring down at him through the window that had been bricked up just moments before. Brutus chuckled and gave a little wave.

Peering back down at the dark shape of Shaun's body, Brutus caught his face reflected in a puddle on the ground. I *must have startled her.* A speckling of red dotted his skin. Looking up at the blackening sky, he let out a satisfied sigh.

"How very beautiful," Brutus said softly, as he smiled into the night.

28 | THE NEW YOU

Pictures danced across the room as red ribbons of text threaded themselves in and out of focus. A narration of the events underway came dribbling out of the Face of a middle-aged woman with a stagnant smile.

"—unprecedented in every way. It will take some time to see if these proceedings will hold, as the trial has hit so many roadblocks along the way."

A birds-eye view of a sterile-looking room came into focus. The court was completely empty save for a row of white Faces sitting in a semicircle, positioned behind a figure in a disheveled suit. The figure was that of a man, but the entirety of his head was blurred so that no detail could be discerned.

"As you can see, the courtroom is closed off to the public due to the obscene and disturbing nature of the defendant, who has been forced to turn away from the assembly in order for the trial to take place."

A rectangle floated up onto the screen with an image slowly fading into view. It was the portrait of a man wearing a smart black suit with a slight smile playing across his sleek white Face and a swatch of dark hair spilling over his brow. A ribbon of text threading its way around the image identified the man as a local City worker with an unremarkable past.

"We are here to ascertain the nature of your transgressions against the City and the deceased," one of the court members spoke from behind Brutus. "Questions will be levied by the court, in efforts to discover why—"

"Because I wanted to."

"What?"

"Because, I wanted to."

A soft chuckle sounded as Lucian watched the events unfolding through glowing lenses. The whole of the City would watch the court proceedings today, and all of them would hear Brutus' words.

Reaching up, Lucian slid the mask from his own face and yawned widely while rubbing his eyes. He leaned forward to lay the half-cut mask on the coffee table, pausing for a few moments to watch the Mouse busy herself in the kitchen as she keyed in their dinner.

Lucian stretched and turned his attention to the view outside the small apartment window. The City sprawled out, the crest of the courthouse barely visible in the distance.

His eyes wandered the cityscape like a maze. It looked too perfect from this vantage, all the dark alleys and crooked mistakes hidden from view. That would change, though, thanks to Brutus. He would show them how reasonable it was, to be alive and to simply live.

Even in death, as that was sure to be his sentence, he would inspire those around him. Rallying thousands, they would copy the man without ever truly knowing why. Lucian could see the paths they would take, knew the words that would be spoken. It was all laid out, it just needed to be done.

He took a final look, not at the City, but of that setting sun he'd so long ago enjoyed. Today though, Lucian did not wait for the sun to set on the horizon. Instead, he turned to see the new Face of the people sitting by the window. The same Face that Lucian had recovered after it had been so carelessly cast aside by its owner. A faint smile played across his lips as he slipped on the mask that looked so very different from his own.

He would return to the streets, and they would welcome him as an old friend. Even though they had seen many images of him reflected on their lenses, there was no lasting memory of the man, not yet. Only the present image that Lucian would show them, night after night.

The City would always be there, but they would never be here again. One day they would look back and see that for once, their present was brighter than the past.

Act III - Into Remission

"As the old age convulsed in its dying spasm, they took off their masks and found that they were quite human indeed. For it was a simple thought of sanity that brought about the new age."

—from "Eve of Discordance"
by Brutus

29 | THE WHOLE OF THINGS

And so Alexander set to work. He began by running the bath. Regulations stated the temperature be one-hundred and four degrees Fahrenheit, but Alexander had often found that was just a bit too hot for his clients. That moment of recoil when their foot touched the water caused them to rethink their contract, and by that point, there was no going back. So he sat on the edge of the tub, running the water a tad cooler as he pulled from his case three silver candles, lightly scented to resemble the old Northern Forests.

Alexander had heard of droppers who let their candles run dry and would perform the dip without them. The idea seemed so very foreign in his mind. It was the candles that created the atmosphere. It was that scent of the forest that kept clients calm when their bodies started to go cold.

Alexander lit the candles and inhaled slowly, trying to picture in his mind a world where trees stood side by side and went on for miles but, like always, he could only ever imagine that fake pine advertisement at the train station. Its olfactory dispensers dispersed every twenty minutes, coating the air in front of it. The candles and that fake pine shared a similar smell.

He shook the memory away and began to strategically place the candles throughout the room, ensuring that their smell would not escape the nose of his client. Alexander removed his skintight glove and gently placed his hand into the water. It was just right. Grabbing a towel, he dried his hand and replaced the black glove snuggly over his fingers.

"Simon, it's time." Alexander used his client's first name.

Regulations stated that the use of the name helped to establish a rapport, and droppers were urged to use a client's name from the very first day of their meeting.

Alexander had met Simon in his apartment, as was custom for many jobs.

This wasn't so much an established rule but more an issue of comfort. No one wants to arrange their own death in a cubicle, where the very emotions of the world that were too much for them were so prominent.

Simon was a meek-looking man, just another salary in someone's growing empire. He had blonde hair, as all Simons seemed to have, and his ears were slightly off-center. His eyes were a messy mixture of green and blue, and when he met Alexander, they were filled with tears. Simon was just another of the many pathetic masses that couldn't deal with the overflow of emotions and sensory baths people faced in this age after the Revolution. So one day, when Simon finally had too much, he gave a call to the Bureau of Assisted Suicide, and they, in turn, sent Alexander.

The initial consultation was not productive, and Alexander spent the majority of that meeting listening to Simon describe his life and how he had come to the conclusion to end it. Such unproductive meetings cost the Bureau money, as the first consultation was free. Alexander usually liked to try and gauge the seriousness of a client during their first meeting, but Simon was a bawler and had spent his first free forty-five minutes complaining.

So when time was up, Alexander excused himself and left his card for Simon to call. Ninety-five percent of all clients called back and were walked through the billing process. This was an open account transfer in which the client gave access, and the Bureau would automatically withdraw the appropriate sum for each meeting. When the job was finished, the remainder would transfer to the City.

When Alexander had met Simon for the second time, their meeting had been much more productive, and Alexander was able to get most of the paperwork out of the way. Simple things for Alexander, but for people like Simon, they would be impossible to understand without the aid of a dropper. There was the Death Certificate to be signed, a Declaration of Intent to end one's own life, and a form in which a client had to decide on the day they would die. The Death Certificate usually took the longest to complete, not because it was complicated but because once it was signed, there was no going back.

After the Death Certificate, there was the license to be applied for. Depending on how Simon wanted to die, he would have to fill out the proper form, which Alexander had triplets of each. The most popular was hanging—or "dropping" as was its name at the bureau—which could be done in the comfort of one's own home, and the license for that was relatively simple to get.

Diving—or "roof jumping"—was also a popular choice but required a different kind of permit. Diving disrupted traffic, and without a permit, a diver could stop things dead for several hours. To prevent that, when a client applied for a diver's license, a date and a very specific time were set. Traffic would be halted, a client would dive, a dropper would supervise, and a cleanup crew would move the body, all within a two-minute period, at the end of which traffic would resume. It didn't take Simon long to find what he was looking for, and at the end of his second meeting, he had successfully applied for a "dipper's" license.

During their third meeting, Alexander went over the Spousal and Relative Grievance form. It required immediate family to sign, confirming their acknowledgment of Simon's wish to die. Simon had no wife and no immediate family, so they checked the box at the bottom and moved on.

The rest of the paperwork included a Leave of Work for Personal Reasons form and various cancellation forms for things of which Simon was a subscriber. The Leave of Work document informed Simon's boss that he would no longer be an employee at their organization. This could be submitted as late as the night before the job, but many, like Simon, chose to submit theirs a week early and tried to enjoy their last few days.

After the third meeting, Alexander said his goodbyes to Simon and informed him that he would return in a week.

Simon entered the bathroom with his robe wrapped tightly around his waist as if symbolizing that its accidental removal would end his life sooner than what he had signed for. Alexander gently closed the door and turned to face him, and Simon looked hesitantly back at his dropper. He had never been naked in front of another man, but when Alexander nodded at him to continue, he instinctively moved, quickly trying to undo the knot he had so carefully tied an hour earlier. Frustration wrinkled across his face, and he slipped his arms out of his robe. Now in desperation, he tried to slip it down past his slightly bulging waistline. His distress was ended when he felt the cold, gloved hand of Alexander on his back.

"Allow me, Simon."

The dropper moved to face his client, making eye contact and seemingly refusing to break it as he slowly untied the knot in Simon's robe. Alexander's gentle stare kept Simon from looking away. He just stared into the eyes of his dropper, finding it impossible to give a name to the color of his eyes. For Simon, they seemed just too far away, just on the cusp of his vision.

"There," said Alexander, "why don't you step into the tub."

Simon blankly nodded, coming back to himself. He picked up his foot and swung it around to enter the tub. Experience reminded him that the water might be too hot, and a moment of hesitation caused Simon to let out a barely audible gasp. He had heard of clients who didn't go along with their droppers and didn't want to be cheated out of his peaceful death by a few degrees of imperfection. Simon struggled against himself and dipped his foot into the water, expecting to feel that familiar burn. Yet when his toe hit the surface, his eyes opened, and his mind swelled with the realization that it wasn't too hot and that he wouldn't be shot in the head for not wanting to get in.

After his foot, he slowly lowered the rest of his body into the tub, until everything below his chest was submerged. Finding a comfortable spot, Simon looked up to see Alexander holding his washcloth. It was neatly folded in his hand, and before Simon could protest, Alexander had placed the folded cloth across Simon's face.

"Try and relax Simon, this will help you." Alexander's words were the rebuttal to a protest that was never formed. Simon had always hated that malformed towel. He'd only kept it because it had come with his apartment, and the landlord would expect to see it when he left.

Little trickles of warm water ran down his face, and for the first time, Simon acknowledged the scent of the candles. He knew what it was he was smelling but, like Alexander, had never actually seen the pine which this scent was designed to mimic. Before long, in that dark warmth of the wash towel and the vaguely familiar scent, Simon began to feel at peace.

He let his mind wander through the things in his life that had driven him here. It was strange, but he wasn't angry anymore, only sad that such peace was found at the end. Simon's recollections were interrupted by a gentle rubbing on his left wrist.

"What are you doing?" Simon said with an unworried tone.

"I'm numbing your wrists, Simon."

"Ok." He took a deep breath, and in a moment, he could no longer entirely feel his hands. Simon knew that he could lift his arms and could feel their familiar weight, but it was very hard to get them to move as they sat on the edges of the tub. Then to his surprise, they were warm, as if they were sitting in the water with him, but he knew they weren't.

Simon smiled and let the muscles in his body relax. He had been tense for so long.

Alexander leaned back onto his seat that was the toilet. A small razor blade was in his hand, and a small droplet of blood was hanging from its tip. He expertly balanced the razor as he leaned down to retrieve a white handkerchief and gently placed the blade in its center. The droplet quickly soaked into the white fabric and spread as far as it could before Alexander gently folded the razor into the handkerchief and then placed it back in his bag.

Now all he had to do was wait for Simon to die. Alexander watched as the blood flowed out of Simon's wrists and into the tub. It looked like a painting that was slowly taking form, the blood flowing and swirling against the background of its white canvas. Alexander closed his eyes and quietly took in the smell of the candles.

Simon breathed slowly and steadily. It was the ticking of a clock, counting down to that final breath, and when it came, Alexander opened his eyes. The still chest of Simon let Alexander know it was time to finish things up.

He checked Simon's pulse and then pulled the cork on the tub, letting the bloody mixture swirl down past Simon's feet. As it drained, Alexander collected his candles, blowing them all out and capping them off as he placed them into his black bag. He then turned the showerhead on and let the water wash away the blood that remained.

When Simon was clean, Alexander sewed closed the wounds that ran parallel on his client's arms. Professionals like Alexander knew that the best way to cut was along the length of the wrist. After he had finished, Alexander pulled out the body bag he had brought along and placed it on the floor beside the tub. Hefting Simon out, his body quickly found its last resting place in a dark plastic bag.

With the apartment already cleaned by Simon and the bathroom finished off by Alexander, he lifted the body-filled bag and his own worn case and exited the apartment. Locking the door, Alexander left the key in the mail slot and made his way back to his car, with miles to go before he slept.

30 | DAVE

Give it enough time, and you can find just about anything. This is especially true if you work in the disposal business. It's often said that a man can find worth in the refuse of others, but Dave knew it to be more than just a saying.

Eight hours every day, Dave operated the Crematorium to service the City's needs. "Incinerator" had been its previous inclination, but the function the facility occupied itself with now would lend to it a different purpose.

A day and change into the Revolution and the group Dave had been marching with discovered the Crematorium. The structure was smaller than he might have expected but still a commanding presence for its size.

The interior was a singular domed concrete structure, two or three stories high. A large, circular vent at the top allowed for the heat produced by the building to burn off and dissipate. A conveyor belt lay atop a grated gangplank that extended out from the entrance of the building all the way to the structure's fiery center. Assumingly, waste would flow from the conveyor to the center and then be pitched over the side to burn up.

When Dave's group had found it, though, the structure had been operating on its own. A severe jam prevented the majority of things from passing over the edge as they collected, stressing the belt and grinding the gears.

Somehow Dave had been elected to maintain and fix the structure while the rest moved on. At the time, it was possibly the worst news he had ever received. To be left behind in any venture was often the crux for the forming of malice and discontent.

Yet Dave did not succumb to the violence that had brought him out into the streets. Instead, he took to his work, as he had his old job in document verification. A few hours later and he had the belt running again. A backed-up selection of items to be destroyed showed the daily life of yesterday's present.

Dirty dishes, cloth napkins, food containers, and the odd broken glass hinted at opulent lifestyles, where everything needed was provided, and everything provided was in plenty.

Unsure of what to do now that he had the Crematorium working, he stepped outside into the cold evening air and watched from his vantage how the City burned. It almost seemed pointless to keep the Crematorium running. There were easily enough other blazing fires, hot enough to burn out the past.

He thought about leaving, trying to find his group to continue their righteous assault, but something made him stay. Even after all this time, he couldn't describe it, that compelling force to stay and keep the fire going.

So that's what he did. Taking a seat, he sat next to the conveyor and monitored the passing refuse. In time, he would learn what all the buttons did and how hot the fire should be, but it was enough at that moment to simply keep the belt from jamming again.

The items came from a dark hole in the wall where the belt returned, always cycling back with more wasted things. As the days passed, Dave became aware of what happened to those who'd been caught in the streets, who'd either refused to take off their Faces or simply had yet to catch on and were caught unawares.

Corpse after corpse slid by on the narrow path of the conveyor. Dave understood now why he'd really been left behind. This system wasn't meant for bodies. They were too large and had too many moving parts. Limbs would snag, spines would bend, and hair would catch.

Every single corpse, Dave would wrestle with. Either snipping at the snags or unplugging the hole to keep the belt moving. This went on for weeks, and every person and every thing in that building would sidle forward, drop, and then burst into flame, the fine flakes of ash riding the heat up and out, to once again travel through the City.

31 | THUMP-THUMP-THUMP

"There's always been thump-thump-thumps. But I had my Face, my Face to smile for me, to look ahead. But now I, I just can't tune them out. So many more thump-thump-thumps…They just won't go away, they won't leave me be. I can hear them wherever I go, thump-thump-thump, I can't sleep, I vomit when I eat, I'm so tired, so hungry.

"I just want to drive the train again, I'm good at driving the train, I know all the stops, thump-thump-thump, I know all the lines, all the times, all the arrivals and departures, thump-thump-thump. They used to make me push the button when I heard the thump-thump-thumps. The Cleaners would come out, they would clean the problem away, and then there wouldn't be a thump-thump-thump. Now there's just too many of them, too many thump-thump-thumps! No Cleaners, where have they gone, why doesn't the button work? Why do they make me clean up the thump-thump-thumps? Why won't they let me drive the train, why won't they let me push the button, why can't the Cleaners stop the thump-thump-thumps?

"They said if I took the mask off, I could be free. I thought they meant free of the thump-thump-thumps. I threw it away, out the window of the train, but then there were more, so many more thump-thump-thumps. I went looking for it, I walked for days and days, I couldn't find my Face. I couldn't tune them out. So many, many more THUMP-THUMP-THUMPS!

"It's ok, It's ok, It's ok. I know how to stop them, I know how to make them go away. Just a minute more. I know all the lines, all the times, all the arrivals and departures."

Jump-Thump-Thump.

George was lucky to get a seat today. Others crammed around and in front of him, desperately trying to hold on and resist the force of those who couldn't grab onto a support strap. The tram jostled about left and right, people swayed, a sea of flesh in a jar. So many had accepted their uncomfortable fate and had given up even trying. Allowing themselves to be thrown about, they trusted that some shoulder or back would catch them before they fell. They breathed, sneezed, and sweated on each other without a care, and George sneered each time the person standing in front of his seat collided with him as the car made a turn.

"So this is why people kill themselves," George grumbled under his breath as once again the man in front of him leaned too close. Gripping his bag, he tried closing his eyes, twitching each time he was bumped. This truly was hell, and George, on this particular day, had realized that because of who he was and where he worked, he would always ride this car, at this hour, with these people, from now until his death. It did nothing to improve his mood.

The rest of his trip was quiet as he walked for another half hour to his building, took the lift up to his floor, and found his office. George's work was like any other. He sat at a desk next to other desks. His desk had papers on it, as the other desks had papers on them. His boss, Hal, had an office, and Hal's boss had a bigger office, and men sat and worked, typed, and printed. This office, however, had one thing different. It operated on the rigors and fine-tuning of the government's bureaucracy. There was not a pay stub or receipt that was not stamped, filed, and reviewed at the end of the year. Not one piece of paperwork was ever thrown away, nor was there a drop of ink wasted on unneeded words.

"Alex," George's boss refused to use the full name of his subordinates, as if his own gargantuan weight prevented him from speaking more than a single syllable while walking, "you got that two-twenty for me?"

"Of course," Alexander replied as he reached down into his work bag, pulling out a folder and briefly thumbing through it until finding the requested paperwork.

"So no problems then?" A question that only needed asking due to the bureaucratic necessities of George's workplace.

"No."

"Good." Their conversations were always the same, never a pleasantry, only business. George watched as his boss moved onto the next desk. The day always began like this, the boss making the rounds, the workers submitting their paperwork, and Alexander just waiting for a call.

33 | JAMES

James watched as the perspiration from his drink rolled onto his finger. Slowly he began to rub the glass, using the water as his lubricant while he tried to find the pleasure that so many did in such things.

The olfactory dispensers in this bar were wearing out, and the lights no longer held their sheen for James. He had been here too long, the stimulation was lost. It used to be that he could barely step foot inside. He felt the kiss on his earlobe as he opened the door and the feeling of ice trailing down to his groin. The muscles in the back of his leg fluttered, and he couldn't help but feel short of breath. Now he came only for the drinks, and even they seemed watered down. This place was nothing but nostalgia now.

He watched as the crowd teemed and swirled in the deliciousness of their own feelings. For them, the effects were still physical. It seemed that only James and the bartender had moved beyond the parlor tricks. Like any drug, you build up a tolerance, except unlike drugs, you don't get the happy ending of an overdose. You simply feel less.

James had heard there was a percentage of droppers who had joined the Bureau because they had overdone their sensory baths. Killing, it seemed, never lost its flavor though. Watching as a man dangled from a rope restored that spasm in the spine. A blood-filled tub returned that icy touch down to the groin, and watching a child plummet to the ground still made their lips wet, or so he'd heard.

His finger caught suddenly on the glass where the moisture had been rubbed away, and his trance was broken, it was time to go. Work would come in a few hours, and some rest was needed. James stood to pay his bill, the copper coins from his pocket stacked neatly on the table. The sneering coin caught James' stare every time.

On one side, a smiling mask, and on the other the face of Brutus himself. James always placed his coins mask down, as was the custom, a way to honor the leader of the Revolution. How ironic it was to honor a man who fought the rules of society by placing his face on a coin.

34 | JOHN

John had imagined that the Revolution would bring an end to days like this. Working long hours, only to have as much or more work to do by the end of the day. He dreaded his evenings as he often brought his work home. It was the only thing he could do to stay on top of things.

When Brutus had been executed, John was among the masses who heard the call. It wasn't a government they rose up against, but themselves. Brutus changed the way people thought. He challenged societal norms and ridiculous practices that were accepted by all. John remembered ripping off his mask and marching through the streets, shoulder to shoulder with his fellow citizens. People, who a day before were tucked nicely in their proper places, were now burning down skyscrapers and raping anything with a mask. A lifetime of confinement came out that night, and John felt alive for the first time.

Since then, he'd overindulged like everyone else, expended every fantasy, and partaken in every self-gratifying act. The world had changed, but he was still working in the same office, doing the same shit work. He just didn't have to pretend to like it anymore, or so he thought.

On the verge of collapse, John finally made it home to his apartment. Setting down his pile of work, he looked around, summing up his life. There in the corner was his flesh sack, really more of a malleable flesh ball than a sack. Parents gave it to their children when they were away. It was agreed upon that touch was important in the new world. The sack could be stretched out and laid upon. It was warm and felt just like you were lying on someone's arm.

John had heard that some people suffocated themselves with it, so at least they could pretend that someone loved or hated them enough to kill them. In a world of delusions, what was one more? What could it hurt to fool yourself in the last minutes of life? To want and need someone else to kill you, because your life was so devoid that no one loved or hated you.

As he looked up, he caught his reflection in the glass that passed for a window in his apartment. He stared for hours, just looking and wondering. What bespeckled visage lay before him, but the hedonistic guise of a lost child?

35 | JAMES

The bar was worse off since his last visit. The lacquered finish was peeling, and the cheap, sickly grey material that comprised its structure was showing through in some places. Someone had clawed away the wood finish, likely in a fit of some intense ecstasy. But really, who would care about something so trivial in a place where the bigger picture is what mattered.

This place was the first sensory bar, and in its day, had shown like a bright jewel. A politely ignored establishment where only the taboo ventured, its owner had sat like a god above those below, smiling upon his domain and the gifts he had given. Now the lord's seat sat empty, and little else had changed, except for the deterioration which had come about after a thousand other sensory bars and booths had popped up over the City. Little had changed, except for the back rooms.

James found the number he was looking for, an ominous red door with an old-fashioned brass handle. There was no music back here, no artificial smells, and no display of lights. Through the door was a small group of people. They didn't look away from the stage in front of them, all were silent as a man dangled from the ceiling. His legs spasmed, and his body gently contorted. James had come in late and regretted missing the drop. Unlike with the Bureau, the back rooms didn't drop people from any particular height. They didn't want the neck to snap because honestly, where would be the pleasure in that.

James rubbed his lips and took shallow breaths as the kicking slowly stopped. He was racing to catch up with the others who'd had almost a minute longer than he to take in the pleasure. Others were finishing up. For them, it was a release, a chosen pleasure. James, however, just wanted to feel. Watching someone die made him feel alive. Cliché, but true. He felt a connection to life, an appreciation for air, and the ability to breathe as the hanging man slowly turned purple.

When he had stopped kicking, two men from the bar unhooked him from the ceiling and laid him down on the stage. They compressed his chest, forcing blood into his heart. They were efficient at their work and didn't lose pace as one man pressed, and the other breathed. In a moment, the man who had been dead coughed, and for James, the moment was spoiled.

Boring, it was all just so boring. Daniel's head rested on the sheets of his bed. The cool fabric had slowly warmed from his body heat. What was relief was now becoming annoyance. He liked cold sheets. No matter the temperature, they always made him feel better.

The woman next to him sighed in her sleep. It was her fault he had gone to bed so hot. She'd been the one who had stolen the chill he'd come to need. He looked at her, lazily tilting his head to the side. In another life, she would have been beautiful. Her face and her body were slim, and the tone of her skin was fair. It was what had drawn the beaters to her.

Daniel could only see the tip of the scar that ran across the majority of her face. She'd never spoken of what they had done, but her face gave anyone with an inclination for such behavior a clear idea. The beaters hadn't cut her, that wasn't their style. Instead, they had crushed her face. Beaten it until it caved. Hammered and hammered away until her skin split under the pressure. In another place, in another life, she'd have been beautiful.

If she had been born earlier, she would have been spared the torture, but still, no one would have ever seen her face. Was that not a torture in its own way? Daniel stirred for a moment, his hand reaching for the nightstand by his bed. Blindly seeking, his fingers touched the familiar shape of his mask.

Like Daniel, she had been born after the Revolution. They had never known a life under the oppression of the masks. They didn't understand the plight of living without identity. Instead, they had all been conceived in the glorious weeks of the upheaval. Born to mothers who'd been raped in the streets. They were the children of freedom, the products of individuality.

No man had been their judge that day, so their children had all come to be known as Daniel. The children were the turning of the page, they were what the world could be without masks. It was for this reasoning that Daniel and his family adopted what was now taboo. Bitter at the circumstances that had birthed them, Daniel had led his people to the altar of Brutus. There they had stolen back the masks of their fathers. Defacing the relics, they carved away the lower halves.

Daniel held the mask above him, staring into its blank eyes. Who had this been? What had they done? Was this his father? Daniel wished his last thought into reality. During the Revolution, how many men like his father had there been? What would they think, seeing their bastard children roaming the City on their cycles, forgoing their individuality, wearing the masks they'd so heroically cast off?

37 | George

George wheezed as he climbed the stairs. This shit-hole lacked a lift, like many buildings of its time. The only thing worse was when a lift lacked the good sense to stay open long enough for a man to enter. Handkerchief in hand, George uncontrollably spit up a cough. Years of bad habits left their mark as he groped for the inhaler in his jacket pocket.

A door opened down the hall, and a woman waved her hand. "I thought that was you, come in before you wake the neighbors."

The woman hobbled out of sight, leaving the door open. George sneered as best he could before inhaling his medicated breeze. He disliked the woman, she annoyed him to no end. She was opinionated, particularly so about his health. George didn't usually mind opinions, but when they concerned himself, well, then it became personal.

"You really should give that up," the woman said as George entered and closed the door behind him. "At this rate, you'll die before me."

George sneered again and mockingly mimicked her face. *Who was she to talk?* She hadn't eaten a meal that didn't come out of a machine since the change, and by the smell of it, she hadn't thrown the trash out in weeks.

George didn't wait for an offer and promptly seated himself, pulling out his paperwork and needed documentation to progress his client's case.

"Well, if you're done hounding me, I've brought the required documents."

The woman pulled out a dark sphere from her pocket and removed the protective seal around it.

"I don't know anymore," the woman said as she peeled off a slice and nibbled gently at its edge. "I was out yesterday—"

"I doubt that," George mumbled.

"—and saw one of those booths." the woman played as if she had not heard him. "A man walked in, and in five minutes, the booth was free again. I'm giving that serious consideration."

"Oh come on!" George nearly shouted. "Those things are a rip-off, they're unsanitary, and they barely, I mean just barely, have a license to be in the City."

"Well what's the problem with them?" the woman snarled at George. "They save time, they're legal, and they don't force me to wait around here for days while you get your fat ass up the stairs at your own leisure."

George shook his head. "I really can't believe I'm having this conversation." Any pretense at trying to follow the Bureaus' guidelines left him. "First of all, *my fat ass?*"

George paused to let his venom sink in a bit before carrying on. "Second, have you ever been in one?" The question was rhetorical. "I doubt you could fit, but saying that you did, and the door closed, you'd be pressed up against a wall, a screen would descend with a full deposit window. Once you sign, all your assets would go to their company. There's no option for family."

The woman grunted while licking melted crumbs from her fingers.

George continued, "Once you've signed, it's done. You die in a small box, your body is atomized, and then the next idiot like you is allowed to step in. Did you know they don't prevent other people from climbing in with you…Yeah! Sure they have some language discussing the max occupancy, but there's no sensor to enforce it. Do you know how many botched jobs we have to deal with because people are cheap and didn't want to pay for two? You know how many jobs *I've* botched?"

George held up his hands in the form of a large zero.

"It's just all these papers," the woman said. "It just seems restrictive is all."

"But that's exactly why there is so much, so you can do whatever you want. You can look at the sun one last time, have a nap in your bed, take a warm bath."

"You'd like to see that, wouldn't you," she said with disgust in her voice.

George shook his head. He was letting himself get baited into another argument with her. He tried to calm himself but began coughing again. He wheezed out another ball of fluid into his handkerchief and quickly stood up and made his way into the kitchen. Reaching into the woman's preserver, he pulled out a sweet, bottled drink to clear his throat.

"Sure, just help yourself," the woman said sarcastically. "You're taking enough of my money anyway, why not help yourself to my food. Would you like me to make the bed for you as well?"

George coughed while he drank, but his hate drilled a hole into the back of the woman's head from the one bulging eye that was still open. He thought about drawing his weapon and just tapping her in the back of the head. It would save him plenty of irritation, but then, that would just be more paperwork.

38 | JOHN

From his window, John had seen the changing of things. Clouds became rain, the sun became night, and masks, a violent crowd. Like everyone else, he'd born his mask as a sign of citizenship. It had given him a home, a vehicle, a job, a life.

His desk had sat by a window, and still did. His view of the world was like many others, a long street with countless buildings in a row. He watched now as cycles raced by, their flags flying high to announce their coming. They hadn't existed before Brutus, or at least he hadn't thought so?

John's attention returned to his desk. A single sheet lay in front of him, along with its corresponding pen. They were somewhat mandatory these days, a party symbol, an affirmation of the righteousness of Brutus. John's hand lifted the small piece of metal and placed it in his chest pocket. The page didn't need the pen, not this one, at least. He brushed the page into a cart that was passing by and took the free moment to look back out his window.

He wondered if anyone had watched *him* when he'd finally stepped outside to join the marches. Had they seen him push open his office door, had they seen him take off his mask, could they say where it had gone?

Another page floated down, and John looked over its contents. A signature was all that was needed. He again brushed the page away from his desk, and his mind.

When he'd awoken in the streets, his face was black with the fluids of the pavement and the gore of many. He hadn't known what to do as he staggered through the City with so many others. He tried going home, but it didn't recognize his new face. He'd tried wandering, but that took him only so far. In the end, he'd gone back to work, like so many others from the night before. He found his desk waiting for him. Several stacks of pages greeted him as he'd taken a seat, and still more floated down.

Outside, the streets were quiet, though, from his window, he could see others at their desks, performing their trained tasks. By nightfall, the marches had begun again, though John didn't join them. In the following weeks, John had watched as the riots progressed and the fires burned, but still his pages floated down for review.

When the snows fell, John had been comfortable in his office. They'd seized the atmosphere stations on the fourth week, but the heat had returned on the sixth. When the food ran out, the riots had subsided. The streets were quiet then, no people, no trains, but still the pages floated down.

For everything they destroyed, time was spent relearning what they took apart. Smaller and smaller bands would continue the riots as sections broke off to work what they had previously destroyed. It went on like this until there was hardly anyone at all outside John's window.

39 | JAMES

The streets were wet, they were always wet. Teardrops formed and dribbled at a thousand different angles around James, with many finding their way to larger and larger puddles. Tributaries formed and faded, they were, of course, anathema to the real thing. The natural course of the world perverted until it was only just recognizable.

A toxic stream, no longer than the length of James' pinky, burst as he carelessly moved through the street, disrupting the formation of a pool in a burgeoning pothole. If a simple step could disrupt the hydrologic cycle of that cubic inch, what had become of the things living that had been unfortunate enough to find themselves under James' boot?

James was long and far away from his current location, greedily anticipating his next trip to the sensory bar. Perhaps, he thought, his next visit would be fruitful, more… satisfying. His amusement with the establishment always seemed to teeter on the edge between gratification and utter disappointment. It was a thin razor to tread, but at least it was a short one.

Muscles, memory, and sinews played across the street, steering the thing that was James. From street corner to street corner he went, walking and stopping, staring and blinking. It was during a brief moment of residual clarity from an unprompted howl in the distance that James noticed something he had never seen before.

It was a burned-out structure, its white walls painted with the patina of age and fire. When the masks had come off, there had been plenty of these, but now, it seemed out of place. Why had it been left so long? Surely there was an entrepreneur who could do something more with it. At the least, it seemed that it provided adequate shelter, and yet, the structure was empty. Empty for all, except the humble flame of candles.

A rush of air slid past James as vehicles began to move again. Unfazed,

James navigated the currents until he was at the precipice of the archway. Gazing in, he peered into the dark corners made even darker by their shared past. James could see nothing, and so he entered.

The structure had been a shop in the time before. He could see stands littering the ground, their metallic sheen blunted by the ash of their previous burdens. Much violence had these walls seen, pockmarked and smashed, chiseled endlessly with the names of citizens. Where the light shown and violent age spared, names of the many could be seen. Their lettering varied, and penmanship danced along the borders of professional to ambisinister. Yet they were all without a doubt…names.

Though, these hidden scrawls were not the object of the candle's light. That honor lay further in along the back most wall. There, at the center, stood the mighty image of Brutus. His deific marble figure emerged from the wall. His Face was the mask of the people, but his stance was the progress of defiance. Beneath him was the long shape of a molded sarcophagus. Its corners and ridges depicted the famous scenes from Brutus' time. There was the march, his trial, his apotheosis in the alley, it was all there depicted in miniature. Next to it, scrawled and embossed in gold, were the words: "Brutus, first among equals, last among failures."

James let his fingers slide against the letters. His oily tips both dusted and polished the script. Were that all, James would have thought it a poor memorial. It was the masks laid atop, and stacked to the sides, and placed at the feet of Brutus that made this a worthy place. Some were cracked, others were bloody. As Brutus' mask was the symbol of the people, so were these the approval of his deeds.

James stepped back, watching the candles melt and fade. Had he a mask to give, he surely would have done so and added his name to the wall. They were the pallid visage of a generation, standing sentinel before their mortal god.

40 | PETER

Peter opened the door. Nervous already, the sight of the man in the black suit startled him even further, and he slammed the door shut. He could hear his heart thumping in his throat when the knock at the door came again. It was a gentle sound, which brought Peter out of his fear. Opening the door, this time, the man in the black suit wore a smile.

"Hello, Peter, I'm Alexander."

Peter stared for a moment before noticing the outstretched hand. The black glove blended into the suit, and Peter only noticed where the white of the man's shirt extended past his coat. Something about the use of his contraction left Peter with the notion that it was somehow disingenuous, almost as if the introduction had been crafted, rather than practiced.

"Forgive me, I... don't know what came over me." Peter took the man's hand. It was a gentle shake, and Peter was glad of it. At his age, he couldn't grip another man's hand as he had when he was younger. A human sign of weakness and frailty, Peter thought.

"Please come in," Peter said as he opened the door wider for the man to enter.

He watched as Alexander took a seat and pulled from his black bag a series of papers and laid them out individually on the table. Peter was afraid to let go of the handle of the door, and so he stood there, just watching.

"Peter, come have a seat."

"Sure thing," he said nodding, "sure thing."

The distance to his table seemed unbearable, but Alexander's stare drew him in. He felt like he had lost control of his own body and was being willed over. Taking a seat, he began to notice things about the table. He'd never liked it before, but for some reason now, he was finding it very difficult to want to leave it. Its wobbly leg needed fixing, the surface re-staining. If he didn't, who would?

As a matter of fact, without any heirs, Peter would be encouraged to check the box next to the word "liquidate." His assets would be assessed for their value and sold off, likely to be purchased by any number of landlords who reduced cost by buying from the dead. Though who was he to criticize, he'd been an equal opportunist in his day. No one who lived through the riots wasn't.

"Peter," the gentle rebuke snapped what stray thoughts laid in the past, "I need your attention." The man's words drew him in and directed him to the contents that lay on his underappreciated table.

"As you already understand, today's meeting is without charge from the Bureau…" Peter's eyes drifted to Alexander's suit as he leaned down to explain what each of the papers on the table meant. The young man had two buttons, counter to what he remembered from his time in the offices, behind his mask. It fit him well, and there were no out of place creases, not even a speck from the outside. There was a slight deformity, though, under his left side. Something large was hidden under his jacket, and Peter suspected it was the signature "whisper" of the Bureau. It was said that those who did not conform to their agreed upon contracts found the gentle whisper of a dropper in their ear.

Why shout when you can whisper? he thought, chuckling to the black spaces of his mind. Only the Bureau would come up with an idiotic phrase like that.

"Peter," the rebuke was the same as the first. He was beginning to hate that name. "It's alright if you don't want to talk about these now. Would you prefer to tell me about yourself?"

There they were again, those seemingly out of place contractions. Crafted and inserted to breed familiarity, to defuse hostility and fear by placing the government official on the same level as the citizen.

"When I marched through the avenues, no one used my name. They just ran, ran from these hands," Peter said, holding them up, their wrinkled guise hiding the murderous weapons they'd once been. "Citizens, officials, bosses, neighbors, all the same, they all ran from these hands."

Peter leaned forward, grabbed the papers in triplicate which Alexander had set down, and began tearing them into pieces. His arms were like the stuttering of a motor that had nearly run out of fuel. It took a moment to get going, but he'd kept enough in reserve for the task. The look of triumph was not so unfamiliar to his rusted face as he sneered from his upper lip.

"I'm not weak like the others, I took my mask off, not the government, me! And just as assuredly as I didn't need you then, I don't need you now. Get out, and tell your bosses 'Peter's done with them.'"

Not once did Alexander blink, nor grimace, nor even recoil. In fact, Peter noticed that a faint grin appeared on the younger man's face. Peter wanted to be angry, to shout more, but the grin wasn't some outward expression of amusement. It felt more to him like the gentle nodding of one's head during a long conversation. When used appropriately, it denoted one's current and undiluted attention. This grin left Peter with the same impression, but more. He saw pity, understanding, and a judgeless listener. He wanted to be angry, but something in that smile defused his short-lived spark. He felt tired, and his will to rebel left him.

When silence grew, Alexander stood, slowing, fastening his case before reaching into his jacket. Hand and the deformity grew into one large mass, and Peter tensed, his own powerful hands turning back into their frail and wrinkled disguise. He realized now how those in the street had felt when he'd stood above them years ago, helpless. But instead of death, Alexander drew out a small three-by-two business card and set it down gently in the center of the table. Its borders and angles were the organization and control to the chaos of papers around it.

"Have a good day, Peter," Alexander said with the same diffusing smile before grabbing his black bag and showing himself out.

41 | JAMES

"Never lose hope, never feel lost. Never lose hope, never feel lost. Never lose hope, never feel lost." The impossible command blinked from across the street into James' eyes. The repetition of the command might have been convincing, if it wasn't set into the side of the Bureau's high rise. He blinked away the rain, his mouth was dry.

James wondered if there was any actual subtlety meant in the sign. It was obvious to him what the sign really meant: "Never lose hope, never feel lost, *contact the Bureau.*"

Were they trying to be clever by leaving the obvious out, or were they clever at all? They'd certainly provoked the thought in his own mind, which he reluctantly gave them credit for.

As he thought about it more, the scope of the sign's meaning grew and the intentions of those behind it. Was it a command or a request? If it was a request, then such a request surely required some type of relationship first, some level of trust. Who was this imaginary being whom he trusted so well as to not despair? As if despair was a thing that could be put off so easily, to be met again at a more convenient time.

What would he gain from listening? Would the person behind this neon sign grant him relief if he did? Was he to be made to not worry simply because they suggested it, leaving him no recourse, but to worry later? James scoffed at that thought. He hated those who disparaged other people's emotions and knew that all should be the same. That if they were fine, then everyone else should be as well. That sorrow could be cast off as easily as hope could be rekindled. Doubtlessly a hypocritical sentiment, as they themselves would seek the comfort of the myriad pleasures the City had to offer the moment luck turned on them.

And yet, if it was a command, could he afford to disobey? A question posed by all radicals, dissentients, revolutionaries, anarchists, and cats. He blinked away the rain from his eyes.

The light refused to turn, and the streets were unusually busy. The gentle hiss of water being obliterated beneath the moving vehicles called out to James. It sounded to him like the rhythm of the sensory bar. He hummed the tune and mumbled the lyrics, finding to his great amusement that they were all in harmony.

> "I'm walking five feet ahead,
> so you don't see what I dread.
> When I look back will I see,
> you still walking behind me?
> You still walking behind me?
> I'm walking five feet ahead,
> so you don't see what I dread,
> I don't want you to see, what is real to me.
> What is real to me."

Singing out beneath the artificial light with the sounds of the City as his music, he felt more than he had at the bar. He would be lying if he said it was overwhelming, awe-inducing, or even pleasurable. It was however, just enough.

Enough to remember better times, immortal moments, and coy feelings that had since crept back into the darkness. When you've lived with nothing, sometimes, enough can be everything.

Within his jubilation, James had finally noticed the man standing next to him at the crossing. He was taller than James by a foot, wider by a half, and more bearded than he'd ever been or could be. Though James didn't study him as some mortal passerby would, but as a child who simply wanted more.

Enough had passed, and opportunity taken its place. More was ever the answer to moderation. It wasn't James alone who felt this way. Thousands had risen before him to take what they could find. They had subsisted on enough, lived in abstinence, and seized upon opportunity when Brutus had presented it to them.

James saw his own moment unfolding, there for him to take. He hadn't quite consciously pulled the knife from his pocket, though he had a vague recollection of a memory that he'd quite intentionally forgotten.

The knife was less of a knife and more of a sharp piece of metal that had retained an edge from its violent decoupling. A strange form of urging and will took over James, like the inexplicable commands which guide a hand or move one's feet.

The knife inserted itself easily into the man next to him as if they were two lost pieces being reunited. There was less blood than he had imagined, as he took a step back, his hand freeing the haft that he'd so recently guided.

The man turned, and the knife followed, spinning perfectly in place. James kept staring at the knife as he got closer, as the man hurled his head against James', as he fell backward, as his head hit the pavement, as the man crossed the street, as the light turned green.

The rain struck him over and over again, each a sting to his broken face. The rest of the song seemed to just bubble out, chortled in mirth.

> "I'm walking five feet ahead,
> so you don't see what I dread,
> When I look back will I see,
> you standing there behind me?
> You standing there beside me.
> I'm walking five feet ahead,
> so you don't see what I dread,
> I'm walking five feet ahead,
> so you don't see what's in my head.
> So you don't see what I dread.
> So you don't see what's in my head."

Never lose hope, never feel lost, contact the Bureau. He blinked away the rain from his eyes.

42 | PETER

"Is there anything you'd like to say, Peter?" Alexander asked as the man stood on his stool. The noose tight around his neck.

"I walked at Brutus's side, I know everyone says that, but I actually did." Peter looked down at Alexander, who only stared back with that grin that told Peter he was listening. "That first night, I was bloodied. A group of Face-less men knocked me down with bats. They broke my Face and left me on the side of the street. I could hear them down the road as they found another. I laid there, I couldn't comprehend what had happened.

"I ached, fluids ran down my face where the bats had broken through. I could only see the fires the mounting crowds had started. I didn't know what to do, I thought about running home, but I was lost without my Face. As ideas ran through my head, I realized that the only thing I could do was to lie there, and die." A tear formed in the corner of Peter's eye, and he tilted his head up to hide it from Alexander.

"But then he came. He leaned over me, his Face was whole and beautiful. He slid my shards aside, and his hand, his hand pulled me, it pulled me up from the street. And do you know what he said to me? 'Come now, let's get you started.' He pointed me in the direction of a group breaking Faces, and I joined them." Peter sighed as he remembered better times and thought on the circumstances that had brought him here.

"I remember I didn't need a bat. I beat the first Face I saw. I cracked it in a single punch, and I didn't stop until he was all over me. I remember smiling for the first time. Really smiling, not my Face doing it for me because it was expected, but me. When I was done there, we went store by store, street by street, all the while by his side.

"When I look back on it now, it seems crazy. I saw Brutus die, we all did, but there he was, walking like any other man there. He spoke to us, told us what to do. He was like a father in that moment, and we his children.

"I remember a man, no one special, met us in the street. He had his mask still on, and he said, 'Why?' Why had we taken our Faces off? Do you know what Brutus said?"

Alexander politely shook his head. Peter knew better, everyone knew Brutus' words from that night but still, he was happy Alexander was indulging him.

"He said, 'Why have secrets, when there is nothing left to lie about?' We killed that man who stopped us, and everyone after. Brutus walked with us till early in the morning, and then, it seemed to happen so quickly, but when the sun had come up, and we were left to look at our work, he was gone."

Peter could not hide the tears that ran down his face, nor would he want to. They were sorrow and happiness mixed together. He had in that brief night found someone to love, truly love, and though the moment was brief, it was better knowing Brutus's love for a fleeting moment than having spent the rest of his life as yet another Face.

"We heard in the pursuing days that Brutus had been seen in other parts of the City, leading other marches. We tried to find him so many times, but he was always gone when we got there. His words were all that remained each night. Before long, his tomb had appeared. Some said a Face had got him, others that a Cleaner had been his end.

"I brought what was left of my Face to his tomb, my humble offering to the man who set me free. I know he's gone now, but looking back, I like to think that in the end, he finally got to take his Face off." Peter wept freely and sniffed as he spoke.

"I only wish I could thank him, that he would take my hand again. That I could walk with him once more," Peter continued to cry but said nothing more.

"Are you ready, Peter?"

The old man nodded, and Alexander pulled away the stool.

"Oh, you poor thing," George said over the corpse of his former client. "You thought you could do better."

George's client had not died well. In the kitchen of her home, where he had last spoken with her not but a few days ago, laid her bloated corpse.

"This is terrible," George said as he stood up, his old knees catching as they straightened out, somewhat buckling at his own weight. George would have grabbed his legs in pain, had his hand not already been sealed around his mouth to dampen the woman's smell.

"Who does this shit anymore?" George croaked as he looked around at the mess.

"She does, apparently," said the huckle bearer from his own vantage, crouching over the woman.

"What?" coughed George as he inadvertently took his hand away to speak, only to be assaulted by that unique stench of old death.

"From the lithograph, it looks like she did it." The huckle bearer handed over the plates to George for his review.

"At twelve, she's in her chair with a kitchen knife at her throat, and at twelve o'five, she has the knife sticking out of her stomach."

George shook his head as he read along, looking at the images as the bearer spoke.

"Why would she cut her throat, and then stab herself?" George said with genuine intrigue.

"Shallow cut," the bearer said, spreading open the gash at her throat, "though she didn't do any better with the punctures at her waist."

George looked away from the gruesome examination. For shallow punctures, she had bled a lot. There was plenty of blood from her chair to the kitchen where she lay. George gagged as he pointed, his words temporarily held at bay by the afternoon's lunch. Regaining his composure somewhat, George pointed again at his client.

"Why, would she cut off her own hand?" The end of his sentence caught in his throat as he made eye contact with the semi-severed appendage, separated only a few inches by the width of the cleaver's blade.

"I don't know," the huckle bearer stated flatly, still crouching over the body. "There's a gap between the chair and here. Could be blood loss affected her judgement, anything more than that, and I don't think I'm qualified to speculate."

George's mind ran with theories. *Why would she do it? Was it panic? Where did the cleaver come from? What had transpired in those minutes between graphs?* George shook his head. It didn't matter really, she was dead, and by her own hands…*hand?*

George gestured towards the body as a prelude to a command, but ended up turning on his heel and leaving the huckle bearer to his task.

Finally at home and sitting in a chair not dissimilar to his client's, George rested from his day's work. A cough crept out of his lungs, and the pain returned. For the minutes that passed, George felt as if a lifetime had come and gone. The amount of pain he was in seemed infinite, and the longer he coughed, the closer it became to choking, and on occasions like this one, choking felt very much like suffocating.

When his pain had passed, George sat back into his chair, taking long deep breaths. It occurred to him that not even divers emerging from the water appreciated air as much as he did now. Only slightly dizzy, George knew that his cough would return, and it could be at any moment.

His quality of life had deteriorated to the point of not really living at all. Beyond his work, he had no real connection with the rest of the City. He had no one, because he was no one. Every morning and every night felt equally as lonely and without hope for anything better. He'd missed his chance to do something with his life. His career, and therefore his life, could easily be delegated to someone newer and without experience.

His work, his life, had left him with only a single truth. It is better to decide for yourself. As terrifying as death is, it is far better to meet it on your own terms and in your own time. Silently and with a gentle rasp, George continued to think in the silence of his home. He had helped a great many people shed the flesh from their soul.

How would he now help himself? His eyes were drawn to the bulge in his coat. He'd never used his whisper unofficially. He wasn't sure he could without filing the proper forms. He knew it was quick, though, far quicker than his last client's mode of exit.

Then again, he thought, what if killing oneself was like tying a tie. With enough practice, you could do it with your eyes closed. But the moment someone asks you to tie theirs, you fall apart and fail over and over again until you finally fumble your way through it.

The thought made George shiver in horror. He didn't want to be like that woman on the floor, maiming herself in an effort to die faster. He might have been a great tool for others in the years past, but he wasn't sure he could be his own.

The night ticked on for George. Like his life, the evening had grown quickly into the dead of night. The noises from the City hadn't ceased, nor had the lights gone out. At times, those had been a comfort to him. When he felt alone, all he had to do was look out his window. It was that truth that had kept him going for many years. Doubts could be easily brushed aside with a drink on his patio. He was past that now.

An awkward phone call to the Bureau was the decided answer. He couldn't wait. Any longer, and he risked it not being his choice. He waited with a patience that seemed preternatural. He watched as the sun slowly crawled into the horizon of the City. He was late for work by this time. He should have been on the train, fighting for a seat, taking up the space that belonged to him.

His call went through quickly enough. The Bureau had more people answering the phone than they did dropping. His request for the line to Alexander was met with contention, no matter how he asked or said who he was. His years of service had not earned him a second of professional courtesy.

Alexander was busy with months of work already plotted out. George knew Alexander would not bend his schedule, even for a colleague. Though he had hoped, perhaps through mitigating circumstances, that he might somehow get through to Alexander. In the end, though, he didn't even make it past the scheduling desk.

They had inquired if they could transfer him to another dropper, someone named Sam, another named Ellen. George didn't know them, but he considered them for the briefest of moments. He had no doubt they could do the job, but would they be as efficient? George had never botched a job, though there had been plenty of times where a patient had not died…right away.

He disconnected the call. Pulling himself out of his chair, he moved to his window and watched how the City moved beneath him. His eye was drawn to a corner he had passed many times. A corner, with a Booth.

44 | JAMES

Standing by the window, James looked from his apartment down into the City. His bruises seemed to stand out in the faint reflection. His benign gaze mixed with his ever-present narcissism as he saw through his reflection, and into the City.

"As you were told, this first consultation is free."

Free, without charge, gratis. Good, James thought. He'd hate to pay for something he had no intention of using. From the time he'd called to the present moment, he concluded that he'd been rash to contact the Bureau. Death had seemed like the answer, the next logical step. Yet comfort and the din of repetition since then had all but banished the thought. To him, it was a sense of clarity, his instincts kicking in, self-preservation at its most malign.

He wasn't sure what he'd expected from the visit, but its current level of practiced dialogue was a bit too orchestrated for his tastes. No doubt meticulously crafted from moment to moment by the officialdom of the Bureau.

Only minutes had passed since James had welcomed Alexander into his home, and already his mind had departed the scene for tastier memories. Truly, who wouldn't do the same when all you'd heard so far were the same stained words of the past, words which could be readily found in the ears of the Bureau's dead.

How could this man ever hope to tempt him now?

"James," his name echoed out in an unfamiliar tone, dragging him away from the reflection. James turned to stare at the man on his couch. He couldn't help but cross his arms, the gentle touch of his fingers sliding down around his collarbone.

The man, Alexander as he'd introduced himself, wore a neat, tight suit.

His clothes, like his face, were creased into sharp corners, and the black of his suit matched the shade of his slicked-back hair. As James studied him, he could find no imperfection. Even his gloves seemed too fresh, uncracked and unabused by the passages of time. Sitting on his couch, the man seemed simply brighter than every faded thing around him, and his eyes…James could find no way to describe them. Though trying to describe them in any meaningful way was redundant to the feeling they gave James when he looked into them. They were gentle and welcoming, as if they too smiled back, from that place in which our soul resides.

"Why don't you tell me why I'm here?"

The phrasing had caught James off guard, though he'd never really been on his best footing to begin with.

'Why don't you tell me why I'm here?' James repeated the phrase in his mind, squinting his eyes and tilting his head down to look at his feet.

Should he tell him the truth, should he lie? Would Alexander understand how truly empty he'd begun to feel? How could a man so full of life and beauty comprehend the dregs which James sifted through on a daily basis? But he'd asked, so surely he must have some sense, some sympathy for the lost?

James paused and then took a seat opposite Alexander. He breathed a moment to push back at what might come crawling out, and then, he spoke.

"I feel more awake when I'm asleep. I know people there I've never met, I've traveled farther than what is possible, and done things in which I might rest my laurels. Every night I am someone new, better. I am devoid of what makes me…" he sighed, "me. And I wonder, what if life is meant to be more fluid, without the burden of memory, conscience, or guilt? What if…what if we evolved long ago, learned to live untethered from reality, to move with fluidity between the rigidity of time. And what if right now is the real dream, a nightmare, bound to the tediousness of what we call life. A hollow, soulless, excruciating, and vague genetic memory of sadness and of being grounded by the weight of expectations and being forced to live one moment to the next.

"And if that is true, am I just another thought in that dark dream?"

James had begun to cry, he couldn't help it, *for a bunch of bullshit about a dream, it sounded pretty good.*

Every tear felt like a kindness he'd long since missed. He breathed, his mouth slightly open, his forehead crumpled, and his eyes looking at the patchwork of his ceiling. Had he been alone, he'd have felt relieved, but he couldn't help not wanting to appear weak in front of a stranger.

"It's okay James, you don't have to hide from me."

That last little bit of kindness broke James. He lost his composure and began to cry like he'd never done before. As he crumpled in upon himself, he felt the gloved hand of his house guest upon his shoulder, a moment later another resting atop his own balled fists. This stranger whom he'd met only minutes ago was kneeling beside him, holding him. His solace was like the warm heat of the sun after a cold morning.

James had always enjoyed the touch of strangers. His body used to warm and tingle at even a chance brushing of hands or gentle jostling of shoulders during a morning commute. Though as he'd grown older, he'd lost that wonderful feeling to the habituals of time.

Alexander's touch at that moment was better than any sensory bar, any drink, drug, or violence he had previously known, and he wished he could exist there forever. Though within a few minutes, Alexander stood and returned to his seat. It was like tearing flesh, as painful as any violence, and woefully more terrible than having never experienced it at all. In any other life, he would have screamed for the man to come back, to hold him forever.

"I'm afraid I have to go, James." Through his fading tears, James looked up to see Alexander withdrawing a card from his coat. The man set it gently on the table between them.

"If you'd like, you may call the Bureau to set up your billing account and a day and time that works for you to meet again. I sincerely hope that you have a pleasant day."

James' voice caught in his throat, there was no way that his consultation had already lapsed. He'd only cried for a moment, hadn't he? Already Alexander was out the door, James meekly clawing at his fading image, trying to find a way to say, "come back."

As the door closed, James sank to his knees, sliding from his chair and flopping on all fours. Anxiety bit at his chest, and he felt as though he might stop breathing altogether. Panting and sweating, James stared wide-eyed at the floor, willing himself to take control. If he strayed by less than a hair, he was sure he'd collapse and fall headfirst into the void.

He was overwhelmed, and while at first utterly terrifying, he slowly began to smile and then to laugh. He was alive!

Finally, after what could have been days, James leaned to his side and sat with a thud. The hum of the City and the garbled congestion of life fell upon his ears. The rancid smell of rotten food and stale clothes filled his nostrils. The desperate need for water after having wept for hours nipped at his throat.

Standing up slowly, he hobbled meekly towards his sink, though as he passed the seat where Alexander had sat, he greedily collapsed again to the floor. This is where the man had been, perhaps there was something left of him, something James could linger in? Laying his face down, he smelled deeply at the soft fabric and rubbed his hands across the surface, looking for any remnants of warmth. What a joy it would have been, if there had been anything there. Though it seemed nothing had survived. No indent, no residual heat, not even a transient musk. James arbitrarily licked the seat, confident that he would find nothing for him, though still bewitched enough to try.

Slumped with his head on the seat, James daydreamed, reliving his experience with Alexander. No one had ever cared for him like that, no one had ever just listened. This was love, he was sure of it. He'd experienced every pleasure the City had to offer, and never had he felt so good, so alive, and so... connected to another person.

James was sure that Alexander had felt it as well. Beneath his gloved and sterile exterior, he knew that Alexander was just like him. They were both lost in this world, both dreamers, shackled in their own ways, and between the monotony of things, they had found each other.

"No one would have held me like that, if they didn't care," James whispered into the cushion.

45 | JOHN

"Just fucking do it."

John had said nothing to provoke the response from the floor chief. He simply had never learned how to hide his expressions.

"At least pretend like you want me to pay you."

John halfheartedly smiled as he walked the pages back to his desk. He sighed as he sat down, his hands caressed his forehead, and he sat focusing on making a blank expression. He had never gotten the hang of it. His voice could chirp out a pleasant comment, but his face, his face always gave him away.

When he'd had his mask, he had never been forced to smile, never forced to act out a false persona. The mask had given him all he needed. He had found that the freedom to be himself was much more oppressive than he'd originally realized.

A page floated down, and John stared at it with a sense of desperation that did not immediately show on his placid face. There was no reason for this, no reason at all. Why did he do this, why had he ever done this? It was pointless, utterly pointless. All he did was sign papers, page after page, day after day. They never said anything different, never seemed to hold meaning beyond their wasteful tediousness.

He had read them once when he wore his mask. The words seemed to have meaning and his signature purpose. Each word he read to himself, mumbling behind his mask. His finger traced across invisible lines that held up each sentence until he reached the end.

"John," he would sign across that last invisible line, his name affirming the document, giving it life and finality. Now though, now he saw what these pages were, he understood better their purpose, and his.

They were a rule, a law, a contract to bind others. It was the cryptic magic that had once held the City together, and his name was the invocation to seal it. His entire life, and purpose, was to be the reaction to an arbitrary rule that the citizens had made for themselves. He was the solution to a self-made problem.

Without his mask, his creaseless face sank away from the document. *Why do we do this to ourselves?* Why, when there was so much freedom, did those above him still hold to account these antiquated rules? Why did they create a false reality to the world, a false belief that this is the way of things?

It was like chaining a rock to the ground and saying the chain is why the rock stays in place. Shaded in false ideals, John didn't see how he could sign another page. Looking out to the street below, John realized that throughout all these years, he could still see his reflection in the window.

46 | KATHERINE

Katherine answered the call with the due haste that was expected of her position. Before the first bell faded into the second, Katherine had waded into her practiced speaking points.

First, an eloquent and personal introduction.

"Thank you for calling the Bureau of Assisted Suicide…" Katherine checked the tags on the line, with a flick of her eyes, discerning a name for the next step, "…James, my name is Katherine, how may I be of assistance to you today?"

Gentle breathing was her response, it usually was.

Second was to wait and to no matter what, not speak until the caller had. With any chance of anonymity removed, the caller was encouraged not to leave the line for fear of embarrassment by inevitably having to call back a second time and being an inconvenience to staff like Katherine.

If they did hang up, Katherine was trained to call them back and inquire as to why they had called and why they'd hung up. Katherine was preparing herself for this outcome when a voice finally came across.

"Hello Katherine, I suppose I'm contacting the Bureau to make a follow-up appointment to my free consultation."

Three, inform them of the contractual obligations of proceeding.

"Of course, James, as you are already aware, further meetings with the Bureau will be charged from your account." Some knew beforehand, some forgot, regardless, treating the decision of payment as if it had already been made was the key to step three. "To proceed, may I please have your four-digit code?"

"4-3-5-7."

From this point forward, the Bureau would be working at a profit.

"Alright, James, the Bureau now has discretionary access to your account and will appropriately deduct from your finances for each subsequent visit. The Bureau now acknowledges its role as trustee and will appropriately administer your funds as you request. Should you not designate a recipient to take possession of your finances after final billing has been processed, the Bureau will transfer and liquidate any and all remaining assets for the City to then take possession of."

Katherine kept her speaking to a steady pace. Questions or any form of reciprocal conversation were kept intentionally at a minimum to discourage "awareness indicators." With the typical systemic imbalance of the Bureau's clients, a stray thought, a bubble in the throat, or even an inappropriate intonation could be enough to see them collapse in on themselves, and most importantly, disconnect.

"Your Bureau representative..." Katherine scanned quickly, her eyes reading ahead of her, acquiring a name, even before she'd finished speaking, "...Alexander will go over in detail with you the documentation necessary to establish any and all beneficiaries other than the City."

Four, arrange the next meeting. After that, the account was left in the dropper's hands. "James, what day and time would work best for you to meet with Alexander?"

"Well, I would like to meet tomorrow, I'm not sure I want to wait much longer than that. Let's say anytime around lunch, before, after, or during? Oh, and I'd like to meet in the park."

47 | Daniel

The wind blew through Daniel's hair as he gripped the handles of his cycle, revving the engine as he blew past building after building. Danielle held onto his waist, her mask hiding only the upper half of her face, leaving her disfigured jaw exposed.

There was no aim to their wandering. Daniel and the other Half-cracks did this every day, their flags hoisted high, beating against the wind as they weaved through the City. They would do this until they were bored, pulling over then to harass passersby until they were bored again, of course.

They were a generation born with everything, freedom, choice, endless indulgence, and spared from the soullessness of the previous era. At least, that is what their parents thought. The Half-cracks thought otherwise. For them, there was no challenge to life, no goals, no ambitions. They had and did whatever they wanted, whenever they wanted. There was no revolution for them, no great triumph—just the endless tedium of a life without resistance.

Danielle squeezed his side, it was their way of communicating when on the cycle. That was how things went, Daniel would lead the riders through town, and hours would go by until finally, Danielle squeezed his side. She was ready to stop, bored with the wind in her hair.

The park was their haven when away from their cycles. Daniel and his people would make their pilgrimage to the center, past the Libro and the lakes. They kept close together, passing the other roving groups without pleasantry. The Half-cracks were known for their ambivalence towards violence. What reason allowed one group to pass unmolested was not necessarily true for the next.

A hand came from behind Daniel and squeezed tightly. This was Danielle's symbol when she wanted something, her hollow black eyes stared ahead with intent. Daniel followed her gaze to a slow-moving elderly woman. Her long coat and pinned hat tottered along with her. She kept her eyes down, but that wouldn't save her today. Daniel looked behind him at his gathered brothers and sisters. He nodded his head, and they tore ahead of him. They'd done this before, it didn't matter that she was old, only that she had it coming.

Daniel and Danielle watched as they beat the woman. Her hand squeezed tighter and tighter, and Daniel thought for a moment about her motives. He'd never been beaten as bad as Danielle, but he wondered why one who'd suffered as she had would want to do the same to others? He knew that the last time her voice had been heard was in a plea for help. She'd called out for someone to save her, she'd asked them to stop, she'd even said, "Please."

That isn't how trauma works, though, is it? When we've been caught wanting, we do whatever we can to feel powerful. Even if it means mirroring our own pain onto others. It's the only thing that keeps the ground from opening up beneath our feet. There is an order to things, and even when we're aware of it, it's often too hard to shake free.

A tug at his sleeve pulled him from thought. Danielle saw someone coming. It was a man in a black suit, with a black case. He was a dropper, a man of the City, a representative of the new government. Daniel felt his hand squeezed again. She wanted him too, and he could understand why.

The man's placid face watched the violence as he approached. He did not change his pace or direction as he walked, seemingly only justifying a look as he passed by.

"Would you care to do anything about it?" Daniel said in a challenge to the man. He, like the rest, knew what was tucked inside the coat of a dropper—its subtle bulge visible to everyone.

Without stopping, the man smiled without judgement or fear.

"It's not my business."

He continued on without another word, unmolested by the Daniels. For a government that was more concerned with killing its citizens than saving them, this interaction seemed right on the nose.

48 | JAMES

It was a gentle breeze that had brushed past James' face, gently pulling him back to where he should have been. James looked around the park from his seat on the bench. Disappointed, he sighed and returned to the torture of time. Even though he'd arrived several hours early, it was beginning to feel as if Alexander might be late. Tapping his foot and sighing, James tried to dilute the conscious thoughts that were slowly driving him mad.

Having been able to schedule a meeting so quickly, James eagerly spent the time between preparing himself to meet Alexander. They'd met at such an inopportune time, James worried what Alexander might think of him.

Earlier in the day, he'd awoken to fading but still bluntly obvious bruises from his minor foray as a beater. He didn't mind so much the purple, he found it to be quite the pop of color, but the putrid yellow and green made his skin look…sickly. He'd lost a fight, after all, not contracted some neo-plague. The proper application of product helped to gently conceal the undesired tones and shades. He was sure to leave some of the bruising, though. He wanted to be aesthetically pleasing while not appearing to be vain.

After he'd cleaned and readied himself, he went to his drawer and selected his best yellow scarf. It had meant something at one point in time, but now was nothing more than a pleasing form couched in a warm color that accented his best features.

Black had been Alexander's colors, and mimicry was the best form of flattery, or so he'd been told. Digging through, he eventually landed on a black jacket that he felt would not only stylishly match his companion's but would not be so loud as to deter from the focal piece of his scarf.

So focused was James with his illusions and vagaries that time had ceased to flow in a manner with which he was accustomed. Being attentive to the problems at hand, James felt as though days and even weeks had begun to pass. Many times had he frantically broken away from preening himself to find that only mere minutes had elapsed since he'd last checked.

Having finished readying himself sometime in the early morning, he found that no matter what he did, he could not stop thinking about his meeting with Alexander. He sidled up to a few activities which in the past had occupied his time, though as he'd suspected, it was Alexander that continued to occupy his mind. Nor could he tear himself away from constantly checking his appearance for fear of damaging the facade he'd so painstakingly created.

After a few stressful attempts, he decided that he would best serve his cause by going to the park early and waiting there. If there was even a slight chance that Alexander might be early, he did not want to miss out for punctuality's sake.

So, sitting by himself, he tried to remember how to talk to another person. Not just speak at them, but talk. To exchange ideas, discuss current affairs, and have a passable interest in what was heard. There was no doubt for James that he would hang on every word Alexander said, but could he find anything to say in return?

He wasn't much of a talker because he wasn't very much interested in his fellow citizens. Sure at one point, he'd had friends, pursued ideas and goals he thought might impress others. But he found that he was always just waiting, waiting to interrupt, to tell his own tale of self-veneration. It was a sad day when he realized that people hadn't cared anymore for his stories than he cared for theirs.

"Hello, James."

Looking up, James realized that he'd missed catching the man in the distance, missed the chance to admire him from afar, to take in those qualities which define his kind. As if perfectly placed, James was forced to squint as he looked up to see Alexander, his head crowned in the glow of the sky.

"I hope you have not been waiting too long. May I have a seat?"

James half nodded, though being unsure of his stuttering bob, gave a greater affectation which he imagined would have looked more appropriate on the shoulders of an eager child. Deriding himself for his foolish gestures, he scooted closer to the end of his seat to allow Alexander space to sit.

"I'm glad we have a chance to continue together," Alexander said as he opened his bag, drawing forth one page after another until he'd formed a neat and polite stack. "Your account has been made open to the Bureau, and after our session, the appropriate funds will be withdrawn by the end of the business day. As you've chosen to progress today, we will focus on getting the necessary forms completed, so the next time we meet, we can focus on taking care of you."

James hung on every word. His voice, his tone, his intonation were all so beautiful. He seemed so confident, so practiced, like he knew where he was supposed to be and how he fit into the City around him.

James longed for that kind of clarity and drive. He wasn't sure he'd ever known who he was, other than just a sensory fiend, strung out and out of stimuli. Seeing Alexander just being himself was inspiring and, in a way, moving. These feelings only further served the ideas in James' mind. They told him that this was a man that he could love and be loved by.

"I'm sorry to interrupt," he said, even though he wasn't, "but do we only have forty-five minutes again?" There was a hope that perhaps if he sounded pathetic enough, Alexander might take some level of pity on him and spare a bit more time than he usually would. James as well couldn't help but wish that Alexander secretly felt the same way about him. Perhaps if they both knew that each of them wanted more time with the other, maybe something could come of it.

"No, James, I'm here for as long as you need me." The air had an odd metallic tang to it, but for James, things were perfect.

It is peculiar in a way that often having hope of a certain outcome is better than the eventual conclusion. Living in that endless moment of possibility, failure, and half-realized goals are only ideas. Where success is a certainty, hampered only by the flow of time and the drudgery of action.

A paper slipped into the space between James' thigh and hands.

"This is your Death Certificate, James. This is an acknowledgment that progressing any further with the Bureau's services will require the willful commitment to utilizing the Bureau's predefined services as requested and to complete any and all processing requests made upon you up unto your passing. This will then mark the conclusion of your contract with the Bureau. Failure to follow defined guidelines and instructions from your representative or to willfully object to final termination will result in the legal seizure of your person, and termination as best defined by your Bureau's representative."

James' eye couldn't help but drift to the bulge in Alexander's coat, though he knew it wouldn't come to that. They both just had to play along, long enough until they felt comfortable telling each other how they felt. After that, things would be different, life would be different. Taking a pen from Alexander, he scrawled his name at the bottom of the page, nodding at his vision for the future. This was just a step towards what he wanted. He just had to stay focused, and things would work out, there was nothing to fear. After all, it was just a name on a page.

"So, should I fill in the date, and the..." James scanned the page looking at the numerous lines which were blank except for the contextual markers beneath them.

"No, that is something I will do later for you." Alexander smiled as he gently took the page back, neatly placing it into his bag. "The next form I would like you to sign is your Declaration of Intent, form 34-b."

James tried scanning the document, which was thick with text, single-spaced, and without indentation. As if sensing his confusion, Alexander slid just a hair closer and leaned in.

"This form serves as a redundancy to further state that you, as a citizen of the City, wish to affirm your intent to take your own life and would do so utilizing the resources of the Bureau of Assisted Suicide."

James nodded in understanding and once again signed his name across the designated line. It was somewhat empowering that his signature carried such weight in this professional interaction. It made him feel very much in control.

Seeing that there was still more documentation, James felt almost better about the process. Something about the fact that there was so much work involved lent to it a legitimacy and an air of professionalism that he had not previously associated with the service.

"This is your DDF, or Day of Death form 26-c. Here you can fill out your requested day of passing. This date will have to fall outside of any necessary or previously scheduled visitations that require your active participation in the processing of your request on the Bureau. Any day may be scheduled up unto three months after the processing of all finalized signatures. I, as your representative of the Bureau, will make myself available on any day of your choosing and at any time that best suits your requested form of passing."

"Alright, uhmm..." James' lip curled in as he tried to think of some date that might be of some meaning to him. Though as his mind ticked away, he could not remember a time when the date mattered. All he really knew was that he hated how his favorite restaurant was closed on a Saturday when clearly Tuesday would have been a better option. Everyone hated Tuesday, it was that bleak reminder that the week had only just begun, a midpoint before a midpoint. The sour soggy day that told you, you had to work because Monday was only yesterday, and that you couldn't quit because Saturday was still so far away. Not that it mattered because his favorite restaurant was closed on a Saturday, forcing him to conclude that he hated both Tuesdays and Saturdays.

That left a series of disjointed days which he didn't particularly care about in any sort of meaningful fashion. So with a sigh, he said, "Next Thursday should be okay," shortly after dotting in the appropriate boxes and signing again at the bottom.

James noticed Alexander's smile again, and he felt somehow special. It was all for him, just the two of them, sitting on a bench in a park, smiling.

"I forgot to say thank you for meeting me out here. I just felt like being outside, you know?"

"It's my pleasure, James. It's very easy for us to be accommodating." James wasn't entirely sure if he understood what Alexander meant, but he smiled and let his gaze drift a bit. Sitting in the park, with company.

"The last item I would like you to consider today is your means of passing. I have with me a selection of permits I can file on your behalf if you come to a conclusion today."

"Ok, sure," James said, smiling with a shrug, "I can't say I've ever really come to a 'conclusion' on any particular end. I've thought about it like everyone in the City, but uh, yeah just, not really sure. Do you, have any recommendations?"

"I don't have an opinion on the matter, James. You should pick something that has meaning to you."

James had for a brief moment felt slightly dejected, but on contemplation, he realized how sweet it was that he wasn't being forced into any particular means of departure. There were some ends that were messier than others and plenty that had to be easier on a dropper like Alexander. Yet sweet Alex didn't want to dilute his decision. That or he was like James and had no intention of going through with it. And if that was the case, then a decision like this didn't really matter at all.

"I do, however, have a brochure which outlines several options that are available to you." Alex held it out for James to take, which he did with a nod.

It was a very interesting and visual brochure, but once again, James felt lost. There were a lot of terms he was unfamiliar with and none of the old slang which he'd grown up using. No droppers, no dippers, no beaters, or leapers. Just a slew of tasteful depictions and words he was unfamiliar with. A diagram of a woman underwater caught his eye. A gulper, now that was a way to go.

Something clicked in him, and the spiteful and morose side of James returned. Death shouldn't be peaceful or transcendent. He wasn't going to pretend to be a bird and jump off a building or have someone help snap his neck. Death was a violent thing, and he'd had too much of the City to die in any way but by clawing and kicking. Sure it was the City that would have killed him, killed him like everyone else, but he wouldn't just lie down. It wouldn't be easy.

He'd struggle for every breath and scream into the muted slurry of spit and water. He'd feel every moment of his death, but it wouldn't be a clean death. The City wouldn't get to pull a switch and just quickly clean up. He'd show the City what it had forgotten in the days after its Revolution.

A pause in his thoughts allowed him to see that the suppositions about his death were quickly becoming the certitudes of a dangerous line of thinking. He reassured himself that at least, that's what he would have done, before Alex.

"James?" Snapping himself out of his own mind, James turned to see Alex patiently waiting.

"I'm sorry, uh, I would like to apply for this sub…submersion permit." His finger pointed at the tasteful image as he handed the brochure back to Alex.

"Since this form of departure can take place in the confines of your home, I will only need a signature. Please disregard the boxes requesting a date, time, and authorizing signature. Those can be filled in at a later date. Everything else you can fill out now."

James quickly noted some preferences that the permit requested, such as temperature, the level of soap, scented or unscented candles. It seemed more like a menu than a permit, but he supposed their level of detail was born of a certain efficiency. Signing again, he passed the permit back to Alex, and the man, with a practiced motion, placed it back inside his bag.

"Do you have to go now, Alex?" James whimpered out, only managing to stop his voice cracking towards the end. He felt terribly vulnerable in asking something like this of his companion. He was expressing his own desires and wants in an appropriately subtle and polite way. Which meant that it would hurt just as much if he heard a subtle and polite, "No."

"No, James, though that is the last of the paperwork we need to sign today. If you'd like to sit and talk for a bit, we can."

James felt his heart flutter as he tried to hide his joy. Looking around with a smile, he tried to spot something worth mentioning, some bit of conversation that might float him to something more substantial and noteworthy.

"Have you been to the Libro lately? I hear there have been some great shows…lately." James gestured to the opened domed structure in the distance.

"No," the answer seemed blunt, but there was that smile on Alex's face that told him otherwise.

"Oh, really? When's the last time you went?"

"I can't recall, James."

"Yeah, well it's not the best thing in the City. I used to really like their earlier stuff. I don't really connect with everything they're doing now. I mean, not everything has to have a deeper meaning. Sometimes just a good fight or lay is enough to be interesting. What do I know though? I mean, I'm the guy who won't be here in a week. Not exactly their target audience, I assume." James chuckled as he shook his awkward head.

"No, you're right, James," Alexander said as his hand stretched to rest on James' knee. "Not everything has to have a deeper meaning."

49 | GEORGE

George supposed that he was lucky to get a seat today. The door closed beside him, and he was pressed against the adjoining wall. A screen descended with a full deposit window, with no option for family. George stared at the screen in front of him. Once he signed, that would be it. His body would be atomized, and he wouldn't even be a speck on the wall.

The thought was comforting to George. Fear and disappointment had plagued him since he'd settled upon this course. He looked around the small and confined room. While he spoke the slanderous material well enough, he had at least expected a smell, a warm seat, even some graffiti. Yet there was none, the room felt new and perfect. He wheezed and coughed, holding the rounded wall to support himself. His spittle speckled the wall and screen in front of him. His red, swollen face bulged as his body once again became his own, settling his fit into a few shallow breaths.

He loosened his tie and breathed freely unhindered for a moment. The Booth was claustrophobic, and the longer he sat, the more stale the air became. It felt uncomfortably similar to the train, and he laughed at the irony of the situation.

George sighed and supposed that not even with all his knowledge and practice that death could be perfect. He was happy, though. His life was ending, and of all the solutions before him, this was the best that he could do. He had failed to accomplish much, but at least he could do this for himself.

George, in his last act, signed his name within the full deposit window. The image blinked away, and the screen ascended to safety, returning to its place out of view. Closing his eyes, George took one last deep breath. The air was still stale, but at least he could breathe. Sitting with his eyes closed, George let his mind go. He didn't think on his life, his work, or his clients.

He didn't fixate on his shortcomings, nor even his few successes. He let it all go, making peace with the past. It seemed sad that this sense of relief and harmony only came at the end, but like a tired dreamer, he felt ready to drift off to the next place.

George would have kept his eyes closed if he could, but the pain forced them open. He didn't see much, as he opened his eyes only to have them burned away, bursting in his sockets before evaporating from the heat. He screamed as his body melted down. His cries and thrashings were muffled to silence for those walking by the street corner. As his legs gave way and his body crumbled in upon itself, the fine specs of ash that were left drifted down through the vent in the floor.

The booth scrubbed itself clean of the man, and in a few practiced moments, the door to the booth slid open, ready for the next passerby.

50 | DAVE

Years passed, and Dave had become an expert in his field. The belt ran smoother, the overall structure was maintained, and he even knew how to stoke the fires during the busy hours. Fortunately, corpses were no longer sent through the chutes, plugging up the system. Instead, the Bureau hand-delivered the dead, tied up neatly in their black body bags.

Since the marches had ended, the Bureau had emerged as the leading cause of death. Granted, they only executed the willing, but it was rare for anyone other than a dropper to deliver a corpse for him to burn.

There wasn't much to talk about whenever one stopped by. A simple exchange, the dotting of a few 'i's, and a nod until next time was the extent of their interactions. Which meant that Dave was alone for much of his life.

He was okay with that though, he'd been alone before, and at least now, he felt as though he served a purpose. It was a slightly empowering feeling to know that the City wouldn't be able to run without him, but he wasn't delusional enough to think that he couldn't be replaced. After all, hadn't he done that to whoever had come before?

Dave busied himself with a variety of interesting games. He would sit and watch as the disposed passed by, eagerly awaiting something new that he'd never seen before. If it was interesting enough, he'd reach out and grab it. Inspecting and learning, sometimes keeping, other times replacing.

Just about the only thing he hadn't seen come down his belt was a Face, or mask as they called it now. People were so eager to take them off but not so eager to forget and do away with them, apparently. The idea of finding one and trying it out was a curiosity he'd maintained since he started.

Beyond that, he would entertain himself with tallies, counting the number of similar items each day—two combs here, seven shoes there. Patterns would emerge, but he wasn't nearly clever enough to confidently draw any revelatory conclusions. No, to Dave, he was quite a simple man who was lucky enough to enjoy his work.

"EMERGENCY STOP! EMERGENCY STOP! EMERGENCY STOP!"

He couldn't find the button. Lost in his games, his mind was far and away from the Crematorium. He stumbled around the chair he'd knocked over in his panic.

His feet tangled with the crisscrossing of the foldable seat. Dave landed on his face before he even realized he was falling. The grating of the floor felt like it had jumped up and cut him in their hexagonal patterns. His head swirled as he opened his eyes, a guttural swear leaked out of his mouth in a soft whisper.

There it was. Peeling his face from the grate, he reached out and slammed the emergency stop. Light twirled, and a violent bell rang in the concrete dome. Using the belt to haul himself up, he staggered to what he had seen passing by. It laid precariously near the end, a mild stutter from falling into the furnace.

Gently Dave scooped it into his hands, marveling at the beauty that was almost destroyed. He stabbed with his shoe at the emergency stop button, disengaging the hold and silencing the swirling lights and ringing bell.

He picked up his chair and took a seat, all the while gently maintaining the treasure. It was unlike anything he'd ever seen. The sense of awe it emitted filled the room, it was by far the most precious thing he'd ever known.

He bit at the tip of his glove, tugging it off and spitting it on the ground. He wanted to touch it, but a better idea struck him as he stood up and marched outside. He felt sucked out by the hot air, stumbling forward towards the rail outside the door. He held the thing close to his chest to prevent it from being carried away.

When the door had shut, and he was confident that it was safe, he held it up to the light. Buried in a small pocket of dirt, was a tiny sapling. Green needle-like protrusions extended from the stem. As he looked closer, he realized that it had the most wonderful scent. Sweet and clean, it felt like breathing in a fine mist.

He didn't know what it was, but he knew that it was something worth saving, something worth caring for.

51 | JAMES

James had spent the entire day cleaning. With a fine brush, he scraped every crack and crevice from his kitchen sink to his adjoining bathtub. James was embarrassed about how their first meeting had gone. With each new scrap of mold and line of dust, James sighed loudly, stressed to think that he'd had such an interest as Alex over to such a filthy home.

Even though he told himself how easy it was to let go and 'forget' to clean, he still chided himself throughout the experience. When you lived alone, it was easy to tolerate anything, so long as it didn't require you to work to fix it. What matter was it that soap scum had piled up into his grouting, turning shades of pink and green? He was the only one that would see that pile of dishes or that sock by the chair.

Who would know that he hadn't showered or washed his clothes? So long as he was comfortable, wasn't that all that really mattered? Besides, it was just a few rooms stitched together for his personal use. He didn't really 'live' there. It was a place to store things, to sleep, and sometimes eat. He lived out in the City, in the sensory bars, and along the ill illuminated back rooms.

So he could be excused for their first meeting and the state of his domicile. Alex would understand, James was sure that he'd seen worse. Even if he hadn't excused him necessarily by circumstances alone, so long as it was cleaner than the first time around, Alex would certainly be…impressed?

James rushed across his apartment, cleaning where he could and hiding things that he couldn't. He couldn't become too caught up in cleaning though, he still had to cook. Which, as he checked the hour of the day, was already past the time he was supposed to start the noodles, let alone the sauce.

"Thank you so much again for joining me for dinner. I'm just so hungry, and I haven't been able to eat all day. I hope it's appetizing for you."

"It's not a problem James. I'm happy to do whatever is convenient for you." Alex grinned and looked at his food. He took a small bite, chewed, and then took a sip from his drink. From under the table, his hand rose with the vibrantly colored napkin James had once received as a going away gift.

Alex gently wiped his mouth and then returned the napkin to his lap, folding it out of view from James' line of sight. "It's very good James, thank you."

He made no mention of the chewy noodles or the lukewarm sauce. He didn't wince at the cheap wine or the coarse and inappropriate swatch of cloth that barely passed as a napkin. Anyone else would have told him that his food was shit and his wine was cheap, but not Alex. James felt a beautiful warmth from the thought and stared at his plate as he chewed his noodles, unable to hide his smile.

"We just have a few forms to complete today, James. Mostly items that will make your passing easier, but won't be a problem if we don't get to them today."

James nodded and smiled. Since his last meeting, he felt calmer and more relaxed conversationally. He wasn't too terribly concerned with the documents, as the services they would be canceling were things he could easily get back after he'd opted out with Alex in tow.

"Sure, can't really complain about work that makes my life easier. Do you need me to move closer to sign anything?" An outside observer would likely have noticed how hard James was trying.

"No, I can fill these forms out for you." Alex nodded before reaching into his bag and pulling out a color-coordinated stack. It seemed that, like last time, Alex came prepared with several copies, each to be filed and stored in separate locations for redundancy's sake.

"This is your Spousal and Relative Grievance form 17-a, immediate family acknowledgement of wish for passing. Do you have any immediate family members or spouse you wish to notify of your intent to proceed with Bureau services?"

James' head twitched slightly as he tried to understand the purpose of the form.

"No, I don't think I do. I uh, had a mother once, but she left when I was young."

Alex nodded and wrote a short note within a defined boundary in the middle of the form. He quickly copied this to the two remaining identical pages and then placed them in his bag.

James ate a bit more as he stared blankly at his stained table. He'd never used a coaster, not for hot drinks or cold ones. A film of rings dotted around his plate, a halo of neglect and uncaring.

"James?" Looking up from his plate, he saw Alex smiling back at him. His eyes and grin were soft as if he knew exactly what he was feeling. Had they never met, James might have assumed the man was tired and politely grinning at a joke that wasn't nearly as funny as was intended.

But James knew Alex, and he knew the man in the suit was more than he appeared. That those eyes hid who he really was and weren't a reflection of his sterile exterior.

"Would you like to continue? I can come back if you would like some time to think."

"No," blurted out James, why would he want Alex to go, they'd only just begun. Though James quickly realized, *oh no! What if he thinks I don't want him to come back?*

"I mean no, you don't need to leave, though I don't mind if you want, uh, need to come back." Sweaty palms itched within the grooves of James' hand. "...I'm sorry, did you say something?"

"I didn't say anything, James. If you are ready, this is your Leave of Work for Personal Reasons form b-2. I have already filled out your information and have retained the necessary copies for the Bureau's archives. Do you have any other employment outside your work as a temp?"

"No, just the temp stuff at a nostalgia shop. Do you need the name?"

"No, that's fine," Alex looked over the forms before filing them away. "Form b-2 can be submitted as late as the night before. You may also choose to submit it any time after this meeting."

James raised his eyebrows, as time off work wouldn't be such a terrible thing. A week of slack time would be a nice bonus to these proceedings. He'd just have to figure out something to do.

"Do you have any standing subscriptions, such as a Libro pass or any other paid entertainment?"

The forms Alex noted on had become substantially smaller. Less than half the size of a standard page. James could just gleam his name at the top of each, written neatly in by hand.

"I let my Libro pass lapse, but I do have a subscription to 'ART-I-FICIAL'… the art of…" James furrowed his brow and looked off to the side. His lip sneered briefly as he failed to recall the name before getting up to find his subscription packet. "Ah, here it is. 'ART-I-FICIAL: *the art of official small talk, and the depth of substantial conversation.*' Kind of a mouthful, isn't it?" A small awkward chuckle escaped James' mouth.

"That's a good show," Alexander stated with a nod. Something was odd about the way he said it, and James couldn't help but feel that he would have voiced his approval regardless of what the program actually was.

"You may submit these cancellations and notifications yourself, or I can do that on your behalf. You may also leave them for me to collect and submit after your passing, except for your Leave of Work form b-2, which should be submitted no later than the night before. Do you have a preference, James?"

"Well, I mean, I'd like some time off, obviously, but would it be alright if I left the subscription cancellation for the day of?"

"Of course, I will also schedule for your citizen's benefits to be canceled after passing. Lastly, do you have anyone that you would like to indicate as a beneficiary? Without doing so, all assets and accounts will be turned over to the City after final billing."

James crumpled his nose as he looked down at his yellow noodles. A few names snuck through his head, but no one he wanted to see profit on his death. They'd never been good enough people for James to want to give them anything. Really though, he didn't need to worry, he wasn't going to go through with this and would still need his funds when he and Alex went away.

"I don't think it matters enough to me to name anyone in particular. Just go ahead and do what's standard."

"In that case, I would like to encourage you to do what you want in the time till our next meeting. Many people take this time to reflect and make peace with what brought about their decision to progress with our service. Others enjoy parts of the City they never had time for. In the case that you might feel lost or need to talk, vent even, please give the Bureau a call. Now, if it is alright with you, James, I would like to look around so

I know how to prepare for your passing."

James half-heartedly smiled and extended his hand towards the bathroom. Alexander rose in a practiced motion as if he'd been poised to do so throughout their dinner together.

James watched him disappear into the adjacent room. His practiced steps allowing him to take in every aspect of the apartment. The man would have been horrifying if he'd ever arrived unexpectedly, cornering you at some back door or alleyway. Even the beaters in all their brutality had a bluntness about them, which denoted a weakness that could be exploited.

A chill ran down his spine as he realized that Alexander had, at one point, been intent on killing him. That was before, though, and James knew they understood each other now. They'd just had dinner, Alex had done his paperwork, he'd smiled. James shook the feeling away and got up to walk around and pump out the chill that had crept into the joints of his body.

The window in his apartment was intrusively small. It seemed to focus the light from the City, casting it narrowly into his room. He hated looking out of it, only barely able to see a sliver of the skyline. Though from afar, the ray of light it let into his room always seemed to draw him over, forcing him to squint as he looked outside.

Now that sliver of skyline seemed so much like just enough. He had always wanted everything, every experience, every sensory bath. He wanted to go out all the time, be with everyone all the time. He figured that's why he'd come to hate his view so much because it could never offer him anything other than a sliver.

These last few years, though, he'd been just burnt out. He didn't feel the joy from his youth, and it was killing him to remember what he'd had. Constantly pushing himself further and deeper into the City so he could get back a little of what he'd lost.

As he looked outside, he felt completely different about his view. This wasn't everything, no, but it was a start, a new, fresh chance with Alex to make something for themselves.

"Thank you, James, and thank you for dinner. I hope you have a pleasant evening, I will see you again on Thursday."

Turning too slowly, James only caught the back of Alex as he opened the door and let himself out. A mild protest had begun to burp out as his eyes widened in realization. Yet by the time he'd managed to say anything at all, the door had already closed.

James had hoped that they might sit together and talk. Maybe Alex would even tell him how he felt, and they could think about their lives past the confined interactions of client and representative.

Gathering the plates up, James reassured himself that everything would be alright. That there would be a life past Thursday and that his life would soon include a new lifelong companion. A song his mother used to sing crept back into his mind, and he felt compelled to sing as he washed down Alex's unfinished meal.

> "Someday will be today,
> today will be every day
> and every day will be always,
> with you."

Danielle hadn't understood why Daniel had let the man pass, nor had she forgiven him. She rode with another Daniel, refusing to even sit with him, and if he was being honest, he wasn't sure that he was entirely upset with the outcome.

He had been born with the freedom to choose, why would he give that up to anyone? No, if there was a later for them, then Daniel wouldn't argue. For now, though, he enjoyed the ride. His cycle, going faster and faster, his flock having difficulty keeping up. Weaving through the traffic, his flag a marker for those behind him.

He wouldn't be told how to live his life. If he was given autonomy, then he would choose heteronomy. Violence, then pacifism. Individuality, conformity. Only the right to choose would he accept as it was. He was a contrarian, and he would always be so. The relic on his face was proof of that.

The sacrosanct masks of their fathers adorned their heads, bisected and defaced by the children they'd created through their unburdening. Nothing was more satisfying than goading the culture that had created him.

As all men do, Daniel thought of the life ahead of him that had yet to play out. The present seemed like it could last forever, but one day he too would be old and weak. Where would his flock be then, would they still be Daniel? Or would time force their wounded souls closed and impart on them a name that better reflected the outcome of their life? Would they still hate their fathers with the same passion, or would old age geld them into an accepting weakness?

Daniel knew now that he would never understand his father and those who came before. He knew how much he hated the City and the people who enabled it. Daniel knew the truths of his life and the facts of the present, but time would change that.

He hated the man he would become because he knew that man would look back with shame and regret on the man he was now. He would see himself as a boy, a boy who knew so very little, ignorant, and lost. Daniel hated that man who would betray him to age and weakness. Whose luxury of time could only criticize the youth who had come before.

As Daniel slowed down, his mind seemed to as well. Overwhelmed by destiny, he returned solely to the streets of the City, the sounds of cycle engines resting behind him. They'd traveled far enough today, Daniel had decided. Pulling over, he and the other's dismounted, taking to the pedestrian lanes.

With glee, many walked softly behind him, hypervigilant for his word and direction. He was not the master but the leash. An imaginary restraint whose bindings were more fragile than any would truly realize.

Daniel's long gaze struck all who passed. The ineffable eyes of his mask, both damning and pardoning those who were unfortunate enough to be within the vicinity of Daniel and his family.

In the distance, the shambling shape of an old woman carrying the day's food teetered back and forth, struggling to ascend what one would assume as a flight of asinine stairs. Their depth and height varied in no particular fashion, all the while managing to be wider than actually needed, with a good portion being dedicated to a path that ascended to a bricked-up wall.

Eccentricities like these confused Daniel. He had learned with plenty of practice how much easier it was to destroy rather than build. It would have taken little effort to shave off the portion of stairs that existed beyond the need of reaching the orphaned door. Yet sights like this could be found all over the City.

As they approached, he could tell that she had seen him, though really, who hadn't? The lane was not particularly wide, and the Half-cracks were not particularly unnoticeable from a distance. Somehow, this woman had convinced herself that if she could but accelerate her ritual of ascent, she might just pass through the threshold unmolested.

Daniel looked behind him at his gathered brothers and sisters. He made to give his accustomed nod, a nod which might put him in the good graces of his scorned lover. They'd done this before, it didn't matter that she was old, only that she had it coming. In the time between turning and nodding, Daniel remembered the man in the suit.

It's not my business. It's...not...my...business. It sounded harsh, but it was true. There was more bureaucracy than there had ever been, hidden in the guise of freedom—the death of the people, corporatized suicide. It was like the mask he wore on his head, just another form of oppression. No one cared that the people lived, only that they were obedient, fooled like they had been before the unburdening. So long as a system was in place, and so long as the people followed it, the City would be happy.

If that was their role, then who was left to help the people?

"Hey!" the bark of his voice squeezed out into the air around them. The woman froze, dropping her bags. Her frail form gently rocking as instinct and experience played against each other.

Daniel approached the woman with his best smile at the ready. Fear would be his greeting, and compliance would be her reply. His posture and demeanor unchanged from his daily routine, he bent over and lifted the bag for the woman.

"May we help you inside with these?" She nodded, her face no different than if she'd been asked to lie down and die. Daniel motioned for others to help as he began to ascend the stairs, holding the old woman's hand.

A Daniel spoke out from behind, no doubt goaded on by the squeezing hand of Danielle, "Why are we doing this?"

Daniel thought for a moment before giving his reply.

"Because no one else is."

53 | JAMES

The smell was unfamiliar, sweet but earthy, with hints of rain. It reminded him somewhat of the park, which reminded him of growing up. Alex had mentioned something about having to prepare, to draw his bath, to prep the room. His black bag, unlike everything about Alex, seemed old and worn down. This, though, seemed to lend to it a legitimacy that might not have otherwise been there had it been new and shining.

James paced around his room as he listened to the preparations for his suicide. He wore a short robe that did not lend itself to the needed modesty of the moment. Chewing on his nails, his mind ran with possibilities and eventualities.

Alex had made no mention of their shared love, he'd given no hint about leaving together. He'd come prepared, going through his dropper motions, leaving James to wonder why. There was an understanding, wasn't there? Alex had cared for him, they'd gone out to the park together, eaten dinner. *Why isn't he saying anything?*

Soft and subtle words began to emanate from his mouth as he began to speak louder. His inner thoughts were too loud, he couldn't hear himself think. He began to mumble as he traced his path backward, looking for something he'd missed.

Maybe Alex was going through the motions so that there would be some evidence, some kind of trail that showed something to his employers. That had to be it, he'd draw the bath, place the scent candles, and then they'd leave together. Anyone coming by would connect the dots and assume that James' contract had been carried out. They'd be somewhere else by then, together, happy, alone.

A smile curled onto his features as he nodded, understanding what was happening. He'd nearly scared himself, thinking about the worst, doubting those he loved. An easy mistake, an easy mistake to make. Now though, now he got it, it was clicking in his mind. He'd just not understood, not understood how clever Alex was.

The rumbling of his tub had changed from that sharp splatting sound of water crashing down on a corporeal surface to the throbbing hum of water rolling down and around itself. He could feel the humid heat coming from his bathroom, like a warm blanket slowly wrapping him up.

James wondered if maybe they might actually use the tub. He'd worked himself up, he could do with some relaxing. Maybe even something a little more fun?

The thought of being underwater filled James' mind, Alexander's hands around his throat, struggling to get up as his own screams were muted around him. Like that night on the street lying in the rain, the notion of dying filled him with a vibrant sense of living.

That's how this had all started, after all. Just a new way to get off. A good time, a sense of thrill and excitement. A wake up from the benign and boring, and he was glad he'd done it. The fear of death, the proximity of violence, it had woken him up, sensitized him enough to feel something for someone else. Alex had walked into his life, and instead of death, had given hope, showing him that people could care for each other. That he could love someone other than himself.

"James, it's time," the leveled voice said as if the tub was calling him and not the man whom he'd soon be spending the rest of his life with.

Peeking in, James saw Alex waiting by the bath. He stood upright with his hands held in front of his waist. Gentle vapors lifted up from the now still water, carrying a scent of nostalgia past James and through the door. Smiling, he pushed the door open and walked up to the tub.

He waited a moment. Now was the time for Alexander to say something like, *'We'll leave this scene here for someone to find after we've gone, now go get dressed.'* He'd be wasting time if he played along, tested the water, commented on the candles. Alex was going to say something, he was going to push him out the door, out of the building, out of this shit life.

Any minute now, he'd cough up a joke, make a quip, validating James' feelings.

"Allow me, James." Gloved hands seized around his waist, reaching for the bow at his side to undo his robe. Panic filled James, something was wrong, this wasn't right. Alex didn't know, he didn't understand. This isn't what they were supposed to be doing.

Realization presented its theory. What if Alex had never known, never understood. What if he'd always just been doing his job. James hadn't been blunt enough, he'd never stated his love!

Action overcame reason as James leaned in, closing his eyes, lips interlocking with Alex's as fear exhaled through his nose. James held himself as warmth and a tingle trickled down his body. He was kissing the man he loved, as someday became today. Pulling himself back, James kept his eyes closed as he savored the moment. His hands tucked under Alex's coat.

"Why don't you step into the tub." His eyes snapped open, and there was Alex, grinning patiently.

"No, no no!" James mumbled as he stepped backward. Alexander wasn't right, this wasn't what he'd seen. This was a dropper, a representative of the Bureau. His eyes, his smile, they weren't soft for him. Alexander didn't see into him, he saw through him. He didn't care about his client any more than he cared about anything else.

How could he have been so wrong, what had he missed? James turned on his heel and ran through his apartment door. His vision was muddied. He couldn't hear anything other than his panting. His foot hit the familiar edge of a step, and he powered through it. His body took over from his mind, and he could sense the pounding of his feet on stairs as his muted screams crept past his ear.

He'd been wrong, so wrong. How could he have not seen it, how could he have not seen the truth in the curves of the dropper's smile? It was for show, just a tool, an affectation of sympathy. How many others had been lured in, died thinking someone cared?

His shoulder hit the edge of the door frame, and he spun out into the open air. A sun brighter than he'd ever experienced burnt its way into his mind, waking him up as he staggered, still trying to get away.

James caught himself as he came to the edge of a step. All he had to do was get past this, and he could disappear. The Bureau wouldn't know how to find him once they'd lost track. He knew the City and all its haunts, every scum-ridden corner. He just had to make it past this step, and he could disappear into the periphery.

James lifted his leg, just a step. His foot gliding over the edge a hair before his eyes did. Below him wasn't a sidewalk. It was a great chasm, ribbed in stone and glass. He was looking down onto the street, hundreds of feet below him. An extreme sense of vertigo took him as he felt his body willing itself over the edge. He rocked to the side, crashed down onto his arm, rolling away from the edge.

His hearing came back to him as the rushing of wind and the sound of cycles in the distance played across his ears. He was on the roof, he'd gone the wrong way. He'd panicked, he'd let his body take over, and he'd gone the wrong way!

James picked himself up and stumbled toward the way he'd come. He just had to get to the street, he just had to…get past Alexander.

The dropper had followed him and now approached slowly towards his client. James just had to get around him, but as he looked towards the door that had led him onto the roof, his heart sank.

There was no door, just a bricked-up frame. His head shook at the impossibility. Looking around, he tried to spot the door that had led him onto the roof. His feet backpedaling to keep a distance between him and Alexander.

There was nothing, just a bricked-up doorway.

James' foot slid as a heel depressed down past the ground and into the open air. He was at the edge again, and Alexander was drawing closer. It was a nightmare, that's all it was. He didn't believe in this, it was all just a dream—one long, terrifying, monotonous dream. When he woke up, he would be a thousand different things, a thousand different people. All he had to do was wake up. All he had to do was believe his own lies.

But that wasn't going to happen. Alexander was real, the Bureau was real, the City was real. He'd acknowledged them. No idiosyncrasy would change that. His depression wouldn't blunt the pain of death or pervert it into some philosophical transcendence. He was going to die, the man he loved was going to kill him.

Why? Why was this happening? Why didn't Alexander understand? Why had he not understood how he felt? There had to be something he could do, something that would fix this.

James couldn't help but breathe himself into a frenzy as Alexander finally came to a halt. The man was still smiling, smiling at James. Threading what was left of his mind into a final plea, James spoke from what he thought was his heart.

"We can go away together, you and me, we can find out what's past this place. We don't have to throw away our lives here. I've spent too much time trying to figure out who I am and what I want. In all this hate and violence, I've found you, Alex!" James curled his lips in a fleeting glimpse where anxiety meets happiness. It was, if anything, an honest smile.

Alexander just grinned, and James saw what he'd already realized. His smile never changed, and he understood now, it wasn't like his at all.

James watched as Alexander unbuttoned his coat.

"This doesn't have a happy ending does it?"

Alexander whispered his reply.

"No."

EPILOGUE

54 | THE NIGHT OF THE REVOLUTION

It was dust that woke Thomasson from forced slumber. Its powdery nature mixing with the saliva in his mouth, forcing out instinctive coughs, which set pain flaming through his head and chest.

He couldn't remember where he was, nor could he piece together the slowly growing roar around him. All his disembodied mind knew was that he was lying against something hard, like a floor.

He opened what he could of his eyes to see a world drenched in a vibrant glow. As if signaling the appropriate channels in his mind, he began to feel an intense heat around him. In all his life, he'd never experienced a fire. Sure enough, he'd seen them through the lenses in his Face, felt the warmth of a hot dish as it ascended from his kitchen counter.

From afar, it had been a beautiful thing. It showed all the signs of life, dancing un-repetitiously, blinking, and moving as if some alien thing was trying to communicate. He'd watched hours of it looping over and over again. Rising from a humble spark to a flashing curtain and back into a softly glowing ember. He'd compared it to life once, a reflection on the cycle of things. He dared say that it had been poetic.

How very wrong he'd been. His Face could never impart to him how he'd react once fire was in his proximity. Its presence ate at his mind, collapsing his reason and overwhelming his senses. Sight, sound, touch, taste, and smell were racked by the hideous groping of the fire. Uncontent to simply exist, it grew from its greed.

The sad thing about fire, which in all his observations he'd only now realized, was that its only real creation was in the glamouring of its own self. To become bigger, brighter, and hotter, it would tear down anything that came near it.

Thomasson realized this with a profound sense of sadness.

"I'm glad we could have this moment, you and I." His watery eyes trailed up the foot of a man who'd stepped into his line of sight. The fire cast a shadow over much of his features, hiding the details behind a trick of the light.

"That heat your feeling, that's life."

The man knelt down, crouching fully into Thomasson's view.

"Not a vague recollection or a dusty thing left in the corner because you're too sentimental to part with it." It was Brutus, he could read the tag now, but there was something not right about him. This man was slimmer than Brutus, his hair a different color, and he possessed none of the awe for the things around him.

"It exists only in the now, and lives for the beauty of that moment."

The man's Face trailed across the store, taking in views Thomasson could not see. Who was this man with the Face of Brutus? Why had he come here, why was he destroying his life's work?

"Oh, where are my manners, let me help you with that."

Strong, lithe fingers wrapped around Thomasson's Face. The seal cracked, and it was pulled away. A gasping noise emitted from his body, and the crackling sounds of fire grew to an alarming intensity.

"And whose Face was this? An old friend? A lover?" He chuckled, tossing it aside. Thomasson did his best to reach out for where the Face had gone.

"Now now, leave it be." The man grabbed Thomasson's hand and placed it back at his side. "Besides, you're bleeding. Certainly, that should be of more concern."

The lithe fingers dabbed at Thomasson's temple, returning back into view with a droplet of rich-colored blood.

Thomasson stared confused, coughing as he tried to briefly make sense of it, though his mind was still focused on his borrowed Face. He again reached out past his view to where the thing had gone.

The man behind Brutus' Face sighed, "You don't need that crutch anymore, you don't need any of this anymore." He motioned with both his hands to encompass the remnants of his store.

"All you have now, is the moment." Standing, Brutus' Face left his line of sight and all that remained was a pair of ivory feet.

"Goodbye, Thomasson. No one will remember you." And then, the feet were gone, and he was alone. Alone with the growing volume of the fire and the ever-present heat that permeated his body, and choked at the thoughts of his mind.

Everything was gone, he could see nothing left, nothing at all. His life was ending, his purpose finished. He thought of his wife, he thought of his boy, and of the life they once had. Thomasson smiled as he drifted off one last time to the memories of his family.

55 | BRIGHTER

Dave set the helmet down gently outside of the Crematorium. He'd saved it from being destroyed. The cycle helmet had an interesting pattern, blue checkers bisected with swirling white lines. Sometimes he would wear it when he was at home, just for fun. The idea of riding a cycle was entertaining to him, even though it was likely something he'd never have a chance to actually do. When the seals were locked into place, though, he found that it made an excellent pot for the sapling.

Every day he would bring it to work with him, and every night he would take it back home. Every week or so, he would notice that it seemed to have grown. Once when he'd given it too much water, he feared that he might have killed the only real special thing in the City. Though a few holes in the helmet allowed the excess water to drain, and the sapling returned to its seemingly good health.

Dave had taken to talking to the plant on his breaks. He would talk about all the things he'd seen and what score he'd given himself for the games he played. He would speak about the City and who he'd been before.

Dave would tell the sapling how special it was and ask how it had come to be in his Crematorium. When the plant didn't reply, Dave would make guesses and postulate with it.

"You must have been sleeping a long time somewhere, tucked away in a corner, only to be blown free by the wind, where you somehow became lodged in the edges under some man's shoe. There I suspect you stayed for quite some time, catching only glimpses of the City as the man stepped heel to toe. Then when the shoe had worn out and been tossed down a chute, you caught a ride on the conveyor system.

"Lucky for you, it's not the old days with every household having its own incinerator. We might have never met then. On the conveyor, you must have finally slipped free from the grooves and plopped right down into a clump of dirt from the park. Sometime later, you passed by, giving me a start. Yeah, that's what must have happened. It's the only thing that makes sense. Unless, of course, you feel like correcting me?"

The plant never replied, but still, Dave felt like he had a companion worth talking to. Months and months went by. The pine would grow, and Dave would sit and talk to it, making sure that it was well-fed and healthy. It was his best friend in the whole of the City, and it was pleasurable to him to feel such a connection.

Slowly the pine grew until one day, it was apparent that it had grown too big for its helmet. Dave knew what he had to do, but he couldn't bring himself to give it up. So he tried going about his usual routine, imagining that the sapling might stay with him a bit longer.

When it began to droop, though, Dave realized that his greed for company and happiness was slowly strangling the only real thing that mattered to him. Resolved, he took up his friend and marched off to the park. Taking the sapling into his hands, he scooped it gently from its container and apologized for the harm he'd caused.

Tears ran down his eyes as he said goodbye, placing it in a small patch of ground that he'd dug up. He planted it near the Libro so that it could still enjoy a good conversation when he wasn't around. When they parted, Dave felt like life wouldn't go on and thought briefly about the Bureau as he passed a Booth on the street, watching it slowly open for its next customer.

Though when tomorrow finally came around, Dave swung by the park. The sapling was still there and looking all the more healthier. Dave felt his heart flutter as he realized that this wasn't the end. That every day he could stop by to see his friend, to reminisce about their days, and play games until the sunset.

As he walked home with a smile on his face, he thought of what the future held for his friend. It would keep growing, its seeds would spread, and one day, he knew, the City would be just a little bit brighter.

Authors' Bio

Christopher and Ellen Huntingdon are natives of the Oregon Coast. Growing up together in the City of Florence, the two have shared many adventures, including attending Temple University Japan Campus and living four years abroad in Tokyo. The two have since been happily married and enjoy life with their dog, Ornstein.

Their life experiences have helped them form their driving maxim as authors: "Strangers in strange lands tell strange tales."

www.ingramcontent.com/pod-product-compliance
Lightning Source LLC
Chambersburg PA
CBHW032023120726
47898CB00002BB/638